SILENT SOURCE

SILENT SOURCE

James Marshall Smith

Aura Libertatis Spirat

SILENT SOURCE

Braveship Books
San Diego, CA

www.BraveshipBooks.com

Library of Congress Control Number: 2016914769

Cover Artwork & Design by Rossitsa Atanassova
www.99Designs.com

Photo credit: Wendy Rouleau
www.PortraitsByWendy.com

ISBN-13: 978-1-939398-69-7
Printed in the United States of America

To Kym, who taught me love above everything; Tim, who taught enthusiasm; J.M., perseverance. And to June, who gave me them and taught us all.

ACKNOWLEDGMENTS

Thanks to Anne Jones, who provided research assistance about places and cultures, along with Angela Cannon of the US Library of Congress. I am grateful to the experts who read parts of the manuscript and provided advice on technical issues, including Timothy Smith, MD, Armin Ansari, PhD, Stephen Musolino, PhD, and John Dixon, CHP. Helpful also were enlightening discussions with Col. Don Sawtelle, US Army (ret.); Sharla Gibson, US Secret Service (ret.); and Derek Pacifico, San Bernardino County Sheriff's Department (ret.).

Many thanks to Sheri Reaves, MA, and David Wright, PhD, who gave me insight into that mysterious field of personalities and their disorders. I am also grateful to Gloria Boyer for editorial assistance as well as those who educated me on a variety of unfamiliar but relevant topics to the story: Tom Owen, Jerry Giesen, Dan Brown, Giles Fischer, and Mick Van Rooy. Although all of those above provided advice, responsibility for any errors are mine alone.

All writers should be so lucky as I to have had a group of enthusiastic readers who not only read and commented on early drafts, but who made valuable suggestions for improvement. They include Pat Minicozzi, Sue Tankersley, Deborah Owen, Jo Sawtelle, Ginny Keller, Chuck Reaves, Andy and Louise Higgins, Sal Minicozzi, and Bill Fokes. Warm thanks to Addison Fischer, who provided not only encouragement from the start, but occasional royal getaways to relax and write in Scotland.

I am especially indebted to Peter Greene and all involved in the Adventure Writer's Competition for the Clive Cussler Collector's Society; together they provided the final boost to publication. A special thanks to Jeff Edwards of Braveship Books whose unfailing enthusiasm and support for the book I am deeply grateful.

Finally, I cannot express my gratitude enough for my Chief Editor and loving wife, June, who has been there through it all, providing not only meticulous editing and wise counsel on every draft, but unlimited love, encouragement, and support from beginning to end.

All men should strive to learn before they die what they are running from and to and why.

—James Thurber

CHAPTER 1

Like fashion, torture comes in a variety of styles. The paramedic shoved the gurney into the ambulance. Why would anyone, he thought, force Father Michael O'Shannon to trample through a bed of burning coals? *And in the name of Jesus?* He'd never heard anything like the babbling of the old priest. There were plenty of outlandish stories about the church and Catholics, but he assumed tales from his drinking buddies were all bullshit.

He tucked the blanket around the priest's vomit-stained collar. His partner with less than two months on the job collected the BP cuff and IV tube.

Father O'Shannon struggled to breathe. He curled his knees into his chest in agony and then muttered as he reached toward his red swollen feet: "They keep shoving me."

The paramedic wiped foam away from the mouth of the priest with a tissue and leaned toward his ashen face.

Words trickled from the old man's lips with his drool. "They hold me back, then push at me again. I . . . I can't take it anymore." He uttered each word as if it were his last.

When the ambulance rolled away with its siren blaring, the paramedic adjusted the IV saline dripping into the frail vein. All would be reported to the cop stationed at Grady's ER after the paperwork was filled out. He leaned back and stared across at his partner. "What the hell's going on around here?"

The rookie shrugged and shook his head.

By the time they arrived at the emergency entrance to Atlanta's Grady Memorial, the Father had erupted into violent convulsions. Yellow foam gushed from his mouth and showered the blanket.

Just like with the others.

*   *   *

Damon Keane crept across the gorge on some hikers' jerry-rigged bridge of tattered rope and rotting timber. It looked like a fifty-foot drop. He gingerly steered his right foot forward as he hugged ropes on either side.

"Careful, Alonzo!" he shouted. Keane was in his third year of volunteering as a chaperone for a week each summer at Dream Valley Ranch for wayward teenagers.

The Pérez boy stumbled ahead over the makeshift span that swayed like a dinghy in a gale. An older teenager in the group behind yelled that Keane wasn't moving fast enough—the same teen who'd tripped him "accidentally" on the hiking path ten minutes before. Keane's first mistake was agreeing with Alonzo that the troop should take the swinging bridge to get back to the campsite. They could've finished the hike on the sidewalk along the highway bridge, the way normal people crossed the ravine.

The contraption spanning the gorge reeled from side to side again. Keane felt like a cat on a chandelier. "Hold tight, Alonzo." At thirteen, the terrified boy was the youngest of the group.

The older kid yelled from behind, "Whatsamatta, Dr. Keane?" Apparently fifteen-year-old Tucker Carlton needed for the others to hear him and have something to chortle about at dinner.

Keane turned to face Tucker, a boy who approached his own six-foot-two-inch height but was too scrawny to match Keane's well-toned frame. At that moment Keane realized the swaying wasn't coming from the wind but from Tucker yanking on the ropes and rocking the frigging bridge. Deep within the darkest cavern of his mind, Keane thought he'd wait for Tucker to catch up and then give him an ever-so-gentle nudge over the side. It likely wouldn't be received well by the Dream Valley Ranch Board of Directors. "Stop it, Tucker! Stop it now—or else. You're scaring the daylights out of Alonzo."

"Help!" Alonzo yelled. He'd slipped and one bony leg had jammed between the wooden slats. From the expression on his face, he was about to puke over the side.

Keane hustled for him as the bridge galloped under his feet. Tucker followed, giggling.

Keane's imagination took over. *I've come before the board this morning to give you a detailed account of the tragic accident last week. What I tell you may differ a good bit from what the young eyewitnesses shared with the news media. But as you might understand, all of the boys were terribly traumatized by the sight of one of their own, flailing through the air, screaming . . . .*

When he got to Alonzo he grabbed him with one arm and jerked on his skinny ribcage to release the trapped leg. With his free hand clamped tightly to one side-rope, he staggered across the fluttering bridge as he timed each step to the bobbing of the slat ahead. They had almost made it to the end when a gust of wind blew the boy's Braves cap away, and he cried out. Three more long strides and both reached solid earth.

Alonzo slid from Keane's grasp and cheered as if he'd won a race. Keane stooped and gripped his knees as he tried to regain normal breathing. Tucker Carlton slapped him on the shoulder as he jogged past and yelled, "It's my turn for the white pieces after supper!"

"No chess for you until you shape up," Keane growled back.

Alonzo ran after Tucker, who was laughing, and both boys disappeared over the hill. Keane then spotted a familiar face.

Jessie Wiley, dressed in a dark-green jumpsuit that contrasted with her delicate features, marched toward him as if on parade. Her carriage and trim outfit covering long, slender legs revealed a take-charge attitude. He was startled to see the elite group following her.

The celebrity among them spoke first. "Enjoying yourself, Dr. Keane?" Sandwiched between two Georgia state troopers, Carl Stillwell moved with the grace of a mature lion. A handsome African American, the mayor of Atlanta grabbed Keane by the shoulder and vigorously pumped his hand like he was greeting a campaign contributor. The mayor's khaki pants and Carolina-blue knit shirt gave him the air of a professional golfer on tour. "My people had trouble locating you," he said. "Thankfully they were put on to Miss Wiley here. She promised to deliver me directly to you."

Jessie shot Keane a wink. She was a freelancer like himself, but a whopping difference set them as far apart as the ravine he'd just crossed: she took to the outdoors as if brought up by a family of Grizzlies on the banks of a wilderness river.

"I wasn't surprised a bit," the mayor said, "to learn you were spendin' some time here at the ranch. Doggone beautiful place, isn't it now? Doggone beautiful."

Keane had found that working with boys in need of a father figure was therapy—another chance at what he'd missed in raising his own two kids, now at the tail end of their teens. His sister had talked him into getting involved at Dream Valley when he was going through his divorce.

Jessie led a group of curious boys away as the mayor's expression turned somber. "You just might be able to guess why I wanted to have a face-to-face with you, Damon. Now am I right about that?"

"I suppose there's a problem?"

The mayor moved closer and lowered his voice. "You're damned right we have a problem." He twisted his head both ways and hitched his trousers. All Keane could think about at the moment was what had happened two years before. Keane had found that working with APD's detectives on the Reinauer case was nothing but miserable from the get-go.

Assignments for small-time operations like APD's Strategy and Special Projects Division were only a public service. He'd been a consulting scientist for the last fourteen years on missions around the country. Unique in his business, he carried degrees in both medicine and physics. But he was best known for his forensic smarts. He could quickly look over the data and evidence; show where the logic was inconsistent or crucial clues missed. Then he'd recommend the best course of action and step out of the way. Let others take action and get the credit. People who mattered knew his capabilities.

It was tough to look Stillwell in the eye and say no, but fortunately this time would be easy. Everyone retires at some point and everybody understands that. "I have to apologize, Mayor, but—"

"Let me get to the point, Damon."

"But, sir—"

"Grady Memorial has had two unexplained deaths on their hands. They tell me both died with the same symptoms but with no obvious cause. Then to beat all, yesterday a priest was brought into their ER with symptoms exactly like theirs. He's not expected to make it. All three came from the Piedmont Park area. No gunshot or stab wounds. Infectious disease docs have found absolutely nothing. People are dropping but no one has any idea what's going on—not a clue. I decided it was a good time to call on you again. I'd like you to work with Chief Walters or whoever he partners you with. Not a lot for you to do here, Damon. Just give us your advice on what needs to be done. I place a lot of faith in your judgment. You know that."

Keane had never met Dallas Walters. The mayor had recruited the new chief of police from Nashville the year before during a political storm over the city's deepest budget cuts in its history.

"To be totally honest," Keane said, "I'm in the midst of moving on. I really can't take on any new work."

The mayor paused as if taken aback by sudden news he damn well should've been forewarned about by his people. That's why you have people. "I'm . . . sorry to hear that. Not leaving Georgia now, are you? There's no reason to leave this beautiful state. Right?"

"I'm planning on it but haven't told anyone yet. I'd like to keep it confidential." He glanced over at Jessie Wiley, who was out of earshot.

The mayor lifted his shoulders and shoved them back as he glanced at the sky. Then he looked down and twisted the toe of one shoe in the grass as if squashing a fire ant. "That will be Georgia's loss. Where you headed?"

"One of the islands around Tahiti. I'd keep the place I have here, but spend most of the year there."

"You're a young man, Damon. Retirement isn't good for young men. 'Specially those with your kinda talent."

"I'm actually looking forward to finally having some free time," Keane said.

The mayor placed a firm hand on Keane's shoulder. "That's what graves are for, aren't they? Why they dig 'em deep. Quieter down there."

Two weeks before, Keane had been combing the warm white sands of Bora Bora with his toes while staring out over towering banyan trees and turquoise water toward Mount Otemanu. The more he thought about it, the more he needed to put Atlanta and the States behind. Family matters out West had complicated his life again. The never-ending demand for his services in the East gnawed at his gut more and more—especially after passing the big Four-O.

But what got him thinking hard and long about his future was his annual physical the month before. Chest x-rays picked up a spot on his lung that was confirmed by a CT scan. Although he'd never smoked, the spot had the appearance of an oat cell tumor, and he knew the stats on that one. Scared hell and perspiration out of him. He hardly slept for three days until they got back the needle biopsy: scar tissue, for no reason the docs could explain. He escaped that one but it was too damned close and got him thinking about life's Second Half while walking out onto a foggy playing field.

"I don't want to sound heartless," the mayor said, "but you know what would happen if CNN began snoopin' around. And you know how they *love* doing that. It's gonna be a real challenge—much bigger than the Reinauer case, Damon. By the way, I'm told instructors over at the academy often refer to that one. Now that's a fact."

"I didn't know that, Mayor, but you see—"

Stillwell motioned for Keane to move closer, and then he leaned over to whisper in his left ear. "My wife and I are members of that parish, Damon. Father O'Shannon—the priest dying down at Grady Memorial right now as we stand here—was the very same man who married Genevieve and me. We were the first black couple to have a wedding in that church. I hope to God Almighty there's no connection. I'd never forgive myself. I owe Father O'Shannon for the courage he showed me. For what he did for the entire African American community in Atlanta."

Keane glanced away to watch the boys running about and then turned back and committed the innocent blunder the mayor was waiting for. "Would the hospital and APD know I'd be checking on them?"

The mayor instantly flung an arm around Keane's shoulder and grabbed his hand to pump again. "I've already put the word out, including to Shropshire at Grady. You'll have full support from everybody, Damon. I *knew* I could count on you."

I haven't said yes. "But—"

"I really owe you one for this one."

That's what you said last time!

"Remember to keep me informed," the mayor said as he squeezed Keane's shoulder. "I need someone like you to give me the straight scoop. Not just what I want to hear."

Typical Southern charm paled in the charismatic glow of Carl Stillwell. "I really can't promise much," Keane said under his breath.

"If you need me to run interference for you," the mayor said, "leave me a message. That's all you gotta do." He handed him his card with his private number scribbled on the back then spun on his heels and took off.

Jessie Wiley and the state patrolmen rushed to keep up. She glanced back with a coy smile and gave Keane a thumbs-up. Keane grinned and shook his head as if to say *I can't believe your chutzpah.* He'd look into the mayor's request. It was certain to be a job out of his arena—one that was more likely for infectious disease specialists at the CDC. He quickly recognized that. The sooner he did his homework and got back to the mayor, the better.

The South Pacific awaited.

CHAPTER 2

Keane drove the freeway toward Grady Memorial Hospital in downtown Atlanta. It had been three days since he'd departed Dream Valley Ranch. In the meantime, he'd been briefed by others on the cases the mayor had shared with him. The first was a face-to-face with Major Stewart Arlington (the Grim Reaper, as he was affectionately referred to behind his back) from APD's Special Operations Section. The second turned out to be a quick but productive phone conversation with Dr. William Rutledge, a long-time acquaintance and top doc with Grady's Emergency Department.

Keane picked up the wall phone in the ICU waiting area and identified himself. The double doors sprang open. A heavy-set nurse with a side-to-side ramble escorted him through antiseptic halls to Father O'Shannon's dark room and introduced him to a young resident who stood reading from a clipboard at the foot of the bed. IV tubes and wires linked to a pale, lifeless body. A plastic cannula delivered oxygen through the Father's nose. An alarm on the rack of monitors at his bedside quietly buzzed on and off while flashing amber.

"They brought him into ER three days ago at 9:21 a.m.," the resident said, referring to his notes. "Sixty-three-year-old male who presented unconscious, severely dehydrated, his temperature hovering at 102. Electrolytes way off the mark. Lymphocyte count fell below 250. He awakened in spurts over the course of five hours. He's had nausea, vomiting, bloody diarrhea, and sudden bouts of delirium. Also severe pain in his extremities, especially the soles of his feet. No sensation to pinprick. He slipped into a coma at 8:35 p.m."

Keane listened only with one ear while he examined the face of the priest. What he was hearing from the resident jibed with the paramedics who brought the priest by ambulance to Grady: delirium, pain in the soles of the feet.

"I was told you had at least two other similar cases," Keane said.

"Don't know anything about them. Wasn't on my watch."

"What's your guess on this one?"

The resident took an audible breath before he spoke. "The worst. His major organs are failing."

"*All* of them?"

"It started with his kidneys, progressed to his liver and pancreas. I thought he was having a coronary at eleven last night. I called Shropshire and reported it and that's when he told me you might be coming in. He told me to brief you. Even though . . . well, you know HIPAA rules as well as I do."

So, the mayor had already gotten to Leslie Shropshire—Grady Memorial's chief administrator—to clear the bureaucratic path. "When will you get back all of the lab tests?"

"In a few days," the resident replied. "Have to see what if anything grows in culture."

"What about tox? What did you send out for that?"

"Urine, blood. Sent out some tissue for path too."

"You collected vomit?"

"That's included."

"Nasal swabs?"

"I didn't think it necessary."

You didn't think it necessary? Or was it another step that took a little extra effort? "I would swab the nose and get the sample analyzed."

The resident glowered at him. "I believe I'm in charge of the case, Dr. Keane."

Keane knew he was going overboard. He needed to be reminded of his role and couldn't blame the kid. "Just trying to help cover your rear. Incidentally, did you take fecal samples?"

The resident stared back at him without answering.

"Let me remind you that you're not dealing with a standard case here," Keane said. "Toxins could have taken any number of elimination pathways."

"Of course, but—"

"We're going to need as much info as possible about what this guy was exposed to recently." He paused a beat when he realized he'd used the word *we*. "I need copies of all lab results as soon as they're returned. Scan them in and email them to me. The path report too." He handed him his business card.

The resident paused to read the card. "Sorry, no can do. We provide those reports to APD. You'll have to get what you need from them. Good to meet you, sir." He turned and walked away.

Keane strolled out of ICU and toward the ER's main entrance. Maybe he'd been too harsh on the kid. On the other hand, maybe the kid was an asshole. More likely, he was right on both counts—he just brought out the asshole in the kid. Couldn't blame him. Who was going to trust a police department *consultant*? People want to talk with those in authority, not a sideshow hustler.

Keane felt for Father O'Shannon; all he could do was help find clues. Little good that would do the priest now. The bigger question: did Grady or APD really *want* his help? The mayor did, of course, but he knew the mayor was totally alone on that.

Before reaching his car in the lower lot, he was distracted by the arrival of an ambulance with its red lights spinning. He hurried back to the entrance and found two brawny EMTs hauling out a gurney from the rear door. An old man with disheveled gray hair lay under a sheet covering him to his shoulders. An IV tube ran from an arm to a drip chamber below the bag held high over the gurney by one of the EMTs. Keane sauntered up within earshot as the other paramedic briefed a nurse. "Don't know who made the call. He's apparently homeless. They found him unconscious on a bench inside Piedmont Park."

He hung around the ER long enough to learn more from another nurse on staff. The old guy had come in with symptoms that sounded identical to Father O'Shannon's, except for one strange detail—an astonishingly raw and blistered lesion on his rear end, as if someone had lit a fire under him.

CHAPTER 3

Our Mother of Mercy stood gracefully tall, one block from Piedmont Park. Early for his appointment, Keane ambled up the century-old steps toward the church's entrance. Mesmerized by the stone archway above the massive doors, he stumbled on the last step. He fell to one knee and let lose a profanity right at the door of the church. Jumping up quickly, he peeked both ways to see if anyone was close enough to hear.

A priest fitting the description of his contact was whispering to a small group in front of the sanctuary. A stout lady among them held a tissue to her nose and sobbed beneath an oversized pair of tortoiseshell glasses. Keane slid into a back pew and focused straight ahead, imagining blue-green water lapping upon a white sandy beach a few thousand miles away. Along one wall of the sanctuary stood the Virgin Mary with her arms outstretched. He squirmed and shifted to avoid her gaze.

The rigid formality of the Catholic Church collided with his own upbringing. Saturday night tent revivals during summers of his youth had introduced him and his twin Danielle to Jesus, theology and live entertainment. The Reverend Sherman McCallister ministered to the congregation of the First Church of the Nazarene in Ridgemont, a town cuddled in the folds of the Blue Ridge Mountains. The Reverend may have been less educated than his city counterparts, but what he lacked in book learning he made up for with born-again gusto. He didn't just preach the Sermon on the Mount, he "brung it home."

Revivals on those fiery Saturday nights of summer were celebrated under a circus tent. He could still smell the sawdust with an aroma of fresh-cut pine that blanketed the ground beneath battered gray folding chairs arranged in tidy rows. The center aisle swept through just wide enough for sweaty deacons to pass the offering plate while standing back-to-back and fanny-to-fanny, their eyes fixed on the money. No service was complete without the singing of *The Ol' Rugged Cross*, followed by a passage from the Book of Revelation proclaiming the Last Days.

Mankind was doomed.

Hellfire and Brimstone, just around the corner.

In that atmosphere of absolute faith Keane adopted his early values. Obey authority—the Bible, the Church, the Teacher, the Coach, the Parent. That meant a set of rules on how to live. *Rules are rules* was stuffed into him from the crib like he was a Thanksgiving turkey. It all made for a black-and-white kind of life. He never strayed until his years at Cambridge, when he found himself smothered in too many layers of gray. But the tent revivals of his youth were down-home religion and damned good drama—no comparison with the straight-laced primness of where he sat at the moment.

The priest turned away from the grieving women. Not much over five feet, Father Calabrese shuffled toward him with the timid gait of a much older man. Stress from the ordeal showed on his oval face. He lightly grasped Keane's outstretched hand, averting his eyes.

"I'm sorry about Father O'Shannon," Keane said, "but I'm told he's still holding on."

"Thanks be to the Lord," the priest replied. He crossed himself. "I'm Father Calabrese. And you are?"

How do you explain consulting work for a police department? That you actually go out and ask questions like some kind of make-believe detective? Keane knew that most people assumed law enforcement agencies had all the expertise they needed. In truth, there were many cases that demanded skilled practitioners in the arts or trades or academics. Even consultants. He also knew you don't try to explain it, you just steer away from the subject in hopes it will somehow crawl away on its own.

"I'm Damon Keane. I work with the Atlanta police. I know it's been a long day, but I'd like to ask a few questions."

When he glared at Keane's business card the muscles along his gaunt cheeks twitched like caterpillars beneath his skin. "I spent two hours yesterday with one of your detectives, sir. He showed me a badge."

"I only do background work." He hoped Father Calabrese wouldn't stop to think about the meaning of that.

"There's an *MD* after your name."

"Correct, but I don't practice anymore. I'd like to spend a few minutes with you to discuss Father O'Shannon's sudden illness."

"They don't suspect foul play, do they?"

"They have no idea." Not *exactly* true, but the lie was a dingy white. "Do you know of anyone who would want to harm him?"

Calabrese stared back at Keane for a few moments before he answered. "Dr. Keane, there's no reason for *anyone* in the parish or in the entire world to want to harm a hair on Father O'Shannon's head." He stabbed the business card back at him. "Now if you'll excuse me."

"I don't want to suggest that—"

"You should know that Father O'Shannon's been a respected priest here for three decades."

Keane quickly switched gears and explained that the paramedics who brought Father O'Shannon to Grady Memorial had said he was murmuring about torture. "Someone forcing him to walk over hot coals. Or worse."

Calabrese folded his arms across his chest. "That doesn't surprise me."

"It doesn't surprise you?" *You mean this is just another day on the job?*

"Father O'Shannon hasn't been himself lately. He's been acting strange, keeping mostly to his study. Quite unlike him."

"When did all this begin?"

"A couple of weeks ago. Every Thursday Father O'Shannon does his duty at the confessional. As I recall, that Thursday was a long one for him. It's the time of year when many of our parishioners want to leave town on vacation, of course."

"They're eager to get away fast and with a clear conscience, I presume," Keane said. His smile wasn't returned. "Might there be a list of those who come to confession?"

Calabrese paused, staring back at him. "I take it you're not Catholic, Dr. Keane?"

"Actually, no. Please, go on about that Thursday."

Calabrese was studying the ceiling again before he spoke. "Father O'Shannon walked from the rectory looking pasty. Moments before I had heard him throwing up in the restroom. He looked horrible, like he was coming down with the flu."

"Or maybe food poisoning?"

"I dine with the Father every day, along with Sister Clarice and Sister Anna. I begged him to go to Dr. Lloyd—he takes care of all of us—but he'd have nothing to do with it. Said he'd been working too hard. Needed rest. He was never sick before then. Never. I hope you don't mind, but if we could wrap this up . . ."

Keane held up an index finger to signal one more question. "How long does the Father usually stay for confessions?"

The priest sighed. "This time of year he might go in at one or two o'clock and stay until four, sometimes five."

Keane nodded, still thinking. "Could I take a look at the confessional?"

Calabrese stood and quickly led him along a hallway to a dark room without windows and with a thick burgundy carpet. One wall featured the same manufactured stone as on the outside of the church. A walnut-grained screen stood halfway across the room to divide it. Because of the louvers on the screen, whoever entered could at best only make out the silhouette of a priest sitting on the other side of the partition.

A chair rested nearby to provide the parishioner with the option of facing the screen while seated or kneeling before it on a carpeted bench. Keane studied the louvered screen, examining both sides and feeling the wood with an index finger. Surface scratches showed along the edges. At one place along the bottom a deeper gouge appeared. He couldn't make out the backside of the stand, but he rubbed a hand along it. A sticky patch partly coated the hidden surface facing the screen.

He shot a *May I?* look at Calabrese, who closed his eyes and nodded. After sliding the stand away from the partition, he brushed the tips of his finger across the sticky patch on the back. He pointed to the spot and looked up. "Do you know what might have been taped here?"

The priest only shrugged.

Keane stood. There was little use in continuing. "Would it be possible for you and I to sit down sometime with the church's floor plans? Not today of course. I'd like to have a feel for the layout of the entire structure."

"I'm sorry, Dr. Keane, but I certainly wouldn't know how to locate those. And I don't really think it necessary."

That was going to be a tough one to negotiate but it could wait for later. Keane smiled and held out his hand. "I appreciate your time. Is there anything else I should know?"

"Like?"

"Anything at all you think might be helpful."

"So, there will be more investigating here?" Calabrese asked.

Keane handed back his business card. "I can assure you there will be. Please, keep my business card handy. Call when you come across any floor plans."

Calabrese stroked the card with his thumbs as if examining it more carefully this time. "Look, Dr. Keane. I'll level with you. I did find something strange. I wasn't sure who to tell—or if I can even believe it happened."

Curious, the way he switched his tone, Keane thought. "Did you say anything about it to the detective yesterday?"

Calabrese slightly bowed his head. "God forgive me."

"You want to tell me about it, Father." *I can't believe I said that.*

Calabrese pointed at the table beside the chair. "One of Father O'Shannon's special rosaries was always there."

"Someone stole it?"

"Not exactly."

"But how—"

"I took it."

Keane wrinkled his eyebrows. Withholding evidence was more a matter for the law than the Lord.

"I knew that rosary well," Calabrese said. "I was always struck by the warm watermelon color of the beads, almost pale enough to see through."

"Sorry, I'm not following you."

"As soon as the ambulance took him away, I went in to pick up the rosary for safekeeping. The moment I saw it, I had to grab the back of the chair." Calabrese slid a hand into his coat pocket and pulled out a rosary. "These beads. They've suddenly changed color."

Keane stared down at the glistening string looped about the finger of the priest. The beads were blood-red.

CHAPTER 4

A mud-splashed white Chevy van without commercial markings pulled into the parking lot of the Norcross Gas 'N Go, just off I-85. A gringo that Miguel Castillo had never seen before hopped out and sauntered toward the front entrance. He ignored the day laborers who approached with that look of *I'm your man*. Tall and bearded, the stranger moved with a lanky stride as if on a mission.

Miguel shifted from the curbside and crouched by the outside freezer that stored bags of customer ice. He waited—the same way he spent most of his daylight hours. His wife Rosalinda stayed at home on Shallowford Road with their son inside a one-bedroom ranch-style duplex. At times she babysat kids from the block or took in neighbors' clothes to wash. Wasn't much money, but it helped, especially when Miguel was having bad luck with pick-up work. The last week had seen only a four-hour yard job.

The couple had one child, three year-old Eduardo, who was born with clubfeet and looked like his dad. Eduardo's life would be different. He'd get an education. Go to the University on one of those Hope Scholarships that Miguel heard gringos talk about. Sometimes Chicano kids got them, too—a gringo told him that once.

Eduardo would be a lawyer. Miguel's people needed lawyers to show Chicanos how to protect themselves from the police. The cops stopped him or his compadres for small things all the time, like a busted brake light—little stuff that gringos got away with. They'd demand to see their driver's license and a green card, or accuse them of having counterfeit ID purchased from one of their spic connections.

After a few minutes the stranger wandered back outside and lit up. He exhaled a ribbon of smoke from a corner of his clinched lips then glanced over to his left where Miguel squatted. The stranger wiggled a curled finger in his direction.

Miguel jumped up. "I work hard. Very fast." He made sure to show his hefty biceps underneath the rolled-up sleeves of his olive-green T-shirt.

The stranger tossed his cigarette onto the asphalt and mashed it with the toe of his boot. He pointed toward the van's passenger side.

Three of Miguel's friends spotted him springing into the van and ran to it. They were followed by a dozen others dressed in tattered work pants and ball caps. Most had waited since sunrise for a pickup truck or van to move in and stop in the middle of the parking area while they crowded around. The drivers would hold up fingers for the number of men they needed, and the Chicanos hopped into the bed of the pickup or opened the side door of the van and shoved their way in, jockeying to be first.

The stranger shifted into reverse and backed away. He ignored the pleas of the other Chicanos outside his window. Miguel sat with a broad grin and a brown paper bag that held lunch.

The driver pulled onto the roadway and turned toward I-85. During the drive, Miguel tossed out comments once in a while but got back only grunts. A few miles down the interstate, Atlanta's skyscrapers leaped into the view above the trees. The van turned off the highway and drifted along side streets riddled with potholes until they rolled into what looked like an old factory. The van curved around a tall concrete smokestack with soot coating one side, and then stopped out of sight of the street.

A rusted chain link fence with an open gate surrounded a brick building no longer used. Electrical wires from a telephone pole led to corners of the rooftop where black crows the size of chickens cawed.

Miguel jumped down from the van.

The driver moved quickly to the back. He'd opened the double doors and was reaching into the van when Miguel approached.

The stranger turned and pointed a handgun at Miguel's chest. He held a plastic strap in his free hand with another strap wrapped around his elbow.

Madre de Dios?

Miguel lifted his hands and backpedaled. As a teenager snagged by human smugglers in the Chihuahua Desert, he'd seen the results of trying to run from a gun. In the desert they had waved revolvers with long barrels—seizing him, his brother, and two other compadres. His brother took off running and was shot three times in the back before he crumpled into the sand and died.

The stranger motioned for Miguel to turn around. When he obeyed, the stranger barked into his ear to put his hands behind his back. He then bound his wrists together with the plastic strap and shoved the barrel of the pistol between his shoulder blades, pushing him toward the door of the abandoned building. Clutching the back of Miguel's shirt, the stranger steered him inside and across the concrete floor of a massive open area and into a small corner room with a tiled ceiling.

Miguel came face-to-face with three other Chicanos, all squatting upon the floor with their hands bound behind their backs and lashed to steel U-bolts sunk into the concrete.

Panic showed on the faces of two of the men. The third sat with his legs crossed and his head hanging limply to one side like a rag doll. All looked to be in their twenties or thirties.

The oldest growled at the stranger. "I have money. *Muchos dólares, amigo.*"

Miguel didn't speak. The stranger grabbed his head and shoved him downward, forcing him to squat by a free U-bolt and face the others.

He slipped another plastic strap inside the one that bound Miguel's wrists and threaded it through the bolt to secure him to the floor.

The stranger stuffed his pistol into the front of his trousers and disappeared out the door of the small room. The four men studied each other in silence. The older one struggled with his bound hands, yanking at them and mumbling in his native tongue about a gringo devil.

After hearing an outside door slam shut, Miguel scanned the walls of his windowless prison. A single light bulb beneath a rusted hood hung above their heads. He thought of happier times in Monterrey, of Papá and Mamá, of his uncles and aunts. He thought of kicking the football on the front grass to Eduardo, watching him stumble when he struggled to kick it back, while Rosalinda laughed and clapped. He thought of his brother's body letting loose a river of blood into the hot sand.

When the door finally creaked open, he turned to look. The tall stranger leaned against the door to keep it open with his hip while he bent over to lift a long metal toolbox off a hand truck. He clenched his teeth and dragged the hefty contraption across the room toward his wide-eyed captives.

CHAPTER 5

After leaving Our Mother of Mercy, Keane drove his BMW toward rural Rockdale County, an hour east of Atlanta's downtown. The road squirmed through the Georgia countryside where a comforting sight greeted him—giant loblolly pines and sprawling fields bordered by split-rail fences. Weathered wood-framed farmhouses sprang up at respectable distances apart. Scattered cattle and horses munched on field grass and dilapidated chicken houses nestled under groves of crabapple trees.

Keane enjoyed his fifteen-acre estate, which lay a healthy distance from the city in the part of the South known best as "Deep." He'd often been told by neighbors that the highway he was following tracked more or less the same path that General William Tecumseh Sherman's storm troopers took after burning Atlanta. He'd heard plenty of tales passed down through the generations about Sherman's army setting fire to homes and cotton gins, stealing horses, and taking the devil's revenge on any bushwhackers. No doubt the stories included the mandatory rape of womenfolk and the drowning of babies. After all, they were Yankees.

His mind wandered back to his conversation with Father Calabrese and to the rosary beads' mysteriously changing color. Before Keane left the church, Calabrese had informed him that the rosary was a sacramental given to Father O'Shannon by a nun from the Sisters of St. Vincent de Paul on the island of Elba off the coast of Italy.

Keane had politely objected to Calabrese's story. "The rosary must've been replaced by another one for some reason," Keane had said.

"At first, that's what I thought, too," Calabrese replied. "But I knew those gemstones individually, each of the five large ones that begin a decade of ten smaller stones. And the medallion at the end, a silver crucifix rubbed thousands of times. No two rosaries are alike, Dr. Keane."

You'd think that a priest would be up front with you. Did he have something to hide? "You're saying this is *not* a different rosary?"

"It's identical. Except for the color of the beads."

Perhaps Calabrese was confused by the question. "Let me see if I understand. They changed from pale pink to ruby-red overnight?"

"They did."

"But that would be some kind of miracle."

"The Lord isn't unfamiliar with miracles."

The problem was that Keane was unfamiliar with miracles, but quite familiar with malarkey. "What could possibly be the meaning of it?"

"Only the Lord knows. But the change in color could be a symbol of Father O'Shannon's life. He was transformed quickly, like the beads. Something's hiding there, buried deep within the mystery of that transformation."

Maybe he'd been too quick to judge the priest—an old habit and a bad one. No, there wasn't anything hiding in that bizarre color change. More likely something festered deep inside Father Calabrese, something he wasn't sharing. Did he even know what he was saying— the equivalent of Jesus changing water into wine? Although Calabrese wore the robes of a priest, Keane didn't. The priest certainly had tried to lead him off track, but why? And why did Father O'Shannon mumble about torture before drifting into a coma? Nothing added up.

One step at a time.

He needed to find a gemologist—someone who knew about gems and their colors. Of course, there was Margot. His older sis was an amateur gem collector of sorts. He hit a button on the steering wheel and waited. After two rings came a soft "Hello," and they exchanged greetings.

"Why don't you come down for the Fourth?" Margot asked. "Mom was asking me yesterday when you and the kids would be here this summer."

"I hope to be talking with Andy one of these days, but Nicole's taking classes this summer. She wants to finish her degree early."

"Maybe you could arrange for Andy to visit with you for a while?"

"Maybe. I'm on the road here, Margot. Quick question for you."

"Shoot."

"What do you know about tourmaline?"

"Tourmaline? It's semiprecious. Not that rare."

"What color is it?"

"Depends on what part of the world you find it. I for one prefer diamonds, if that's where you're headed."

"Have you heard of tourmaline changing color?" he asked.

"A gemstone changing color? You know, Damon, you've had more education than ten people, but I really think you need to get out and about more often."

"Got it. Running into traffic. Love you, Margot."

Margot herself was a gem. Three years his senior, she'd been a haven of loving support at times of mayhem in his life. Her first love was music and she played the flute regularly in a Sarasota chamber orchestra. But she had nowhere near the talent that the young Danielle his twin sister had shown on the piano from an early age. How had these genes skipped Keane himself? Margot had sometimes joked about that error in DNA coding. But for Keane, thoughts of Danielle were too painful.

His gut told him that somehow the rosary had played a role in Father O'Shannon's sudden life-threatening illness. But a rosary of tourmaline beads that changed color overnight?

Keane checked for messages on his cell phone. He hadn't heard from his son in a month. Although there was nothing from him, there was a message from Jessie Wiley. After putting down the phone, he massaged both sides of his face with his palms. He really didn't need this right now. But she wanted to "urgently" meet the next day. He had no idea why.

CHAPTER 6

Keane followed a sidewalk around to the back of the building at suburban Peachtree-DeKalb Airport. Jessie Wiley's Bell helicopter had just landed on a concrete pad, and the chopper's blades were still whirling. He sat at an outdoor table to wait while sipping sweet tea. The table's umbrella tossed a narrow strip of shade but could give no relief from the stifling humidity.

When Jessie joined him, they high-fived and she slammed down her cold bottle of Bud Light on the table. She tilted her head downward and straightened out her ponytail with alternating hands as she spoke. "Gotta question for you. How long have we been working together anyway?"

He pursed his lips and winced. "I'd say, about two years, maybe—"

"It's been over three years now, Damon."

She was probably right. On and off for a good three years. They'd met when both were doing contract work for FBI field ops—a case of smuggling from Havana to the Keys. She had piloted the chopper used for the aerial photography.

"How's business lately?" he asked. After leaving the military, she'd built her own helicopter-for-hire firm from scratch.

"Could be better. Some cop or sheriff work now and then. Helped with firefighting down in South Florida last month and I've been on a couple of search-and-rescues so far this summer."

Too bad she hadn't been busier. She damned well knew her stuff. Over the time he'd spent working with her, the one thing that stood out in his mind was her stubborn determination to stay focused and on task, no matter what.

"You're a Pisces, right?" she blurted.

"What's a Pisces?"

"Your sign, Damon. Weren't you born in March?"

How did she remember that? "Yeah, I suppose that's my 'sign.'"

"For you it's an ideal time now. For all of those lucky enough to be born a Pisces. Great time to be starting new adventures. It could lead to a new you."

I need a new me?

"Tell me something," she said. "What kind of project does the mayor have you on anyway?"

She could shift gears in the middle of a thought like a driver at Le Mans. Now he knew what this was all about.

"And don't try to give me that classified bullshit." she quickly added.

"So, at Dream Valley you were eavesdropping on my chat with the mayor?"

"No, I wasn't. Eavesdropping means listening on purpose, Dr. Keane."

"There's a difference?"

"With that booming voice of his . . . well, you don't have to give me all the details for chrissakes."

"If I let you in on some info, can I count on you to keep mum?" he asked.

She raised her eyebrows. "Can I count on you to trust me?"

He held up a hand to acknowledge his sin. "Hard to tell what's going on, Jessie, but people in the Piedmont Park neighborhood are coming down with a strange syndrome. It's deadly."

"Some kind of disease?"

"Who knows? Not getting straight answers from everybody."

"Maybe that's more of a mission for the docs at the CDC," she said.

He paused to choose his words carefully. "I'm hitting the usual stone wall when I go around asking questions. I need cooperation when I come into a project. It doesn't have to be jump-up-and-down 'Go Team' stuff, but I want people working *with* me."

"So, I gather you're thinking about throwing in the towel because they're grabbing at your toys in the sandbox. Sounds like a perfectly good reason to wipe the sand off your butt and go home."

They held their stare at each other. Sure, it all looked simple to her. She didn't need to know all that was going on in his life at the moment.

She took a swig of beer and massaged the bottle. "Tell me more about this famous Reinauer case. I'd read about it in the papers a couple of years ago. You've never talked much about it."

"Interesting case," Keane replied. He remembered that his reputation as a forensic consultant was spreading around the country at the time. "Martin Reinauer was a supervisory engineer with Georgia Power and Light. APD detectives quickly pinned him as the prime suspect in the murder of his wife. Whoever did it split open her skull with a meat cleaver."

"What was his motive?"

"His wife had reportedly discovered his affair with a coworker."

"But . . . murder?"

"His coworker was male. That added an extra layer of rage. APD detectives thought he had a perfect alibi. Reinauer said he'd taken off with his five-year-old son to the Okefenokee Swamp. When they returned home, he said he was shocked to find his wife's bludgeoned body in the kitchen. Obvious home invasion gone haywire, he claimed."

"Couldn't anybody say they were down in the Okefenokee when they're accused of whatever?" Jessie asked.

"Sure, anybody could say it. But before I was called in to consult they'd already analyzed the layers of soil trapped in the tire treads of

Reinauer's Subaru. Going layer by layer, from youngest to the oldest and deepest layer, they analyzed the types of minerals and particle sizes. They linked that to characteristics of the mud and soil in places wherever the Subaru had been driven off the highway. That verified his account."

"They can do that?"

"You bet. Done routinely in high-profile cases when forensics have to determine or verify where vehicle tires have been."

"Okay, but look. When a meat cleaver smashes a skull, it splatters a little more than a bit of blood around, I would think. But I'm just an amateur. What do I know?"

"You're on the right track. Not a trace of his wife's blood was found on Reinauer or his clothes."

"Then how am I on the right frigging track?"

"My first tip was that they test his nasal hair. It wasn't possible for the murderer to avoid *inhaling* blood droplets."

Jessie's eyes lit up and she smiled. "That nailed it?"

"Reinauer's nose hairs revealed a boatload of his wife's blood cells and her DNA. But things aren't that easy in police work."

"Because?"

"Manny Shepherdson."

"The former police chief?" she asked, surprised.

"Exactly. He wouldn't buy it."

"Why on earth not?" she asked.

"Oral sex."

"*What?*"

"He argued that in court the defense would point out how oral sex around the time of her period could easily explain the test results."

She slapped her forehead. "Another damned good reason he's the former police chief."

Keane explained how he held his ground at the time. At least he and the detectives were convinced Reinauer was the murderer. That was a major breakthrough. Keane then pressed for returning to the alleged campsite at Okefenokee. He reasoned that Reinauer would've wanted to get rid of the weapon at a place he knew well. And he admitted he'd spent a lot of time there when he was younger. He likely figured it impossible for anyone to recover the meat cleaver in a swamp.

"At the tent site," Keane continued, "they found a natural trail to a murky body of water. Divers explored it—a swamp infested with gators and cottonmouths. I remember sitting on a folding canvas chair at the edge of the water. My feet were as high off the ground as I could keep them. I promised myself then and there it would be the last time I'd get out into the miserable *field*."

He added that it only took the divers an hour to find the rusted meat cleaver. "The lab later identified traces of skin and hair from the scalp of Reinauer's wife. They were still attached to the cleaver. In court, it was an open-and-shut case."

The Reinauer case was in Keane's distant past, and he'd learned to forget about victories and press on—the next challenge could totally outwit him and whack a few inches off his ego. He peeked at his watch then tossed his napkin down and scooted his chair back. "I'd better be getting along."

Jessie grabbed his arm and squeezed. "I want to help out, Damon."

"Help out?"

"Help with the case the mayor put you on."

He glared into her perfectly set steel-blue eyes. Was she joshing him or was she serious? And where had their casual friendship been going, anyway? Somewhere other than business? He and the Good Lord knew she had her choice of men. And she'd never given him any hints that she wanted it otherwise.

He realized that he'd never come clean with her about his South Pacific plans. Not that he owed her a heads-up. He hadn't even mentioned them to Mr. J yet. But no deal had been struck. The real estate agent in the islands was still working on it and the whole thing could fall through. He dragged his chair back to the table. He had to be absolutely blunt. "I need to take care of this case quickly now. I'm planning to—"

"I can help you make that happen. Two can work twice as fast. That's mathematics you know."

"Come on, you've got a business you're still launching," he said.

"You're damned right! And I'm in charge of my coming and going. I'm the CHO."

"What's that?"

"Chief Hauncho in the Office. There ought to be *something* I can do to help out, Damon." She tossed the paper sleeve from her straw at him. "I wanna be like you when I grow up."

She was a restless maverick, yearning for adventure. That desire wasn't going away anytime soon; he'd known her long enough. She could check out a few leads. If anyone had the people skills, it was Jessie Wiley. "I suppose you could do a little snooping around for me."

She did a double take and beamed.

"Not a lot, mind you," he added. "Just asking some questions. Maybe getting a little background. That's the key word here, Jessie. *Background.*"

"I know what background means . . . and I'm totally hooked!"

"Did you ever spend any time in Piedmont Park?" he asked.

"You mean sober?"

He had to admit that he could use her help. His only hesitation was bringing the two of them together on another project. She was too eager and that could lead to a place deep within that could upset his bigger plans. He wasn't sure how he would eventually deal with that, but he could at least put her onto checking out the city's popular park. She'd be able to handle that task—and he suspected there was some tidbit of info waiting to be uncovered there.

For now, he needed to follow up with the Big Viking at Grady Memorial. He'd put that off too long.

CHAPTER 7

Keane moved swiftly past the naked men in the locker room of Grady Memorial's sub-basement. He kept his chin high and focused straight ahead. The reek blended with cologne and sweat and mildew played havoc with his sinuses as men toweled off from showers, some throwing on scrubs for duty.

"Tough day, Dr. Rutledge?" Keane asked.

William Rutledge, MD, yanked at his king-size underwear and looked up in surprise. "What brings you around here, Keane?" The shaggy hair that plastered his head was a mix of strawberry blond and strips of white. With the Nordic skin and auburn highlights, Dr. Rutledge's look suggested a Viking in control of a longship instead of just a doc in charge of a Level One trauma center.

"I was hoping to find out about a few recent cases," Keane said.

Rutledge tied his shoes as he panted. Even bending over challenged a man who looked seventy-five pounds overweight. "You mean those cases the mayor himself has taken an interest in?" Rutledge asked. "Funny, but I just got off the phone with his office about you."

"So, you're okay with me asking a couple of questions?"

"I've already talked with two APD forensics—a guy and a gal. She's a tox expert. Frankly, I'm kind of talked out on the subject. No offense, but you don't do police work for a living, do you, Keane? Leave this stuff to the pros."

33

"The rest of the foursome waiting for you at East Lake?"

"Golf's a fine sport, you ought to take it up. You need a life . . . or a woman. A man should choose one or the other. What the hell *do* you do out there in the boondocks, in that estate of yours?"

Keane didn't have a snappy answer, but he did have a practice par-three hole and a putting green on the grounds, but he made more use of his gym. A jock he wasn't, but he secretly hoped that he still looked the part, with his thick blond hair and square chin adding to his charade. Rutledge did have a point. "You're right," Keane said. "I need a life."

"Okay, what's up?" Rutledge asked. "I don't have much time."

Especially for me. "What did you find from the Piedmont Park patients?"

The head doc paused to think, then rattled off his list. Besides the priest, there was a blind African American who ran a newspaper-and-magazine stand on a corner across from the park, and a retired dentist, also black, who lived alone near the park. Each died after a lingering illness. The priest's parish included the neighborhood on the west side of the park. The latest was a John Doe found in the middle of the park. A white guy. He gave him forty-eight hours, at most.

"I know about the John Doe," Keane said. "He came into Emergency while I was down there. What did they all have in common?"

"I've reviewed all of their records. Three had ataxia, tremor, cranial-nerve palsies, seizures, bouts of hallucinations. Two showed patchy hair loss on the scalp and eyebrows. All of them showed peripheral nerve involvement, mainly on the soles of the feet. But the real kicker: all four developed major organ failure—for absolutely no apparent reason."

"And your diagnosis?"

Rutledge waited for two interns dressed in scrubs to pass by, and then he leaned forward and lowered his voice. "My best guess is thallium."

"Rat poison?" Keane asked, surprised.

Rutledge pressed a finger to his lips. "Don't know for certain. We've sent blood and urine samples out to the lab. Should have the first results in a few days."

"But why do you think it's *rat* poison?" Keane whispered back.

"It's been popular throughout history, hasn't it? Thallium sulfate's water-soluble. You can't smell or taste it. I saw what thallium can do during my residency. Had a patient die on me with the same symptoms as these guys. He was a line worker at an industrial site that used tons of thallium as a catalyst."

"Have you talked with APD about this?"

"I briefed a forensic over there, a gal by the name of Fowler. She's all over it. But I warned her that nothing was firm—at least not until I get lab results back. Last I heard, they had a suspect."

Oh, really? No one had told Keane. Fortunately, police headquarters was close by.

*   *   *

Keane studied the porcelain face of Suzanne Fowler as she plucked file folders from jumbled stacks on her desk. Behind her was a bookcase of textbooks and references scattered on the shelves like firewood. He'd been briefed about her by APD's Chief Dallas Walters—a quick session between the chief's phone calls. Keane took advantage of the meeting to tell the chief he'd appreciate being let in on developments as the case moved along.

"Our doors are always open to you, Dr. Keane," Chief Walters had said. "Come around more often."

When he'd asked the chief about Fowler, he learned that she'd been only recently hired by APD. The chief thought her no-nonsense manner made for the perfect go-between with forensics and the detective squad. And she was the only one in APD with a graduate degree in toxicology.

As Fowler stood to retrieve another file folder, Keane noted that she wore a beige pantsuit in addition to what seemed like a perpetual scowl.

He wondered if she was unhappy, either with his presence or her life. He glanced at her finger for a wedding band. There was none.

She tossed down a photo of a clean-cut kid with olive skin. "His name is Leon Ziad, a twenty-six-year-old chemistry grad student at Georgia Tech. He graduated from the University of Chicago. We learned from Chicago PD that six weeks after his girlfriend broke up with him, she was taken to the ER with a high fever and hallucinations. The doctors held her for a week, saving her life. The crime unit there discovered a small lab inside his apartment. He was extracting belladonna from nightshade berries."

"Not many know about belladonna," he said.

"It only takes a few berries to be fatal," she replied. "But they'd pulled in a real sleuth for the case. It turns out that this kid majored in history as an undergraduate. His specialty was Medieval Europe, a time when assassinations with belladonna were in their heyday. Along with this last psych report, that link put the finger on him. But they could never mount the evidence to connect him."

She shoved the report in his direction.

He pushed it back. "Not particularly interested right now."

"You should know all the facts."

"Let's say it's a long story." He'd read enough psychiatric reports to know they could be as subjective as a novel.

She ignored his comment and glanced down at her notes. "The shrink in Chicago said he has all the marks of a psychotic. He's admitted that he's been to Piedmont Park more than once. His dorm buddies say he's a loner, goes around acting weird, dressing strange. No one ever gets into his room."

"The questions on my mind would be how many hundreds of Georgia Tech students are loners, look weird, dress crazy, and have visited Piedmont Park. How did you come up with this Georgia Tech kid so quickly?"

"I started working with a new partner. A department veteran, Detective Sergeant Selsby. He volunteered to help out."

A bit of enthusiasm arose in her voice and eyes as she spoke about Selsby. "I have to give him the credit," she said. "Turns out, that kid's been on our watch list for the last year, since he arrived in Atlanta."

"So, you and he think this grad student is delivering belladonna again?"

"He would've switched to another poison for any number of reasons."

"Like thallium?" Keane asked.

"Possibly. Dr. Rutledge at Grady made me aware of that—based upon symptoms he's seen in the patients."

"Have you found traces of it in his dorm room? Or on his clothes?"

"Not yet. We're still analyzing fibers and swipes."

Not yet? He wondered if she'd keep on analyzing until she got a positive for thallium. Both she and Rutledge could be going down the path he saw time and again—a classic fault in logic. Come up with an hypothesis early on then search until you find evidence to support it. *Voila!*

She returned to her paper shuffling and appeared not to want him there, only pretending to be busy.

"Remember the case of the Russian spy a few years back?" he asked. "The guy in London who defected from Moscow. He claimed before he died that he was poisoned by the KGB."

"I remember the case vaguely, but I forget the details."

Keane recalled the picture of the man—the forlorn face, the ghostly look. All his critical organs failed over time. "It took him a month to die. The British doctors thought thallium poisoning was the culprit at first too, but it turned out to be a different kind of poison—a radioactive poison."

"I don't do left-field toxicology, Dr. Keane."

"I'm just trying to think out of the box."

"I only stay *inside* boxes and approved protocols. Absolute requirement in my specialty."

Chief Walters was right. She was all business. But something in her nervous look bothered him. He thanked her for her time and she responded with the only hint of a smile he'd seen out of her since they'd met.

*   *   *

That evening Keane walked toward the drawing room, a glass of Douro port in hand. He stopped by the chessboard resting on a mahogany hall table and glanced over the pieces. The game had been going on since the night he returned from Dream Valley Ranch. He agreed to let his teenage nemesis, Tucker Carlton from the swinging-bridge fiasco, take as much time as he wanted on every move.

Putting down his drink, he picked up the white bishop and carried it across the board. He sat down in a club chair and took another sip of port before texting the move to Tucker.

The cell phone rang.

"Dr. Damon Keane?" a rugged voice asked.

"Correct. Can I help you?"

"As a matter of fact, not at all sure you can. This is Detective Sergeant Crawford Selsby with APD. I've just been handed a multiple homicide. I'm told I should bring you in on it."

Holy crap!

"Put 135 York Avenue in your GPS," the detective ordered. "I'm inside the warehouse on the corner."

CHAPTER 8

In less than an hour Keane reached the Bluff, the neighborhood known for its outstanding efficiency in serving Atlanta's narcotics traffic. He pulled up behind a column of squad cars with their blue lights swirling. A patrolman escorted him inside an abandoned warehouse large enough to hold a football field.

Built like a linebacker and looking like he'd just lost the game, Sergeant Crawford Selsby stood at the door of a small room in the back corner. He inhabited a wrinkled tan suit at least two sizes too big. His unbuttoned shirt collar wilted beneath the knot of a loosened blue-and-gold tie with a coffee stain. After a quick handshake, he asked Keane to get prepared then opened the door to the room.

The stench of decaying flesh punched Keane in the face. Four bodies were propped up in a sitting positions with hands tied behind their backs and linked to steel bolts embedded in the concrete floor. Each faced another directly across from him beneath a single naked light bulb that hung from the ceiling. All four appeared to be Latinos in their twenties and thirties. Eyes bulged from the sockets of one victim, his teeth clenched and lips stretched tight. A dried mix of vomit and saliva coated his chin and neck. Another's face resembled melted wax, with ulcerations covering both cheeks. The others showed similar swollen lesions leaking pus.

Nausea struck Keane's gut at the very time he needed to think of something intelligent to say. "How long have they been dead?" The question sounded stupid as soon as he asked it.

Selsby stared at him before answering. The bags under his eyes sagged to his cheekbones. "That's why we have forensics."

"So, why did you call me in?"

"I'm totally surprised. I thought you'd be able to guess that when you saw the scene."

Nausea and a smart-ass. It wasn't shaping up to be a good evening.

Selsby reached inside his jacket and pulled out a ballpoint pen as he walked to one body and stooped. He pointed the pen's tip at the victim's face. "Each died while gagging on his own puke. Do you see as much as a drop of blood on anyone? None of them has a sign of a bullet or stab wound."

Like a student in anatomy class, Keane listened and watched.

"Look at this," Selsby said. He pointed to one victim's bound hands. While he gestured, Keane peered at a blurred purple tattoo just beneath Selsby's shirt collar—the image of an iron cross. Strange for a cop.

Selsby stood. "Apparently they were marched in here, probably with guns to their heads, and each forced to squat down by the U-bolts in the floor. Whoever did this wanted these guys to watch each other die. But there's no sign of the cause of death."

Too traumatized by what he'd confronted, Keane couldn't think rationally. An experienced homicide detective could cut through a god-awful scene like that, ignoring the foul odor and ghastly image of shriveled corpses. That was one of many hard-boiled differences between a professional cop and an amateur like himself. Selsby's gut feeling about him was right. Keane knew science, medicine, forensics. But he lacked the detective's instincts, the acquired skill to ignore a scene's shock and revulsion and to focus like a coiled snake on possible clues. Keane knew he had no business being there—getting himself involved was idiocy of the highest order.

Selsby took out his penlight. He stooped and pointed to a scrape on the floor—scuff marks on the concrete in the middle of the square of death. "These are recent. What do you make of them?"

"Truthfully?" Keane asked.

"I'm waiting."

"I haven't the slightest."

The detective turned to catch a phone call. "Be back in a minute," he mumbled over his shoulder as he shuffled away.

Keane paced behind the victims while an APD forensic flashed pictures from every angle. He imagined what must have occurred days before. At least two—maybe three or more—perpetrators had to be working together. They had dragged some kind of heavy device into the death square's center under the hanging light. But what was their motive? It couldn't have been robbery. Drugs? But why would they go to so much trouble carefully positioning each victim? What statement were they trying to make? Nothing in the scene made sense.

When Selsby returned, he tugged at Keane's sleeve to move him away so that the photographer could have clear shots. After they walked back to the door, Keane said, "I met the lady over in the lab who's working with you on the Piedmont Park cases."

"You mean the toxicologist?" Selsby asked.

"Yeah, Suzanne Fowler. She said that you put her on to a Georgia Tech chemistry student. Is he still a suspect?"

"I had to release the sonofabitch. Not enough evidence to hold him. I've got a tail on him though. We have a few bugs strategically planted, plus a tracker on his Kia."

He wondered if Selsby got a court order for that. Keane turned back to the victims. Something was strange about the single naked light bulb hanging from the ceiling on a frayed cord.

"I'd like to take a look at one more thing before we leave," Keane said.

"Don't take long. And be damned careful where you step inside my crime scene. I'll be checking my messages outside."

After Selsby departed, Keane searched the area and found a grimy but heavy-duty plastic bucket next to a wall. He brought it into the center of the square, turned it upside-down, and stepped up onto it to get a closer look. The bulb was a one-hundred-fifty-watt GE frosted white, but with a brownish hue. A yellow tint at the base of the glass bulb gradually turned into darker brown.

He rubbed a finger across the thin glass and examined his fingertip. Although dusty, nothing apparent had been deposited on the bulb's surface. But something had caused its weird appearance.

                        *   *   *

Later that evening Keane rested on a leather recliner in the honey-oak-paneled study. His four-year-old St. Bernard, a gift from his sister Margot, lay with his nose on the ottoman and flat against his master's feet. It was Wilbur's favorite posture and he relayed that message with a low growl every time Keane rustled his legs or wiggled his feet. There were times when Keane unwittingly allowed his legs to cramp up because he'd held them in the same position for so long, refusing to upset Wilbur.

Mr. J knocked then entered with a leash in his hand to take the dog outside before retiring for the night. A broad-shouldered man of fifty-six, Mr. J habitually dressed in a dark suit with a solid-silk necktie. Theodore Baxter Johnston III was a true Jeeves—the trusted assistant, butler, and confidante who managed a faithful staff of four. He had graduated from Brown with a civil engineering degree. Given his utter lack of enthusiasm for the major his dad had chosen for him, he dillydallied in a number of jobs as a personal assistant for a number of wealthy entrepreneurs and retired CEOs throughout New England. Keane eventually got word of him and his specialized talent and Mr. J accepted the generous offer to work for Keane 24/7. The only drawback in the job was that Atlanta wasn't Providence—"However you want to take that," Mr. J always said.

Keane pointed to a chair across from him. "I've been meaning to talk with you. Please, sit down."

"Something wrong, sir?"

"No, no. Not at all." Keane scooted to the chair's edge and clasped his hands around a knee, searching for a way to say it. "You remember that I've brought up my long-term plans a couple of times."

"I do, but I have to admit, I've never taken them too seriously. Is something brewing?"

"I'm talking with a realtor down in the Tahitian Islands."

"Yes, sir. A Mr. Roger Frazier, as I recall."

"The kids are of age now," Keane said.

"I know, but . . . well, it's really none of my business, sir."

"Please, go ahead," Keane said.

"I think a time may come when Andy and Nicole may need you. And the South Pacific seems . . . so distant."

Mr. J was right. There'd be times when he'd have to return, to check on his son and daughter. The West Coast was probably where they'd stay and develop careers. At least he hoped that Andy would have something resembling a career. Nicole would no doubt take off and flourish.

"I should've talked with you more about the possible move," Keane said. "How would you feel about that? Not for the entire year. Maybe for just eight or nine months each year."

"Sorry, sir, but I'm afraid I'm confined to the East. You know my sister in Pawtucket has not been doing well lately. I'm the only one she has."

"Don't begin making any plans right now. I'll go ahead and take Wilbur out for his walk. Let's chat some more in a few days."

A stroll around the garden gave Keane a chance to wrestle with his thoughts while Wilbur attacked a scrappy chipmunk. People were dropping, as the mayor had said, and for no apparent reason. Their organs failed, one by one, until they died. Could it be rat poison—thallium? Or a new emerging virus?

After the dog had done his business, Keane sauntered up to the study. There was a lot of speculation about what could be going on, but no hard evidence. The idea he'd expressed to Suzanne Fowler at her office haunted him. He rushed to his desk, where he flipped on the computer. He linked into the electronic journals of the Emory Library and entered all of the keywords he could think of into the search engine:

Ex-Russian spy Poisoning London

Eleven articles popped up. The principal author of five was a physician by the name of A. D. Becker at the University College of London Hospital.

Keane closed the lid on his laptop and punched "1" on his quick dial. "Please give Taylor a call, Mr. J. I'd like to prepare the jet for a trip to London, ASAP."

CHAPTER 9

Sidney Lanier's head was missing.

Jessie Wiley remembered from her Georgia history that Sidney Lanier was a native son and prominent Southerner who'd fought in the Civil War. His monument in Piedmont Park stood over seven feet, but in the distant past vandals saw fit to remove his granite head. She sat with a bag of fast food at a green metallic picnic table behind the monument, thinking about Damon Keane and what might be going on between them. She wondered how tight their bond was anyway. You could never be sure with him.

His spontaneous ways excited her. It was fun to mess with him, tease him when he didn't know it. Often the ribbing flew over his head like a bat at dusk. She had to admit he was in damned good shape for someone eight years her senior. His intelligence and wit had enticed her from the first time they'd met. At times she pondered whether he ever planned to actually ask her out—like on a *date*? He'd never come right out and *ask,* of course. That would be too pedestrian.

A variety of men had wandered into and out of her life. She'd come close to marriage once, to a handsome Marine she met at a sports-car rally in Charlotte. In the beginning she was blown away by him, but in the end, he was blown away by an IED somewhere in the Kunar Province. She plunged all out into her work and career that much more—a way of healing herself, if such wounds ever really healed. They did, but left with ragged scar tissue.

The entire discussion was moot. Keane was never going to get that serious about another woman. She never planned to push the issue, had to hold back, dammit. After working now and then with Keane for three years, she still had no idea what she meant to him. Maybe nothing. Maybe no-frigging-*nothing*.

She ripped open the miserable box containing a cheeseburger. When a man with stormy hair and flabby trousers ambled past her for the third time, she nodded in his direction. He stopped and eyed her, a cigarette sticking out from somewhere within his rumpled beard. She'd learned to ignore what a man might be thinking and to get on with business. She wasn't concerned about her safety and knew that Keane wouldn't be either. She'd told him about her combat training, but few were aware of the Mini Recon knife concealed in a sheath at the small of her back. Those who became aware included a first lieutenant when she served in Afghanistan—plus those who witnessed the court martial. The officer tried to rape her on patrol in the desert, outside Kabul. She slashed a gouge in his groin the length of his erect penis, but then had to endure the humiliation of the ugly court martial. Her self-defense plea won out, and he got the ol' bobtail—dishonorable discharge. She was always on the lookout for the son-of-a-bitch, a Georgia native.

Trying to act nonchalant she said, "Looks like some weather moving in."

"Moving in, moving out. Sort of works that way."

She yanked another wrapped cheeseburger out of the bag. "Don't know why I ordered two of these. Thought I was hungry, I suppose." She held up one burger in his direction.

He flipped his cigarette to the ground and grabbed the sandwich with a polite nod. After he'd gulped down half of it, he wiped his mouth on his sleeve and looked up. "Ain't seen you around here before."

"Haven't been here for years. I used to walk my dogs around the park on weekends."

"Watcha do for a living?" the stranger asked.

"Fly Apache attack helicopters." She smiled.

He stopped chewing.

The retort was usually a conversation stopper, so she didn't use it much. "Well, I used to when I was in the Army."

He began to chew again and then swallowed. "Why you hang around here?"

"Fresh air. What do you do?"

"Construction. Like you, I used to anyways. Nigh onto thirty-two year."

"Interesting. What kind of construction?"

He took another bite of the burger. "You name it, I did it. Sheet rock, plumbin', roofin', landscape. Did it all, by God."

"You worked in town?"

"All over the damn country! Tallahassee . . . Hattiesburg . . . Memphis. Spent a couple of year up north."

"Up north?"

"Boone County, Kentucky. Bossed a three-man crew. Made good money for those days, but I finally wore out. My knees first and then my lumbar. Old Arthur took over my joints last couple year. Drifted down here lookin' for easy."

She held out her hand. "I'm Jessie Wiley. Sorry, but I don't believe I caught yours."

He let her fingers hang in midair. "Didn't catch it 'cause I didn't toss it out."

"Okay . . . yes." She withdrew her hand and used it pull hair back from the side of her face. "I'm just here looking for information."

"Figured that when you started gabbing. Look, I don't do crank or crack or—"

"Not that kind of information."

"You dressed up all fancy and stuff. We don't get offered any shit less'n someone wants—pardon my French, ma'am. You a cop, right?"

She spread out her arms onto the top of the bench and leaned back. "Not even close."

He wiped his right hand on the side of his trousers and offered his hand. "Dorsey's the name."

"To tell you the truth, Mr. Dorsey, I'm looking—"

"Dorsey's my first name."

"Sorry, Dorsey. I'm working an assignment with the staff over at Grady. Their EMTs picked up an unidentified man here in the park three days ago. He's been in a coma ever since. I'm trying to help them find out who he is."

Dorsey mopped at his beard with the napkin and used the tip of his tongue to clean his teeth. "Heard he died." More cleaning with the fingernail of his pinky. "Trash Ben was a good man. Better than most who call this place home."

"Trash bin?" she asked.

"*Ben.* Trash Ben's his tag. We suppose he got into some kind of decayed shit in one of those garbage bins over on McCleary. Always told him to stay out of the stuff but he never paid no 'tention to me."

"Did you know his last name?"

"No need for last names in our little community. Not like we're gated, you know."

"What did you know about Ben?"

"If anything, he was a loner. A while back he was gone at nights. Said he was making good money as a watchman."

"Night watchman for a business?" she asked.

"A junkyard, if you call that a business. But it didn't last long."

"Could you tell me where he spent most of his time here?"

He pointed toward a wooded area surrounding a lake in the center of the park. "Follow me."

Dorsey struggled in the heat as he ambled down the walkway, occasionally stopping to wipe his brow with a ragged shirtsleeve. He waved at one of the regulars across the way who toted a green plastic bag slung over one shoulder. Three lone figures in shorts jogged along the oval running track beneath the background of the historic Piedmont Driving Club that stood on higher ground—elevated, haughty. Beyond it, dark clouds glided over Atlanta's towering skyline. A well-buffed couple on Rollerblades and sporting matching T-shirts skated briskly by. Printed on the front of his was *Nudism isn't about sex*, and on hers, *Get over it.*

When she and Dorsey came upon a park trashcan, he stopped and stuck a hand down inside and swished it around. He then pointed into the distance. "That bench over against the tree? He'd nap there from time to time. Often spent the night on it or under it."

Black wrought iron supported the wooden bench that could hold four people, but one bar ran through the middle. Made it tough to get a good night's sleep. Whoever slept on the bench would have to wrap one leg around the outside of the bar and curl the other over it. Otherwise, nothing out of the ordinary for a park bench. She peeked under it. A swath of duct tape dangled from the slats and remnants of a newspaper and an empty bottle of Bacardi rum lay in the dirt.

"Where did you say that garbage bin was?" she asked.

"Behind the apartment building on McCleary."

Fat drops of rain splattered the walkway. "Thanks for your help, Dorsey. It's been a pleasure." She held out her hand to shake.

He grabbed it and smiled. "Take care of yourself. Remember, we ain't promised tomorrow."

Jessie rushed back to the car just before a cloudburst struck. She opened the browser on her cell phone and found four salvage dealers and junkyards within a five-mile radius of Piedmont Park.

CHAPTER 10

The blaze of a rising sun greeted Keane's Gulfstream G550 as it flew out high over the Atlantic. At times Keane felt a smidge of guilt over the size of his carbon footprint—guilt over that plus his wealth, earned only in small part by his own sweat. The bulk of his fortune came from his dad in the postwar boom years of the fifties and sixties.

Damon Keane's grandfather, Richard Norman Keane—a God-fearing, evangelical Southern Baptist—had inherited ten thousand acres of premium grazing land and fruit orchards in the Shenandoah Valley. With the vision of a twentieth-century Columbus, Damon's father and his small lot of speculators developed the land into first-class real estate, including vacation retreats and private golf clubs. Although the land handed down was prime, the genes passed along were tainted. Keane's dad died at age forty-six from pancreatic cancer. His assets were just shy of a billion, all of which he left to his family.

The sun beamed through his window and Keane reached up and pulled down the shade. The jet continued winging across the Atlantic as he drifted off to sleep.

*   *   *

Keane sat deep within a plush high-back chair the next afternoon in the lobby of the Grosvenor Hotel in London's Hyde Park. On the far side of the lavish room, an Indonesian pianist played softly. An Arab man and a woman covered in a light-blue burka enjoyed tea on a sofa nearby. Seated across from Keane was Dr. Anderson Becker, a principal author of many of the articles he'd found in his computer search. Keane had reached Becker's office on the flight across and arranged to share high tea soon after he arrived.

"I'm somewhat familiar with your country," Keane began. "I spent four years at Cambridge."

"I was a graduate of the dear ol' place myself," Dr. Becker replied. "King's in '93. What about you?"

"St. John's, class of '90," Keane replied. "Studied physics."

"My word. We may have raced together 'round the Trinity clock at some point. Then you went on to medical school?"

"In the States, at Duke. Switching fields after Cambridge was more a matter of curiosity. My real passion was hard science."

"Interesting combination of degrees," Becker said. He smacked his lips and exhaled. "A fine English tea. Deep, rich aroma."

"I believe I'll go for the coffee," Keane murmured while he poured from a silver pot.

"Spoken like a true Colonist," Becker said with only a trace of a smile.

Neither spoke for a moment as Becker sat with his head resting back against the top of his chair. "Do you recognize the piano music?" he finally asked.

It seemed like some kind of cultural test. "I'd guess a piece along the lines of a French dinner party."

Becker set his cup back on the table between them and reached for a scone from the china tier. "Excellent! You know the piano well?"

"Only by accident, really. I had a twin sister who was a musical prodigy."

"A twin, huh? That has to be an intriguing relationship. Maybe challenging at times?"

Keane took a sip of his coffee. "She's gone."

"I'm sorry. She died recently?"

"Twenty-eight years ago. An accident." *Twenty-eight years come July the second.*

They sat in silence again until Keane spoke up. "We were fourteen and did everything together. Except for some reason I never got into piano. Her brain was wired differently. She could play by ear."

She had begun learning the piano at age six on a Baldwin Grand. Keane could still see their mom sitting on the bench beside her each evening as they grew up, listening to her run the scales while Keane lay on the floor nearby, reading books or playing rummy with older sister Margot.

"I'm sorry I got off on a tangent there," Keane said.

"But I was the one who brought up the piano. Tell me, Dr. Keane, how did you learn of my involvement in the Litvinenko incident?"

Keane finished a bite from a dry blueberry scone, lubricated with a pat of butter. He swallowed hard. "I try to do my—" He coughed into a napkin before he could get out *homework* and quickly took a gulp of coffee.

"A most remarkable case," Becker said, ignoring his visitor choking to death. "Happened back in 2006. Mr. Litvinenko was a former Russian intelligence officer who defected. He became a British citizen and too frequently, I'm afraid, openly criticized the Russian government. I was told Litvinenko was in the midst of investigating the death of a Russian journalist at the time he fell seriously ill. She was about to publish a series of articles criticizing Russian practices in Chechnya."

"As I recall," Keane said, "she met an untimely death as well."

"I think it's fair to call four gunshots to the head when she stepped out of an elevator untimely. I was told that a meeting was eventually arranged with Litvinenko at a sushi bar in the Millennium on Piccadilly. The meeting was supposed to be between Litvinenko and another former KGB agent, a chap whose name I don't remember. He found a way to spike Litvinenko's tea with radioactive polonium."

"And where might you acquire that?"

"You don't, I'm told. Not in the amount and purity needed to kill anyway. You need dedicated nuclear reactors, made available by a state or national effort. That's what it takes to make the required amount—even though it's less than a teaspoon."

"Powerful stuff."

"I call it the Mother of all poisons."

"How did Litvinenko present at the hospital?" Keane asked.

"He thought he had food poisoning when he arrived at the A & E the next morning. The staff found that his entire GI tract was inflamed, as if his insides were set afire. You could pull his hair out in clumps. All the symptoms were that of a thallium poisoning. The docs started him on large doses of Prussian blue to get him excreting as much of the poison as possible. Lab results took a while."

"And you found?"

"There was no possible way it could have been thallium. Not a trace of it was found in the lab work-up. The symptoms also looked like acute radiation exposure, but how could that be? Exposed to an intense beam of radiation, without even knowing about it?"

"I assume Vauxhall Cross was pushing for an answer."

"Indeed, MI6 was lurking over our shoulders. You must be familiar with their culture?"

"I've done work for them in the past," Keane said. "Fascinating group."

"We were forced to consider a radioactive substance at that point, maybe something secretly injected in him. We used the most sensitive radiation detectors we could get our hands on. Found nothing."

"Nothing?"

"We were stumped. But we kept on chasing the evidence," Becker said. "We had the good fortune to call on the scientists in Aldermaston, one of the key labs in our nuclear weapons establishment. They analyzed his blood and urine. The results were unbelievable. We'd been looking for the wrong type of radiation."

"Wrong type?"

"Litvinenko indeed had something emitting radiation throughout his body, but it was pure *alpha* radiation. Totally different from what you would normally think of as radiation, like gammas or x-rays."

Keane knew the physics. Alpha radiation couldn't travel more than an inch or two in air. A single sheet of paper could block it completely. It wasn't possible to detect it with ordinary instruments, like Geiger counters. On the other hand, gamma rays were the easiest of all to pick up with almost any type of detector. Like a butcher knife slicing through butter, gamma rays could penetrate organs, bones, and stonewalls. In air they could travel a football field or more.

"He was killed by polonium-210 lodged inside every organ and irradiating every cell of his body. Since it emits only alpha radiation, it's totally undetectable with any instrument *outside* his body. We didn't verify it until the day after he died, three weeks after he drank the polonium-laced tea."

"What happened with the suspect who laced his drink?"

"Russia would never turn him over."

Keane had gotten a heckuva lot more information than he'd planned. He thanked Becker for making himself available on short notice. "Would you be my guest at the Fat Duck for dinner this evening?"

"My Lord! You got a reservation?"

"I believe I can arrange it."

Becker tossed back his head and let out a spirited laugh.

"Perhaps my next trip," Keane said. He stood and shook hands. He'd been looking forward to a side trip to Berkshire and the Fat Duck's saddle of venison and mock-turtle soup—but he'd no desire to eat alone. When his taxi arrived at London City Airport, he met up with his pilots and downed a quick snack of fried cod and chips.

During the flight home, Keane called Dr. Bill Rutledge at Grady and left a voice message. Did they check the urine from any of the victims for radioactive isotopes? Not a standard clinical check by any means. He walked to the cockpit and stuck his head in to greet Taylor and

Roberto. The weather looked terrific for the rest of the flight, and a smooth ride was in the offing.

Taylor was an ex-navy pilot with the carved stone features of someone in charge. His tan gave away his favorite pastime on the golf course and his spare-time sailing. His copilot was Roberto, a youthful, small-framed guy with slick black hair that spilled over his forehead and grabbed his ears. Both men looked relaxed and confident at the controls of the Gulfstream.

"Could we make a slight change in the flight plan?" Keane asked.

"You're the boss," Taylor responded, with a wrinkled eyebrow that reminded Keane the flight plan had already been filed.

"I'd like to go on to Oregon to see my son." Phone calls and emails alone were never going to hack it. Face time was more valuable than Facebook.

"No problem," Taylor said. "I'll call in a mod to the plan as soon as we start talking to Gander Control near Labrador. We'll stop in Chicago to refuel. Your daughter's still in Portland, too?"

"Nope, she's in her sophomore year in California—Pomona College."

"Taking classes in the summer? The peach doesn't fall far from the tree, huh?"

Keane smiled and strolled back through the cabin. No, the fruit didn't fall far from the tree, at least not in Nicole's case. She had her mother's perky nose and slender frame, her fair skin, but she'd acquired her dad's love of learning and his relentless curiosity about the world.

And then there was Andy, a different matter altogether. He maintained above-average grades and showed aptitude. But then came the call from the Portland police during his junior year in high school. He'd been caught with another kid vandalizing a new Lexus in the Pearl District. He was put on probation for six months. Keane assumed he'd learned an important lesson. But the worst was the call from Keane's ex saying he'd been gone overnight. She finally found him wandering near the Vista Bridge, the site of eight suicides in the past year alone.

Although Andy had recently graduated from Portland's Catlin Gable High School, he was still "looking for himself," a phrase Keane could never comprehend. He didn't know how to deal with it. How could he explain Andy's guerrilla war with his family? But he had to face the truth. A coldness separated the two, no doubt. It was a chill—one that clung to their relationship like a heavy fog in winter.

After Keane kicked off his shoes, he lay down on the cabin couch and closed his eyes to the image of the city of Portland. It was always risky to surprise Kat, but if he phoned ahead, he knew what the response would be. He squeezed his forehead with his right hand. A gargantuan headache was coming on.

*   *   *

Jessie Wiley had faced combat in Afghanistan, but this was the first time she'd been threatened with disembowelment. The danger was real and imminent: a pair of drenched Rottweilers barked and growled as they scrambled behind a chain link fence in the downpour. Only three feet separated her from a close encounter of the worst kind. She'd arrived at the gate of Morrison's Auto Salvage with umbrella in hand. The owner ran the operation himself and had done so for twenty-six years. He had never used a night watchman, although he'd reconsider if she was "interested in the job."

After slopping through puddles and mud back to the car, she drove three miles to locate Midtown Auto Parts and Towing. A woman dressed in camouflage and with a thick scar on one cheek stuck her head out the guardhouse door. Above the bluster of the pelting rain, she shouted that she "didn't know nothing 'bout night watchmen." The woman studied Jessie from head to crotch. Then she turned her chin to the side and spat out a thin stream of tobacco juice.

Jessie next found Karl's Salvage Yard and Wrecker Service in sight of the tall condo buildings overlooking Piedmont Park. The deluge had slowed to a steady drizzle, and occasionally the sun flashed through the swift-moving clouds. Someone who looked like the owner emerged from his rusted trailer by the gate. His sculpted body, on the far side of middle age, glistened beneath a completely shaved head. Strapping biceps were decorated with sleeve tattoos celebrating some type of voodoo worship. Tattooed on the left side of his face and neck, a tribal devil's mask warmly welcomed everyone who greeted him.

"Looking for spare parts?" Karl asked with a soft sneer.

Jessie pushed her wet and matted hair back from her eyes. "Actually, I need a little information."

She smiled in an effort to relax his icy expression. It didn't work. She nodded toward the junkyard. "That's quite an inventory you got there."

The proud owner motioned with a sweep of his sizable arm toward his collection of junk. "Seven years' worth."

He strolled down the main path through the mechanical graveyard as Jessie followed. Red mud splattered her leather pumps as she pretended to be interested. Ancient wrecked cars lined the path like monuments to a sleazy past. A blue Pontiac choked by kudzu vines hid in the weeds with a shattered windshield and missing hood.

"Now, exactly what sort of information are you looking for?" he asked.

"I have an uncle I'm trying to find," she said. "He left his wife two years ago and she hasn't heard from him since. The last she knew, he worked in a downtown junkyard as a night watchman."

"Then you've come to the wrong place."

"How's that?"

"I don't do junk."

"Sorry?"

"I do treasures."

"Oh . . . I understand."

"Not sure you do. What you call junk, I might call antiques. Take a good look around at these trashed pickup trucks and rusted-out washing machines. They're testimonies to people's lives. Symbols of family struggles."

"Never thought of it that way."

"We don't stop to consider the meaning of what we see around us, do we? These treasures lie here, but they don't *lie* here. They tell us who we are. Or who we were. Our dreams, our failures."

Okay, Professor, but I'm soaked in mud up to my ass and I'm only here asking a simple question.

"You gotta picture of this guy?" he asked.

"Only as a much younger man. Wouldn't do much good now. His first name was Ben. But he used a host of aliases trying to escape alimony." She was surprised at how fast she could invent stories.

"Gets my dander up to think about all the drunks and dopers I've had as night watchmen. Who would want a job like this anyway? I remember a guy by the name of Ben from a year or so back. He guarded for me."

With a palm he buffed the top of his gleaming head, in thought. Then came an apparent flash of light. "Ben Thornton. I remember the name because I had cousins who were Thorntons. He was supposed to be a devout Catholic. Whenever he'd arrive late, he'd claim Mass went overtime. His problem was staying awake on the job. Found that out with a couple of spot checks, along with empty bottles of Early Times. Finally had to up and fire him."

Right on the money.

Damon Keane wasn't the only one who could play Sherlock.

CHAPTER 11

When the doorbell chimed those three hideous tones, Keane's stomach muscles stiffened as if a colossal hand from the past clutched his chest and squeezed. He'd driven to Englewood Heights from Portland International in a rented Lincoln Navigator.

Dressed in a white tennis skirt, Kat opened the door, her brunette hair tied back with a scarf. Sunglasses rested uneasily above her forehead. "*Jesus*, Damon, you could've called."

Of course he could have called and politely asked to drop in. She would've invented some rickety excuse, or Andy would have had some lame reason not to be there.

"You always loved surprises," he said with a mock smile.

"You wasted your time and jet fuel. Andy isn't here."

She'd set up for battle, just like old times. He gritted his teeth and returned her glare. "I suppose he'll come home at some point today?"

"He's out with friends. Lord only knows when he'll be home. We have *lives*, you know." She hung onto the doorknob as her emerald eyes wandered up and down the street.

He stuffed his hands into his pockets and glanced over her shoulder into the house to see if he could spot any telltale signs.

She lowered her head and pursed her lips. "Come on in," a command given in the spirit of an SS sturmfuhrer. Backing up, she opened the front door wider and avoided his eyes as he entered.

As he followed her to the back patio, he inspected the sway of her tiny pleated skirt. Old thoughts. The divorce had been finalized two years before in the spring. Kat had first brought up the idea of a separation. He argued passionately with her in the beginning and talked at length about the impact on Nicole and Andy. He couldn't eat or sleep for three weeks. He began his own concocted medication of Zoloft and Scotch in an attempt to heal himself. That effort was given up when the mayor called him into the Reinauer case. In the end, the settlement provided a home for Kat in her native state of Oregon. Keane felt that he at least owed her that. Within three months—87 days—she remarried.

On the patio he shoved a lawn chair into the shade of the roof overhang. She slid into a chaise lounge in the sun and pulled the designer shades down onto the ridge of her nose. He had avoided rehearsing—couldn't stomach the thought—and wasn't sure where to start.

"Have you been okay?" she asked. "You don't look well."

That was unexpected. She'd spoken first. A good omen. "On the other hand, you still look great."

She waved a dismissive hand.

"Like a model out of *Vogue*."

"Give it up, Damon. We're not going there."

"I wasn't headed anywhere. What do you think I am?"

"With twenty-three years of you behind me, I know who and what you are. The question is, have you grown up?" She probed her fingernails.

"You mean, have I finally gotten a regular job?"

He'd often asked himself why they'd drifted apart after so many years together. There was no one to blame but himself. He was starting med school at Duke when they wed—he was twenty-two, and she, the older woman at twenty-six. He'd met her a year before they traded vows. She was assertive, smart, an administrative assistant to the Dean of Arts and Sciences.

Eventually, with Keane's unique educational combo, his consulting work and travels began in earnest. He wasn't looking for the income. His inheritance had taken care of that. What he needed was cerebral challenge—apparently more than he needed family, a lesson learned much too late in life.

"I assume that tall Georgia peach shares your bed by now?" she asked.

"Georgia peaches are sweet, juicy. Tingle the tongue."

"So now you screw fruit. How quaint. What other thrills do you and your Southern buddies enjoy?"

"You mean, other than rattlesnake roundups and guzzling moonshine?"

"Shut up, Damon. You're not funny."

He scooted his chair over to get an inch more shade. "Have you heard from Nicole?"

"Not often enough. She's loving Pomona though."

"I knew she would," he said.

"Of course. She acts like you so much sometimes I want to smack her. I guess you'll be dropping in on her while you're out here?"

"Would you go with me?"

She lifted her sunglasses with a finger and stared back at him from beneath them. "Share a meal with both of you and chat about DNA or the Hubble telescope? I'd rather—"

"How's Andy?" he asked. *Keep quiet about our daughter. I've had enough.*

"He loves his new Nissan."

"His Nissan?"

"Maybe you forgot since you missed his birthday."

"How many times do I need to apologize for that?" he asked. "I did make his graduation."

"That's where his current problems began. You told him he should see the world. That this summer was the best chance for the rest of his life to do that."

"Certainly. To trot the globe discovering people and places with nothing pressuring him. I told him I'd fly him wherever for the summer. He could volunteer for aiding hunger victims in Kenya or—"

"He doesn't want your bribes, Damon. And Kenya already has plenty of missionaries, thank you. Paul said he's had trouble trying to talk to Andy about college since you were here."

"Paul's not his father."

"Paul is *here,* dammit."

Darling Paul owned a ball-bearing-distribution company on the outskirts of Portland. Conversations with Paul had always been interesting. He really knew TV reality shows and was a virtual genius when it came to ball bearings.

"I did my best to bring him into the conversation," Keane said, "but he ignored me."

"That's bullshit—and you know it. Paul told me you wouldn't give him the time of day."

"The graduation was all about our son, Kat. I hadn't seen Andy for three months."

"That's right. Three lousy months. Do you hear yourself?" She jerked her sunglasses from her head and tossed them onto the table. "Now he's thinking of becoming a monk."

"What's *that* all about?" Andy had never in his life shown the slightest interest in religion.

"He's planning on visiting a Buddhist monastery. To check it out."

"He's going to Tibet?"

"Damon, did you learn anything in your ten years of college? Or was it twenty? He's going to California. I wish it was Tibet."

She shot up from her chair and paraded inside. Typical ending to their chats.

He sat stroking his head with both hands and pondering how things might have been. After a few minutes, he rang Andy on his cell but got only his voice mail: "Hi . . . just thinking of you. Hope you're doing well. Give me a call."

He walked back through the house and out the front door, closing it gently.

*   *   *

As Oregon's snow-capped Mt. Hood retreated from view, Keane sat at his desk by the jet's window. Why hadn't he stayed in Portland to wait for another day to see his son? Why was he in such a damned hurry to leave? In one way, Keane was like Andy—he sought something undefined. Although he had the wherewithal to do as he pleased, he only meandered toward some kind of fuzzy horizon.

Using the jet's special-service band, he made a call to Bill Rutledge at Grady Memorial. "I picked up a key clue in London, Bill."

"Why would the damn Brits have any special insight?" Rutledge replied. "You're always looking for excuses to fly that jet of yours. Did you take a couple of women with you? Getting in on a twosome and into the Mile High Club. Now that's living!"

"No one I'd tell you about. Do you remember the Russian spy who defected to London—the guy who was poisoned a few years back?"

"No and I don't have time for a history lesson."

"I mentioned it to Suzanne Fowler over at APD. His tea was spiked with a radiation poison—polonium."

"With *what*?"

"Polonium-210. It's radioactive but only emits a special type of radiation. You can't detect it with typical instruments."

He could sense Rutledge's exasperation from the pace of his breathing into the phone.

"Can you tell me exactly what the hell you're suggesting, Keane?"

"It's simple. Collect more urine specimens from the priest—"

"The lab's already got his piss, looking for thallium and whatever else they can find."

"Have it analyzed for polonium, Bill. They can do it at the CDC labs. Do it today."

"I'm not going to add any more burden to the CDC labs on this, Keane. They've got enough to do. And I don't want to look like a fool when they take this extra effort and show up with nothing. I've played that game too many times."

"You've got to do it. I'm betting it will make you look like a genius."

"Or a damned fool. I'm not putting my reputation on the line for this just because some Brit—"

"I'm staking my reputation on it, Bill. Do it."

Rutledge paused. "You'd better be right on this one."

"One more thing," Keane said. "I need to talk with Father O'Shannon as soon as he's able to speak."

"That's not going to be possible."

"What isn't possible?"

"Talking with the priest."

He paused to gather the right words, to make certain that Rutledge understood he wasn't giving in on this one. The pig-headed fool was too stubborn. It was time to let him know that he'd had enough. "Do I need to go to Shropshire and make the request to his face?"

"You can go to the Pope and make your damned appeal for all I care. Father O'Shannon was pronounced dead six hours ago. He never woke up from his coma."

Keane held the phone to his shoulder and exhaled. He was an ass for not asking about the priest before he waded in. "What about that John Doe, the vagrant from the park?"

"Hanging on, but not responding to his drug regimen. Look, Keane, I got a call today from Emory Midtown. They have a patient dying with the same symptoms—the first female. Her prognosis is downhill and quick. My counterpart at Emory didn't know what we were facing until he learned about it in grand rounds."

"Latino or black?" Keane asked.

"She's white and in her fifties. A receptionist at a rental storage facility."

"What kind of motive would there be on that one? You have a name for the lady?"

Rutledge paused for a moment. "Fergusson . . . Kay Lynn Fergusson. Lives in Midtown with her mother."

With everything moving so fast, he wasn't sure Rutledge got the big picture. "Okay, collect urine from her as well as the John Doe. Have the coroner get chunks of kidney and liver from the priest at autopsy. And get all this over to CDC. I think we're finally nailing this down."

"I'll see what I can do."

"One more thing," Keane said. "Tell everyone to be careful how they handle the urine and the autopsy tissue. Treat each victim as a radiation hazard to the staff."

*   *   *

When Keane's jet landed at Peachtree-DeKalb on the outskirts of Atlanta, he was met inside the terminal by Jessie Wiley. He kept walking as she strode beside him.

"How did it go in the park?" he asked.

"Very Interesting day," she replied, keeping up with his pace. She told of learning about "Trash Ben" from one of the regulars and how she narrowed the name down to a "Ben Thornton," a Catholic and likely connection with the priest.

"You did all that in a day?" he asked.

"I fly choppers fast, too."

While they stood by his parked car, he spoke about the possible new victim Rutledge had told him about. "She's on a ventilator at Emory Midtown. Stay away from the hospital, but see what you can find out.

I'm told she lived with her mother in Midtown. Vinny can find an address for you."

CHAPTER 12

Jessie sat on the flowered sofa, holding onto the plastic frame of the five-by-seven photo of Kay Lynn Fergusson, the victim still drifting in and out of consciousness in the ICU at Emory's Midtown Hospital. Jessie had located Mrs. Lily Fergusson's home through Vinny Carruthers, the IT genius and human search engine. She'd met Vinny at his place once before. He made his way around his Virginia Highlands apartment and his neighborhood in his high-tech iBot wheelchair, thanks to a generous donation from his number-one client, Dr. Damon Keane.

Sitting by Jessie's side, Mrs. Fergusson sorted through old photos to share on the coffee table while occasionally blotting her eyes with a crumpled hanky. After a few minutes of conversation, Jessie realized that she was devastated over her daughter's plight and had no other family in town. She was eager to talk with anyone who stopped by.

The pictures spread across the table showed a woman with features resembling her mother's, a plain face with hair pulled back behind protruding ears. Over coffee, Jessie learned that Kay Lynn had been married, but her husband had died from a rare kidney tumor six years before. After that, she moved in with her mother and began working full-time at the storage facility.

"How old is she, Mrs. Fergusson?" Jessie was careful to use the present tense.

"Kay Lynn's fifty-two. Beautiful girl, as you can see."

"May I ask a personal question?"

"Of course," Mrs. Fergusson replied.

"Is she Catholic?"

"Oh, my gosh, no! My husband would dig himself out of the grave if she ever converted to that religion. She always wanted to be a model, though. Her dad wasn't real fond of that either. In high school she worked one summer for Neiman Marcus, modeling fall fashions."

"She grew up in the Highlands?"

"We raised her there. My only child. All of this has come on so suddenly. She couldn't eat and was always nauseated." Mrs. Fergusson wiped at her eyes again.

"Did she spend much time at Piedmont Park?"

"Well, she went there for a concert a year or two ago. I suppose I could find out if that's important."

"Not necessary. When was she taken to the hospital?" Jessie asked.

"One week ago tomorrow." Mrs. Fergusson paused and lowered her head. "I would be at her bedside now, but . . ."

"I know this hurts, Mrs. Fergusson."

"I'm afraid you don't know the half of it."

"What do you mean?"

"Seven vases of fresh flowers were delivered to her room. All sent in by well-wishers. But yesterday some . . ." She raised a tissue to her nose. "Some beast poured turpentine into each vase. Killed all the flowers. Every last one."

Jessie rested a hand on her shoulder and kept it there as she gently probed about other family members, friends, hobbies, travel. "Could you tell me about her job at the storage facility?"

"She worked the office alone. Often someone would bring in a truck full of furniture or odds and ends to store. She signed up new renters and occasionally collected the rent money. Brad Jennings owns the place. He's an older man, pushing seventy. I can tell you he's shattered by all this, too."

"Had he hired any new people recently?"

"Kay Lynn never mentioned it. We often talk about each other's day when she comes home. You'd best speak to Mr. Jennings about those matters."

"In the last few weeks, did she mention any new customers? Anyone strange coming to the office?"

Mrs. Fergusson thought about the question for a moment. "Kay Lynn did mention something funny," she finally blurted. "But it was only a cute story. It turned out to be an old acquaintance, that's all."

Jessie smiled. "I was thinking more along the lines of someone acting strange or different. New employees, new maintenance workers—"

"He was an air conditioning repairman," Mrs. Fergusson interrupted.

"Pardon?"

"The old acquaintance I mentioned. He showed up one afternoon and told Kay Lynn that Mr. Jennings had called him in for maintenance on the A/C. He was a polite gentleman, and she had no idea who he was at first."

"They talked for a while?"

"Not really. As I recall, Kay Lynn said he went straight to work, bringing his tools in from the van. She thought she recognized him right away, even though he had on a cap that was too big and wore tinted glasses. Then it suddenly occurred to her—that guy was an old classmate from Highlands High! The one who always had a crush on her. Now that was over twenty years ago."

Jessie smiled. "I think we all remember old boyfriends."

"Oh, no, that certainly wasn't the case. He tried back in those days to ask her out, to the prom and things like that. He kept badgering her for two years. He was like what you might call a stalker. Kay Lynn had a terrible time avoiding him. It's a horrible thing to say now, but it was true."

"Do you recall his name?"

"Oh, goodness me, yes. The Thornton kid. Could never remember his first name."

Jessie leaned forward and lightly touched Mrs. Fergusson on the forearm. "You said his name was Thornton. Did you know him?"

"Honestly, not so much. It was a tragedy what happened when he was in middle school."

She then recounted the murder of Matilda Thornton in the early eighties, an event that her generation in Midtown would always remember. Mrs. Thornton was strangled with a lamp cord during a gang rape. The number of attackers had varied in the neighborhood stories over the years, but there were as many as seven, a mix of young blacks and Mexicans. The number floated in the telling because the rapists were never brought to trial. The exception was one black man, acquitted when no semen tests could link him with the crime. The whole affair had always been a source of quiet anger within the small community. "The police never solved that brutal crime."

Jessie asked Mrs. Fergusson if she had known any motive for the attack.

"Hardly one that would justify that kind of atrocity," she replied. "Rumor had it that her husband was a head honcho in the KKK. I don't know how true, but I vaguely remember the defense exhibiting a hooded gown."

Evidently, both the victim's husband and son witnessed the rape and murder. The son would have been thirteen at the time.

"Do you recall the dad's name?"

"Heavens, yes. It was Benjamin. I couldn't forget that, even after all these years."

Jessie's mouth opened wide.

"I'm sorry, Miss Wiley. Did I say something wrong?"

"No, not at all." Then in a flash of inspiration, Jessie asked, "Would you happen to have Kay Lynn's high school yearbook?"

Although she was certain Kay Lynn had one, Mrs. Fergusson wasn't confident she could put her hands on it quickly. Jessie assured her that she had the time and accepted a third cup of coffee while Mrs. Fergusson searched her daughter's room.

Jessie had taken her last sip when Mrs. Fergusson returned with wet eyes and clasping a large book with a blue cover closely to her chest. She opened the well-worn book and scanned through it until she found the picture and proudly rested an index finger on it. Under it was the name "Kay Lynn Fergusson" and beneath her name were her activities:

Majorette, III, IV; Secretary, Starling Club, III;
Helvetia Honor Society, III, IV.

Jessie flipped through the book, glancing at the rows of confident, smiling teenagers. She slowed at the T's, stopping when she got to:

Felix H. Thornton
Football, I; Wrestling, III, IV;
Chemistry Club, IV.

The picture revealed a skinny boy staring straight into the camera as if ready to take on the world. Jessie pointed to the picture. "Is this the Thornton boy you were talking about?" She handed her the book.

Mrs. Fergusson tilted her head and studied it. Then she grinned. "Of course. That's him—Felix Thornton. What a horrible tragedy that family endured, Miss Wiley. Simply horrible."

CHAPTER 13

"Dr. Rutledge, I presume," Keane bellowed, when he strolled onto the golf range at East Lake Country Club with all the panache of someone who actually belonged. It took an hour and four phone calls that morning to track down the head of Grady's Emergency Department.

"You can give a man a heart attack sneaking up on him like that, Keane. How the hell did you get on the range?"

"Charm, my good doctor. Unabashed charm. You wouldn't know much about that, would you?"

Rutledge raked a ball through the grass with his five iron, carefully aligned his shot, and then hit a slice far off to the right. "I suppose you're here for a status report."

"Only if you're not too busy with your . . . *work*?"

Rutledge reached for another ball and paused to look back at him. "That John Doe from the park. He died yesterday. There was nothing we could do for him. All his organs had failed."

Keane paused. He remembered when the guy was brought into Grady's ER. "As I recall, he had a burn or some kind of lesion on his rear end when he was first brought in."

"And others on his legs and back. We never really got much of a handle on those. The path guys are still looking at it."

"Do you know how old he was?" Keane asked.

Rutledge stopped his waggle and looked at him. "What I remember from the condition of his teeth and hair, he must have been around seventy-five. Maybe eighty." He got back into his stance.

"I remember you telling me that the only thing on him was a chain around his neck."

Rutledge lowered his head to think for a moment. "You've got a good memory."

"Only trivia, for some odd reason. Genetic perhaps. My sister was like that too."

Rutledge hooked a shot far to his left and quickly turned to slam his five iron into his Callaway bag. He yanked out a pitching wedge.

"By the way, was there a cross on the chain?" Keane asked. "I mean, did it have a medallion or charm on it?"

Rutledge stuck out his lower lip and brought a hand up behind his head to scratch and think. "A cross might've hung from it, now that you mention it."

"Was Jesus on the cross?"

"*Jesus Christ*, Keane."

"Exactly who I'm talking about!"

"I can't believe you sometimes. How the hell should I remember that?"

"Because you're very bright. Think about it for me."

Rutledge stared at the ground for a moment before lifting his head. "The charm looked like a plain cross when you first glanced at it. But maybe it did have a crucifix. Had an old gold color, worn black over time. Might've been a talisman for the old man."

*   *   *

Whispering parishioners milled about the vestibule of Our Mother of Mercy Catholic Church. Keane found a hardback chair by Father Calabrese's office door and waited. When the priest completed his duties, he moved toward his office. Keane quickly stood and approached him, expressing his sympathies about Father O'Shannon's death.

Calabrese only nodded politely. His shoulders showed the weariness of another grueling day.

"I won't keep you," Keane said. "I have a name for you. A family name. It may have some connection with the Father's death."

"So foul play is definitely suspected?" Calabrese asked.

"At least until it can be ruled out." He pretended to be working under APD orders.

The priest sat by the wall outside his office and patted the chair beside him.

Keane sat and leaned toward him. "How about Thornton? Benjamin Thornton?"

Father Calabrese planted his elbows on the arms of the chair and rested his chin on his hands. "Thornton? I don't know a Thornton family. At least not one that's currently active on the rolls. I do know a Benjamin. A Benjamin Donnelly. He's a banker downtown and a faithful parishioner."

"I'm looking for a Thornton."

"I know another gentleman by the name of Ben, but honestly, his last name escapes me."

"Is he a regular?"

"I wouldn't say *regular*."

Look, Father, I need a little help here. "Would you say he—"

"Ben comes from a lower social status in the church."

"Ben is poor?"

"He's somewhat of a vagrant, you might say. He's always alone whenever I see him."

"Do you recall the last time you saw him?"

Father Calabrese glanced at the far wall for a moment then shook his head. "I don't remember. It's been a few weeks at least."

A couple with an infant in the arms of its dad waited nearby to get the priest's attention. Keane expressed his sympathies again and thanked Calabrese for his patience.

When he passed by the last pew on his way out, a woman under a black floppy-brimmed hat lifted her head and smiled. He did a double take.

Jessie Wiley brought an index finger to her lips to shush him. "We need to talk," she whispered. "Sit down." She scooted over to make room as he dropped into the pew beside her.

"Where did—how did you track me here?"

"Take that silly look off your face and listen up. You need to hear about my visit with the Fergusson lady."

An older man meditating several pews ahead turned his head in their direction. She lowered her voice. "Lily Fergusson was distraught, Damon. You can imagine, her only daughter dying in an ICU with the doctors totally mystified."

Keane thought about his own Nicole and how he'd react if she were trapped in the sterile cage of an ICU while her life sank into oblivion.

"But guess what I found out from Mrs. Fergusson?" Jessie asked. "There was a Thornton in her daughter's high school graduating class. A guy by the name of Felix. His dad was Benjamin. His mom was raped and murdered by a gang of blacks and Latinos. He'd have plenty of reasons to grow up with one helluva chip on his shoulder."

"And his dad would be Ben Thornton—the homeless guy from the park?"

"The last piece in the puzzle."

Felix Thornton was now connected to three victims directly: Kay Lynn Fergusson; the dead park vagrant, who turned out to be Felix Thornton's own father; and Father O'Shannon, the dead priest from the church where Felix grew up.

When Keane returned to his car, he had two phone messages. The first was from the real estate agent in Tahiti—he ignored it. The second came from Detective Selsby, asking to meet the following morning. Keane reached Selsby's cell phone on the first ring.

"Let's get together after the news conference," Selsby said.

"News conference?"

"Tomorrow morning at eight in the courthouse. The chief's briefing reporters on the warehouse massacre."

Keane held the phone away and shook his head. *For crying out . . .* "I really need to be kept in the loop on these things."

"Sorry. I meant to call you yesterday," Selsby replied in a matter-of-fact tone. "I've been busy working on wrapping things up."

Wrapping things up?

CHAPTER 14

Keane slipped into a seat in the back row of APD's briefing room just before the press conference began. He recognized TV newscasters seated in front from three local channels and a reporter from the *Journal-Constitution.* No sign of Detective Selsby. The mayor entered from a side door, followed by Chief of Police Dallas Walters. The two were the tallest in the room and presented an imposing air behind the podium. Just as the mayor stepped to the microphones, Selsby took a seat beside Keane and nodded without speaking.

Mayor Stillwell gave only a few words of introduction about the bodies found in the back room of an abandoned warehouse at York Avenue on the west side. He turned the podium over to Chief Walters. As the lights from the TV cameras lit up his face, the chief began by praising his police force for the grisly discovery in such a remote and decaying area of the city. He gave the approximate ages of the victims and described in vivid detail how they were found, adding that there were no obvious injuries, no gunshot or stab wounds. They were apparently day laborers, picked up and brought to the crime scene with the expectation of work. No relatives could be notified because none had ID. All were assumed to be illegals. When the chief opened the session for questions, the *Journal-Constitution* reporter stood. "Did the victims show any signs of drugs or poison? Anything?" she asked.

"I'll repeat what I said before—there were no obvious injuries. All four bodies are in the coroner's hands. We'll wait to see what he finds."

A Channel Six reporter stood next. He stretched out his arms and shrugged for dramatic effect. "Chief Walters, can you understand how unbelievable all this sounds?"

The chief skipped the question and pointed to a reporter for the *Atlanta Voice,* who was waving her hand from the back of the room. "I understand there were other deaths with a similar MO. Have those cases been investigated? If so, what have you learned from them?"

"We haven't had any other case like this one."

The chief was technically correct, Keane thought. The other deaths were separate crimes. But one thing similar among them all—each died in agony with absolutely no visible signs of murder.

The reporter shouted back, "But emergency department staff at Grady said they've had similar isolated cases."

"Again," the chief said, "there've been none that I am aware of like this horrible murder spree. Now I want to thank all of you for coming out this morning. We have nothing more to say at this time. I want to remind anyone who may have knowledge of this terrible crime, please call the Atlanta Police Department at 404-555-7777."

After the press briefing, Selsby motioned with a head jerk for Keane to follow him. When they were outside of the room, Selsby leaned against a wall in a far corner, away from the hubbub of reporters. "Whaddya think about what you just heard?"

"A lot was left out. The chief didn't mention the other deaths."

"Drug warfare," Selsby said.

"Beg your pardon?"

"Narco shit. That's what it was all about in the warehouse."

Keane shot back a puzzled look. "Strange way to fight a war."

Selsby shook his head as if Keane were too naïve, a kid in school. "These scumbags don't have any rules on killing. The more brutally they kill, the bigger their balls look to their rivals."

"And you've learned these tidbits because . . . ?"

"There's no knowledge like field knowledge."

"You mean intuition."

"No, dammit. You gotta be observant in my line of work. Rookies just try to think and scratch their asses. I observe."

"And what did you see?" Keane asked.

"Spider webs."

"I don't follow."

"Three men had spider webs tattooed on the back of their hands. Jomi—gang brothers. Locals who deal in Special K."

"So, as far as you're concerned," Keane said, "the warehouse case bears has no relationship to any of the others."

"I'm saying I don't know how they died any more than you do. But the perps had to be in the narc trade. Or paid off by narcs. I don't care what symptoms those guys tied to the floor had. That's narco warfare, plain and simple."

Keane pondered the comment. "No knowledge like field knowledge?"

"You got it."

"How you going to go after it?" Keane asked.

"I'm recommending the narc squad take the case." He dropped his voice to a whisper and nodded toward Chief Dallas Walters trotting down the staircase. "My report's on his desk."

Selsby was off and running.

Keane checked his phone messages. He'd received a text marked "STAT" from Dr. Rutledge at Grady.

*   *   *

Keane entered the sprawling office on the fifth floor at Grady Memorial. The office loomed colossal. The framed certificates on the Brazilian cherry–paneled walls suggested an esteemed occupant, someone who deserved whatever authority was granted him.

Dr. William Rutledge sat frowning in his white lab coat, worn in the style of the black robe of a high court judge. It was fitting. Sunlight from the shuttered windows cast broad stripes across the imposing desk, bare except for a picture of a sizable group of loyal staff and residents posing at Grady's main entrance and squinting into the Georgia sun.

"The next time you have a big-ass hunch," Rutledge growled, "would you do me a favor? Keep it to yourself."

"What are you talking about?"

"We got the preliminary analyses back from the CDC," Rutledge replied. "Absolutely zilch. I don't know why you wanted to send us chasing a wild goose."

"Zilch?"

"Nada. There's no polonium-210 or polonium-other-shit. In *no* victim did they find any kind of radiation. And I put my reputation on the line for you on this one, Keane."

"What about thallium?"

"No thallium. No poisons."

"They analyzed for biologics?"

"They're the CDC, for gods sake! Of course. They cultured the urine and blood samples and found nothing. No bacteria, no virus. Let me summarize their report for you, since I know you're a slow learner. We're no damn further along in this investigation than the minute you walked into it. We're back to square one."

Keane stared out the office window overlooking Atlanta's skyline. He'd never seen Rutledge erupt like that. Something deeper was bothering him. Neither could he believe that nothing was panning out. Too many people were dying without one hint of a cause. But if Rutledge had all the facts, how could Keane argue?

He himself had made the same error in logic that both Rutledge and Suzanne Fowler had made with thallium. They'd searched for data only to support their preconceived notions, blinding themselves to the facts. But now, Selsby had made him look like a fool and Rutledge had lowered his image to stupid. An amateur one-man think tank, he'd never had any intention of getting so frigging involved in police work. Why did he pretend to be some kind of genius who could solve any intellectual puzzle brought to him?

"Look, Keane, we have to let the cops do what cops do best. I've worked with forensics a helluva lot myself over the years. I wanted to let you know where we stand before giving you the rest of the news." Rutledge paused and rubbed the back of his head. "I just left the ER before you came in. We've got another victim. Christ Almighty, he's only a kid who was being treated over at Emory Midtown. Started going downhill quickly, so they transferred him to us. He lived in the Piedmont Park neighborhood in a foster home."

Keane recoiled. Some of the kids sent to Dream Valley lived in foster homes within a stone's throw of Piedmont Park. "You have a name?"

"Davenworth. Davenport, maybe. I can't remember."

The name *Davenport* knocked the wind out of him. He knew a Davenport kid. He quickly thanked Rutledge for the info and rushed out of the office, heading for the ICU. He used the stairs instead of the elevator.

CHAPTER 15

When Keane arrived at the ICU waiting area, he immediately spotted familiar faces: the foster parents of twelve- year-old Ronnie, who was Tucker Carlton's best friend at Dream Valley Ranch. Ronnie had been on the infamous swinging bridge, one of the group following Tucker— Keane's over-the-phone chess opponent.

He knew Ronnie to be a frail kid, raised by a single mother. Georgia's Children and Family Services took almost two years to recognize that an uncle had sexually abused him since the age of six. They found a foster home for him near Piedmont Park.

Ronnie's foster parents told Keane that when Ronnie was brought to Grady he was suffering from total lethargy along with relentless diarrhea and pain in his arms and legs. Even more frightening was the sudden reddening of his hands. They even swelled and blistered.

"May I see him?" Keane asked.

The mother led Keane into the unit where Ronnie lay. He wasn't greeted by the boy he'd known, but by the ghostly image of a boy lying pale and limp, a kid feeding electrical pulses into a rack of monitors. A life that had become digits on display. An endotrachial tube snaked into his windpipe and a feeding tube was crammed through his nasal passage into his stomach.

Keane stood by his bed, watching the little chest heave up and down and gasp for air. The boy's eyes followed Keane's, and a faint smile lifted the corners of his mouth. His eyes then shifted to his foster mom, who stood on the opposite side with both hands pressed against his.

Keane stepped back to make room for a nurse who entered to replace an IV line into the boy's tiny vein. She opened the dressing on the other arm, revealing blistered humps of flesh oozing a green fluid. Keane placed a hand on Ronnie's shoulder, squeezed it gently, and tried his best to give a reassuring smile while tears welled up in his own eyes.

Ronnie held tightly to the woman he knew as Mom, his eyes fixed on hers. Keane said good-bye and promised to return when Ronnie was up to it. When he moved for the door, she gently pried Ronnie's fingers away from her hand. His lips mouthed, "Don't go, Mommy."

The boy had no way of knowing what had happened to him. He wasn't even old enough to have an inkling that he wasn't going to make it.

On his way to the elevator, Keane stopped in a men's room marked *Staff Only* and closed the door behind him, locking it. He splashed cold water onto his face then pounded with both fists again and again and again on the porcelain sink.

A riveting knock interrupted him. "Hey! Are you okay in there?"

Keane opened the door and walked down the hallway to a bench by a window. Sitting down, he called for Mr. J and told him to get in touch with Roger Frazier, the real estate agent in Tahiti. The deal was off for now.

*   *   *

Vinny Carruthers greeted Keane with his habitual smile. His jolly round face matched the shape of his tiny frameless glasses.

"It's been a while, Dr. Keane."

Keane followed the wheelchair into the living room of the compact apartment and took a seat on the couch as Vinny wheeled around.

"Who do you like in the Series this fall?" Vinny asked.

"I *like* the Braves, Vinny. But I'm not putting a dime on them."

Vinny was not only a sports stats specialist, he likely knew more about search algorithms than most on staff at Google. Keane had spent plenty of time with him, learning his background. Born and raised in Waycross, Vinny was a graduate student in computer science at MIT when his accident occurred. He was driving home from the Media Lab when his Ford Escort was T-boned by a Cadillac Escalade. His spinal cord was severed at the eighth thoracic vertebra, resulting in paralysis from the waist down. He was confined for life to a wheelchair.

Afterward Vinny's desire to understand the world of software became the full-time focus of his life. Keane understood few of the terms that Vinny sometimes tossed out from his abstract universe of computer software: hash tables, binary search trees, public-key cryptosystems. But Keane knew the bottom line: if you wanted any tidbit of information, no matter how remotely available in the world of the Internet , Vinny Carruthers was your man.

"I've got a hot one for you, Vinny," Keane said. He placed a paper scrap with handwriting on it into Vinny's hand. "I need deep background on this guy. There's his age and the names of his parents. I'd like everything you can get on him."

"Just give me a deadline."

"I'll grab a quick lunch, but I'll be keeping my cell phone close and waiting on your call."

*   *   *

Keane circled the parking lot at the Fulton Clinical Oncology Center, looking for a white van. Vinny had not only located Felix Henry Thornton's employer, but he'd confirmed Thornton's home address and that he owned a white Chevy G20 van. All the info was publicly available on the Internet, "If you know where to look," Vinny had said. "Sometimes you might have to be a little creative to sneak inside the gates."

Vinny also found the death certificate for Matilda Thornton, Felix's mother. It listed the medical code ICD-9-CM E963, assault by "hanging or strangulation." But Vinny couldn't find a death record of his father, Benjamin Malcolm Thornton, who'd be eighty-one.

Keane entered the office of William Titus, the Oncology Center's chief administrator and deputy director. Beneath a dark toupee that was combed with a surgeon's precision, Titus stood to shake hands. The look of contempt frozen on the administrator's face signaled total skepticism. He'd made Keane wait outside his office for ten minutes while he called and checked out his credentials with APD.

Keane understood what was going on inside Titus's head. Discussing an employee's personal matters suggested foul play. Nobody wanted to hear that a former employee was a suspect in a crime. The supervisor was often the one who hired or promoted the guy and would naturally be his chief supporter under most any circumstance.

Titus said that Thornton was the best worker the center had ever had on staff. He knew every detail of clinical services. He added that Thornton's personnel folder contained outstanding performance evaluations and he pulled from the folder a copy of an award certificate issued two years before that read *Technician of the Year*.

"Unfortunately, we had to release him three months ago."

"He was fired?"

Titus said that Felix Thornton always had problems with the orderlies and nurses, never with anyone else. Then Thornton told one practical nurse she was an imbecile, but "given your heritage, I'm not surprised."

"She was African American," Titus continued. "That was the last straw. I finally realized I had tolerated the man much too long. No matter how good a worker, he wasn't going to be changed by counseling or warnings or whatever. Sorry to say, but we considered him a lost cause."

"What did Mr. Thornton do for you?"

"He was a rad therapy tech."

"He delivered radiation therapy to cancer patients?"

"He assisted. Our oncologists prescribe the treatment—radiation, chemo, or both. If radiation's involved, a medical physicist designs the treatment regimen."

"How long had he been a rad tech?"

Titus scanned through the manila folder before looking up. "Close to seven of his twelve years here. Would you like a tour of our facilities, Dr. Keane?"

"Please. I don't have anything else to do this afternoon."

While they walked, Titus explained their two models of LINAC machines—linear accelerators for firing electrons or x-rays into a tumor to destroy it. Also on hand were two types of radioactive isotopes: cobalt-60 and iridium-192. Each could deliver high-energy gamma rays that penetrated deep into the body to kill tumor cells.

"You keep a supply of all these isotopes on hand?" Keane asked.

"The radiation decays away over the years. We have to order more isotopes from time to time to keep a fresh stock on hand."

"You said they're a source of intense gamma radiation."

"Correct. That's why we keep them confined within thick lead shielding."

"How do you release the gamma-ray beam?" Keane asked. He wanted all of the details.

"By remotely cranking open a narrow tunnel through the lead shielding."

"And what if you were to expose someone's entire body to the beam?"

Titus shook his head and smiled, as if to dismiss an asinine question. "I can assure you, we have numerous safety locks to prevent that."

"But what if—and I'm only speaking hypothetically here—what if someone were to lie on the table below the business end of the machine. Then you release the gamma ray beam."

Titus stopped in his tracks. "But that could *never* happen."

"Just a hypothetical, Mr. Titus."

"Of course, if that did happen, they'd get a lethal dose of radiation in minutes. But it could still take weeks to die. On the other hand, if the exposure lasted longer, say for hours, the victim could die, bleeding internally and convulsing, by tomorrow."

Titus led him back to his office and offered his hand to shake. "I hope I've answered all your questions, Dr. Keane."

"Almost. Is it possible that you might have any radioactive isotopes missing?"

Titus glanced at his watch and then fixed a thick clump of hair that had tumbled down, brushing an eyebrow. "Absolutely not. We maintain the tightest security with our entire inventory. The feds and the state insist on it. Otherwise, we wouldn't have a license to possess these sources."

"Who maintains your inventory?" Keane asked.

"Currently that's Rebecca Whitaker. She's a tech and our designated rad-safety officer under our regulatory license. She has many other duties as well."

"How long has she been the radiation safety officer?"

"Since May."

"You mean, since Thornton was fired."

Titus coughed into his fist. "Yes."

"Did Thornton hold that position before her?"

"He did, but I gave him thirty days' notice. I assumed he would get a job at one of the hospitals in the area or at another private clinic. They always have a rad tech shortage."

"Could you do me a big favor?" Keane asked. "Check on your inventory of radioactive isotopes."

"That's hardly necessary, I mean—"

Keane leaned forward to interrupt. "Let me explain something. I suspect Felix Thornton is connected with criminal behavior tied to his employment here—and to your isotope inventory."

"I've heard nothing about this."

"Not yet. This is an undercover investigation by APD. I'm only a member of a big team."

Titus took a deep breath and exhaled slowly before replying. "We keep very close tabs on our isotopes. If we found any source missing, we could lose our license. That would be devastating for our patients."

"A word to the wise, Mr. Titus. You need to check your inventory. If a radiation source is missing—"

"I'm certain, Dr. Keane, that we have accounted for them all. But we'll double-check . . . as a favor to you."

*   *   *

That evening Keane took a grumpy Wilbur for an extended walk around the garden while he reviewed all he'd learned during the day. As they strolled, two text messages came in from Tucker Carlton. He'd made his move on the chessboard and was waiting for Keane to make his. Keane wondered if Tucker had learned about what had happened to his friend Ronnie Davenport.

Keane drifted into his study where he spotted the chessboard. Picking up his knight, he moved it toward the center and captured Tucker's white pawn.

Mr. J rapped a gentle knuckle on the open door. "A snack or refreshment, sir?"

"No, thanks."

"If you change your mind I'm—"

"Is there music playing somewhere, Mr. J?"

"I hear nothing. Absolutely nothing."

"A piano, perhaps?"

Mr. J paused and lowered his head a moment. "No, there is no piano music playing, sir. I can assure you of that. Do call if you need me."

After Mr. J quickly departed, the corner of Keane's eye caught the tangerine wine decanter from across the room on top of a cart. The decanter, given to him by his sister Margot for birthday number forty, was a piece from her small assortment of Blenko vases and glassware. What he remembered most about her collection was the wide array of colors. He studied the decanter again, focusing on the tangerine color and the odd tint. Something was vaguely familiar.

The light bulb in the warehouse.

He yanked out his cell phone and pulled up Detective Sergeant Crawford Selsby's number.

CHAPTER 16

Jessie Wiley walked the side streets of East Point, two miles from Atlanta's Hartsfield-Jackson Airport. The neighborhood's average income likely hovered just above poverty level. She was having second thoughts about Keane's assignments.

A jet whistled in for a landing.

Vinny was able to dig up the name and address of an ex-girlfriend Thornton had lived with for eighteen months; he'd also co-signed a car loan for her. Neither she nor Keane knew what kind of evidence they could get out of the woman, but both thought it was worth a try. House numbers appeared occasionally on rusted mailboxes or painted on curbs. A field of weeds girdled one house where a group of teenage boys sat quibbling on a porch. They stopped chatting when Jessie passed.

She felt their stares. The address of the Cartwright home was a narrow, one-story structure with peeling paint and barred windows. Neatly arranged beds of marigolds and lilies lined the base of the raised porch, a spectacle of color in a world of drab. She treaded carefully up the steps to avoid plunging through a gap in the warped boards and then she knocked on the door and waited. After half a minute, the door creaked open.

The head of an elderly woman popped out. Sadly bent over, she rested one arm on a cane.

"Hello, ma'am. I'm Jessie Wiley. Is this the home of Krystal Cartwright?"

"No! It's *my* home," she protested. Her white hair wrapped around a craggy brown face that spelled anger. Lowering her head, she backed away and began to cough.

"I'm sorry, I must have the wrong address."

A younger woman moved in from behind and laid a hand on her shoulder while the coughing continued. "Are you okay, Momma?"

The older lady nodded and turned away. Her daughter looked at Jessie. "Momma will be fine. Please come on in."

Vinny had made a big mistake with the address. The features of the woman inviting her inside—caramel skin and braided hair—were more African than Caucasian.

"I'm sorry," Jessie said, "is this 305?"

"You have the right place. I'm Krystal Cartwright."

Teenagers from the nearby porch meandered by on the street. She stared back at them as if communicating in a silent code then turned and motioned toward the living room.

Jessie moved ahead and took a seat on a sofa across from a chair covered with an orange-and-black afghan.

Krystal squatted on the carpeted floor and crossed her lanky legs that were covered by bleached jeans with slits in the knees. High on the opposite wall hung the serene face of Jesus of Nazareth looking toward heaven.

"May I offer you anything to drink, Detective?"

"Truthfully, Miss Cartwright—"

"Please, call me Krystal."

"I'm not a detective, Krystal."

"That's not what I understood when the gentleman phoned." Her diction was strong, punctuated, her voice soft and warm.

"I only do some interviewing for others connected with the APD."

"Maybe Dr. Cane did mention that—"

"Dr. Keane. My colleague Damon Keane made the call. Let me make sure I understand. You were at one time a live-in girlfriend of Felix Henry Thornton?"

"That's what I said on the phone," Krystal replied. "Just be straight with me. What's the problem?"

"The police are struggling with some puzzling deaths around the city."

"Why am I not surprised?"

"At puzzling deaths?" Jessie asked.

"No, that APD is struggling with them. You don't think Felix has something to do with it?"

"I'm trying to understand if he has a connection with any of the victims. The docs at Grady Memorial are stumped. They asked APD to check out the possibility of foul play."

"I didn't know Felix worked there now. He was a technician at a cancer clinic when we were together."

"That's where there may be a link with some of the victims."

A loud knock at the front door startled them. Jessie quickly stood. Krystal jumped up and rushed to the door, cracking it open to reveal another teenager. A low-rider hip-hop coupe moved down the street with a rap tune booming from a set of colossal speakers. Krystal and the boy stood whispering to each other. The burly kid glanced into the house. Jessie wasn't sure whether to stay put or run for a back door.

When he departed, Krystal closed the door and returned to squat on the floor again. "You shouldn't be concerned, Miss Wiley. We have a neighborhood watch. Is that your red Porsche at the end of the block?"

"That's mine."

"No worries. Tell me more about your suspicions of Felix."

"I'll be honest with you. APD considers him a person of interest in the deaths."

Krystal cocked one knee up and rested an arm on top of it. "He's not a murderer. I can assure you of that."

"How long has it been since your separation?"

"Six months. We lived together for a year and a half."

"He worked at the cancer clinic the whole time you lived together?"

"Yes. Hated it though. Including everyone he worked with."

"You lived in his house? The one on Purser Street?"

Krystal paused and smiled, cocking her head. "You don't think he'd want to live in *this* neighborhood, do you?"

"Did he ever talk about his work?"

"Just the bastards he worked for and the assholes around him."

"Did he go out a lot?"

"Rarely. If he did, it was to a bar. That's where I met him. The Blue Rag on Finney Street, near the CNN building."

"A regular hangout for him, I suppose?" Jessie asked.

"For me too—the first few months after my divorce, anyway."

"Did Thornton ever talk about his other friends or his family?"

Krystal stared at the ceiling as if in a trance. "He preferred to chat about all the trash he would read in the newspaper or watch on TV."

"He watched TV a lot?"

"Only the evening news and the History Channel. Loved world history, especially war. Anything that came on about war, he'd sit as if he'd been tied down in his favorite chair."

"Did you learn anything about his family or friends?"

"He didn't have many friends."

"Ever mention his—"

"Let me correct that, Miss Wiley. He didn't have *any* friends."

"Did he ever mention parents? Siblings?"

"He was raised in the Catholic Church, but he worshiped his mother more than the Lord. She died when he was young under strange circumstances. At first I thought it was some kind of accident, but I couldn't get much out of him. When he didn't want to talk about something, he just clammed up."

"What about his father?"

"Felix hated him. I never understood why."

"Did you ever have any disagreements?" Jessie asked.

"Oh, hell no. Why would a man and a woman living together ever have any disagreements?"

"I'm sorry, Krystal, let me try again. What things did you argue about?"

"People."

Jessie raised her eyebrows.

"I happen to like people," Krystal said. "He usually saw the worst in everyone. If he received the wrong change at the grocer's, he thought the guy was cheating him and would steal from him if he turned his back. He would think it was all because the grocer was Italian, a worthless Dago raised with the values of a Mafioso. Do you mind if I smoke?"

"Please, go ahead."

Krystal whipped out a pack of crushed cigarettes from a back pocket and a lighter from the other and lit up. Exhaling slowly, she weighed what to say as she picked a tobacco speck from the tip of her tongue. "Frankly, his real problem was that he hated what Atlanta had become."

"Meaning?"

"He thought the city began going straight to hell when Maynard Jackson was elected mayor."

Jessie said, "Quite an event in history—the first black mayor of a major city."

"Felix was only a teenager, but he said it was the day Atlanta disowned the white race—the day when all the whites fled the city for the suburbs. Marietta, Dunwoody, Gwinnett County. More and more blacks moved in from all over the country, followed by the Mexicans and all the other coloreds, as he called them. He believed the city totally decayed after that.

"When Maynard Jackson died, the City Council had the 'goddamn nerve,' he would rant, to change the name of the Hartsfield Airport to *Hartsfield-Jackson*, as if Maynard Jackson should be remembered. He called it godless stupidity. I never saw him so angry over something so petty."

"But, Krystal, I have to ask—"

"How did I ever get in the picture?"

"I can't understand it. Why?"

"He didn't see me as black. He saw me as half-white. He said that mulattos were proof that there was a way for America to begin putting an end to the black race."

"You *stayed* with this man?"

"You don't understand. He was an absolute charmer. When he wasn't pissed off about politics or the world, we'd talk about jazz and literature. I'm into Nicholas Sparks novels. He's read them all, if you can believe that."

Krystal's mother shuffled into the living room on her cane, coughed, and turned back around.

"I'm afraid I've kept you too long," Jessie said, rising from the sofa.

Krystal showed her to the door and strolled back along the street with her to the Porsche.

While they walked, Jessie said, "May I ask one more question, Krystal? A personal one."

"Try me."

"Did Felix ever hit you? Was he ever violent?"

"Never. He loved me. It was the world he hated."

Jessie stood silent for a moment, puzzled. "Do you miss him?"

"At times."

Unbelievable. A malignant link between a man and a woman. History was probably filled with the likes of Bonnie and Clyde.

Krystal waved good-bye and smiled when Jessie pulled away from the curb.

CHAPTER 17

The aroma of coffee blended with that of popping sausages inside the Waffle House, a place for convenient grub within easy walking distance of APD headquarters. Waffles baked on an iron griddle where batter overran the edges like lava and formed a hard crust somewhere between golden brown and burnt black. Keane sat across from Detective Selsby, who'd taken a seat at a booth with his back to the wall and in view of the entrance.

Each man arranged his tableware in silence. Keane had called to request the meeting but he wasn't sure how to begin. Selsby's demeanor broadcast that he didn't take readily to people he didn't know, as if he wouldn't want anyone to get too close.

After getting coffee and placing their orders, Keane asked, "How long have you been in this business?"

"Joined the department twenty-four years ago." Selsby stared out the window and watched street traffic.

"You're a Georgia native?"

Selsby flipped his attention from the traffic to Keane. "A redneck through and through. Born in Moultrie and went to college at Valdosta State where I got a degree in criminal justice. After academy training in Columbus, I started as a street cop in Macon."

Now that's where you get real fieldwork—a street cop. You start at the bottom and work your way up. That's how you can say you've been there and seen it all.

"Married?" Keane asked.

"Do I look like the type?" He added that his momma had died when he was in college and that his dad had passed away from a heart attack "eleven years ago next month."

"Where were you born, Keane?"

"A small town in the western mountains of Virginia."

"You don't wear a wedding band."

"I was married once," Keane said. "Have two kids."

"How often do you see them?"

"Not that much."

"So, you're not exactly a believer in home and family?"

"I didn't say that," Keane replied.

"But you don't have a real family. Like a wife to come home to. Looks like you and me have a similar situation."

Keane raised his cup to the waitress behind the counter to signal a refill. "You gotta get far away from your job at times, I would imagine."

"That's why God made weekends," Selsby said.

In the background a waitress with graying hair tied in a bun belted out orders from behind the counter. "Three eggs smothered and covered and a side of grits!"

It was a good guess that Selsby wasn't going to lift any weight in the conversation.

"Are you an outdoorsman?" Keane asked.

"Yeah. Outdoors. Belong to a club."

"Hunting club?"

"Sort of. We get plenty of shooting in."

The waitress brought the orders of eggs and toast and both men dug into their food. Eating was easier than talking. When Keane's food was half gone, he took another sip of coffee and set down his mug. "I've been doing some homework since the press briefing."

"I assume that's why we're having this little meeting."

"I've been thinking about the corpses in the warehouse," Keane continued. "And I've come up with a theory."

"Theory is fantasy. My job rests upon hard evidence, Keane. Facts. Any real detective worth his salt avoids theory. There's no knowledge like field knowledge."

"I prefer to use both—evidence and theory. They go hand in hand."

Selsby turned away and shook his head with a smirk.

"Tell me something," Keane said. "Do you use a GPS or do you still stop at gas stations and ask for directions?"

"I learned maps in the Scouts. With a GPS, you just use satellites for navigation instead of radio beacons like the old days. Everybody knows that."

"But did you know that using satellites for GPS wouldn't work unless we applied the theory of relativity? Einstein said that gravity affects the passage of time."

"That's impossible and you know it. Total bullshit."

"Time moves slower on the earth's surface than it does in orbit. That's because gravity gets weaker as you go up."

"Textbook bull crap."

"It's not crap and it's not science fiction," Keane said. "It's reality. GPS systems have to correct for it. If it didn't, your GPS soon wouldn't know whether you were in your driveway in Atlanta or flying over Chattanooga."

"Where in the hell are you going with this?" Selsby asked. He stuffed a piece of buttered toast into his mouth.

"I've come up with a theory to explain what you and I are facing right now." He knew Selsby didn't want to hear what a rank amateur had to say about anything. But he was going to put it all on the table. He pointed out first that the look on each warehouse victim's face was that of a gut-wrenching death—as if he'd been forced to eat poison, with either a gun to his head or a knife to his neck. "But that couldn't have happened. At least one would've been shot or had his throat slashed to convince the others to go along."

Selsby arranged his eggs and grits with his fork without looking up.

Keane's second point was that the victims were in a square facing something in the center that had been dragged in from the outside. Heavy enough to scar the concrete floor, it had to be in some way connected with the deaths.

"Finally," Keane said, "consider the light bulb hanging from the ceiling. My guess is that whatever caused their deaths also had some kind of effect on the bulb above their heads."

The yellowish tint on the bulb wasn't a chemical deposit. He'd climbed a ladder and checked it out. But the most looming question of all: could the color change in the light bulb be related to that of the rosary beads?

"Rosary beads?" Selsby asked. "What's that all about?"

"The assistant priest at Father O'Shannon's church told me the beads on the Father's rosary changed color almost overnight. The rosary always stayed in the confessional with the Father. Yesterday, a link between the light bulb and those beads suddenly hit me."

Ignoring his breakfast Keane, recounted his idea. The day before, when he was studying the wine decanter, he remembered what he'd learned years earlier. Fraudulent antique-glass collectors built a racket around exposing glassware to gamma rays. The radiation produced the color of amethyst. The gammas can't make glassware radioactive, so it didn't give off any radiation itself. The racket worked beautifully for the con artists. There was simply no way to tell that the pleasing antique-like hue was a hoax. The crooks charged premium prices for their handiwork. Even diamond dealers got into the act by having some of their gems exposed to heavy doses of gamma rays to give them a blue or green cast. Then they sold them as a rare find from Tanzania or Sri Lanka.

"All the victims we've been investigating," Keane said, "died by *extreme* exposure to radiation."

Selsby shook his head. "You know damned good and well that the lab results ruled out any radiation in the corpses. Why are you bringing this up again?"

"They may not have had anything radioactive and giving off radiation *inside* them. But what about the possibility of a source of radiation *outside* the body? A source that emits a beam of gamma rays?" He paused as a waitress passed by, carrying a plate covered with an oversized waffle decorated with powdered sugar and a massive glob of butter.

"If I'm on the right track," Keane said, "then blood samples from the Latino victims—and any of the others—should easily confirm it. Intense radiation exposure damages the chromosomes in blood cells. You take a blood draw from the victim and do a little prepping of the sample in the lab. The damaged chromosomes are easily seen under a microscope. The more damage you see, the greater the radiation exposure. That's how you measure it."

Selsby held his stare for a moment. "For this kind of advice we pay you the big bucks?"

"You don't actually pay me."

Selsby shoved his coffee mug to one side. "Then I suppose you're one helluva smart volunteer, aren't you? I think I'll buy your breakfast this morning." He grabbed the check lying on the edge of the table and started to stand.

"Wait a minute," Keane said. "I know who carried all this out."

"*Jeezus*, Keane! You think only one guy is responsible?"

Keane leaned over the table and lowered his voice. "He might've had help, but I've identified him."

Selsby whispered back. "Maybe we should turn over all our homicide cases to you. I'm working on four others right now."

"Listen, I've talked with some of the victims' relatives and friends." He wasn't about to mention anything about Jessie Wiley.

Selsby narrowed his eyes. "Who authorized you to do that?" He tipped his empty mug toward the waitress.

"A guy in Midtown by the name of Felix Thornton keeps popping up."

Selsby lifted his chin. "Who?"

"Thornton. Felix Thornton. He has a clear connection with each victim."

"A connection? You've found a connection, have you? You mean something like the one between Robin Hood and Friar Tuck? Look, Keane, we've already got a suspect list as long as my dick."

"I visited the place where Thornton worked for the last twelve years. He was fired three months ago. It's a clinic where they do radiation therapy. He had access to radioactive isotopes."

"Am I supposed to know what the hell that means?"

"Radioactive isotopes emit radiation. They're used for destroying tumors. He had access to enough of it to deliver a killing radiation dose to people, not just tumors. Silent and deadly. He's the man we're looking for!"

Selsby stared back at him and shrugged. "Okay. You made your point. We'll check him out." He pulled a notepad and pen from his inside coat pocket and scribbled.

Check him out? "You need to *stake* him out," Keane said, "or somehow get his cell phone." He knew what they could get off of Thornton's cell—everywhere he'd been for at least the last two years with the resolution of one hundred fifty yards. Possibly every call and text message he'd placed during the same period. A swab of the phone's microphone would pick up his DNA for confirmation.

The waitress poured more coffee for Selsby, but Keane waved her away. "You really need to get on it now."

"Don't try to give me orders, Keane. You think we have a whole division of cops just sitting around waiting for a goddamn consultant to come up with theories to check out? On top of at least three murders a week, we've got narc cases up the ying-yang."

A text message came in on Keane's phone and he glanced down. It was from chess buddy Tucker Carlton: *Don't want 2 finish our chess game. Sorry. Hav u heard bout Ronnie in hosptal?*

He should've called Tucker or paid him a visit, told him about Ronnie Davenport directly to his face. But he kept putting it off. All of the Dream Valley kids probably knew by now what had happened to their friend at camp.

Keane shoved his plate away and took a gulp of coffee that spilled over the sides of the cup and ran down his chin. He wiped off the coffee with his fingers and stared back at Selsby. The chance the detective was going to follow up on Felix Thornton was somewhere between zero and an ant's ass. He stood, pulled cash from his wallet, and slapped it on the table loud enough for others to turn around and gawk. "That should take care of both of us." He headed for the door.

CHAPTER 18

Keane had an hour, maybe two, of sleep. Throughout the night, and the night before, he couldn't get the recurring dream of Ronnie Davenport out of his head. A giant oxygen mask crawling over his mouth and nose. IV lines sprouting from his limbs like kudzu. Angry numbers dancing and flashing on green screens in a dark cathedral.

The previous afternoon he'd received a call from William Titus, the director of the Oncology Center. Titus had checked his isotope inventory as Keane had ordered. For reasons "totally beyond comprehension," Titus had found that one of the rods containing highly radioactive cobalt sources was missing. It was a sealed and double-encased stainless-steel rod—eighteen inches long, a half-inch in diameter—and consisted of a dozen cobalt-60 slugs. Each metallic slug was a deadly source of radiation, unless it was kept shielded by thick layers of lead or steel.

For the second day in a row, Keane had driven to Midtown, passing grassy strips of land anchoring hundred-year-old Southern red oaks that lined the narrow streets. Many homes dated from the late nineteenth century. The house belonging to Felix Henry Thornton was at 4091 Purser Street—the address Vinny had provided. A white two-story Victorian with a round turret rose to a point high above a steep roof.

Keane pulled to the curb and stopped. Broken concrete steps led up to Thornton's wraparound porch. A starburst pattern of yellow and

103

burnt orange shrouded the front door's stained glass. Tall columns in need of paint supported the roof. He drove away and slowly circled the block. When he came around to the house again, he parked across the street and down a half-block then shut off the engine. The day before he'd performed the same maneuver. He hadn't yet spotted Thornton or any hint of him.

Does Thornton actually live here? It would make perfect sense if he'd disappeared.

*   *   *

Groggy and half-asleep, Keane looked up in time to see Thornton's garage door opening and a white van backing down the driveway. He sat up and froze.

The van entered the street and turned in his direction. When it approached, he dropped back down into his seat with his eyes just below the dash. He got a fleeting glance of Thornton's bearded face. Thornton had pulled away in the opposite direction that he was parked. Switching on the ignition, Keane made a rapid U-turn.

The van drifted along Morris Street and headed toward the freeway. Keane stayed a few cars back as Thornton took the Interstate ramp and sped north in traffic. The van stood out among the host of other white vans on the highway because of its bumper: bent downward at an angle on the right side, as if it had been rear-ended. After half an hour, the highway split and Keane continued to follow Thornton as he picked up I-985 North. When the road narrowed to two lanes, it rambled on through the foothills of the North Georgia wilderness. Acres of pine replaced homes and development. Approaching the town of Clayton, Thornton turned off the main road and into a Denny's restaurant parking lot.

Keane veered into a strip mall next to it.

As Thornton strolled inside, Keane focused on his bearded face and tall, lanky features that resembled a lumberjack more than a technician in a clinic. Keane drove back to the sign he'd noted for Enterprise

Rent-A-Car. He'd followed Thornton for too long. He was bound to become suspicious.

*   *   *

When Thornton departed the restaurant, he stopped to stretch his arms before getting back in the van. Keane slowly took off in his rented Chevy Cavalier, in control of roughly eighty-five horsepower. Not far beyond the town, Thornton turned onto a gravel road leading into pine forest. The van's trailing dust settled in the distance as Keane thought about the risk of following him. He guessed that the crude road meandered deep into the forest and was the only way back to the main highway. He pulled to the side and called Mr. J on his cell. With a weak signal that drifted in and out, he explained that he'd be late returning home and told him not to hold dinner.

"May I ask how far away you are, sir?"

"Near the North Carolina border, just outside Dillard. The sign here says US Forest Service Road 57."

"Sounds like the Chattahoochee Forest. I don't understand why you're all the way up there."

Neither did Keane. "I'm on a case. Can't go into details right now, but I dropped off my car and got a rental."

"Was there a problem? I could have arranged a car for you, sir. I hope you got a decent one."

"A Chevy Cavalier."

"Why on earth would you—"

The connection dropped.

Where was Thornton headed? And why? Maybe he'd follow the van a short way along the forest-service road, keeping at a distance.

The dust billowed up in a haze in his rearview mirror, and gravel popped under the tires. Georgia clay spewed from passing vehicles over the years had painted the pine trees a brick red. Now and then, remnants of old logging roads trailed off into the woods. The sun, now a giant ball of orange burning low on the horizon, occasionally flashed through pine boughs. When the road turned into rut after rut, Keane slowed to a creep and searched for a spot to turn around. But there was no space to maneuver. The ruts grew deeper and the passage narrower. Low-hanging branches thumped against the Cavalier's roof as he steered to avoid ditches that could swallow the tires. He crawled along, squeezing the steering wheel and carefully rolling through smaller ruts to dodge the bigger ones.

The Cavalier ground to a stop. He hit the accelerator, but the right-rear wheel only spun, spraying dirt high into the air. After he got out to examine the undercarriage, he found the drive shaft firmly anchored in the ground. He moved to the rear end and rocked the chassis.

No luck—the tires were buried.

He wiped sweat from his forehead and swatted at a horsefly. The dense canopy of trees hid the sky. When he turned around, the figure of a man stood a few yards away. Keane quickly recognized the bushy hair and well-trimmed beard of Felix Thornton.

CHAPTER 19

Keane recoiled at the sight of the man he'd been tailgating for three hours. "I didn't know anyone was there," he said. He tried to sound matter-of-fact, but his pulse was racing.

"Looks like you got a problem," Felix Thornton replied. His eyes hid deep inside their own dark burrows.

Keane chuckled nervously and shook his head. "Stupid of me."

Thornton walked closer to the Cavalier. "Don't think I would've taken this road driving a toy like that." He bent down to examine beneath it. "What you doing all the way out here, anyway?"

Keane cleared his throat. "Just scouting for some good fishing on my day off." His mind was racing supersonic, churning out aimless words. How do you analyze the danger in the presence of a senseless killer and at the same time carry on chitchat like he was a next-door neighbor?

Wearing a pair of tattered leather working gloves, Thornton stood and walked to the other side of the car. "Whatcha do for a living?"

"Retired."

"You're taking a day off from retirement?" Thornton asked.

"I meant a day off from the usual stuff. I farm some acreage down in Cumming."

"Want a tow?" Thornton asked. "Got a van parked in the woods a quarter-mile back. Four-wheel drive with oversized tires. Should do the trick. You want to follow me?"

If Keane stayed behind, his only reason would be to grab a spare tire tool from the trunk and hide it close by. If he ran, Thornton could quickly track him down. No doubt he knew the area.

"Let's walk," Keane said, holding out his hand to shake. "The name's Watkins. Jake Watkins."

Thornton shook without giving a name.

As they walked the rough terrain, Keane was careful to avoid twisting an ankle. He kept watch on his companion, searching for any bulge in his clothing. Thornton moved with a clumsy gait, paying no attention to the flying bugs, when he suddenly halted and raised his hand.

Keane flinched and ducked away. Thornton looked down at him with a grin then pointed ahead. Two coyotes scurried across the road.

"What do you do for a living?" Keane asked when they began walking again.

"Used to work in the medical field," Thornton replied.

"You're a doctor?"

"Not quite. A medical assistant, you might say. Got out of the field."

"Tough job?"

"Medicine's not what it's cracked up to be."

Keane swung at another horsefly. "What do you mean?"

"Everybody's treated who shows up. Whether they deserve it or not." He spat out his words. "Blacks and spics get it for free." He stopped and pointed toward a grove of pine trees at a path where a vehicle made tracks through the weeds.

"I'll wait on you here," Keane said.

"Suit yourself." Thornton shoved into the thicket, pushing back pine limbs as he stooped under the trees.

When he was out of sight, Keane quickly guesstimated how far he'd have to run. He'd stay away from the road, but he wasn't about to move blindly into the thick underbrush. If he took off, Thornton wouldn't know his direction. He began jogging down the road, looking for a path on the other side next to a stream.

An engine rumbled in from behind. He turned to see the white van emerge from the trees. Thornton's forearm hung from the edge of the rolled-down window.

"A lot a wild strawberries around here," Keane yelled. He pointed to a phantom patch along the roadside and forced a smile. When Thornton pulled up alongside, he hopped in and settled into the seat. The van crawled over the humps and around and through the ruts. A crushed Styrofoam cup rested in the corner of the driver's-side dash. In the coffee-stained divider between the two front seats was an assortment of receipts from gas stations, shredded notes, and a wrinkled leaflet advertising the Southern National drag racing competition.

Keane kept one hand on the door below the handle. With the other, he squeezed the seat next to his knee and fixed his side vision on Thornton's hands grasping the top of the steering wheel. When they arrived at the Cavalier, he jumped out before Thornton could turn off the engine.

Thornton walked to the back of the van and opened it. He brought out a steel cable and moseyed to the Cavalier, bending low to hook the cable under the frame. He attached the other end to the front of the van. "Put her in neutral and make sure the brake's off."

It only took a minute for Thornton's van to yank the Cavalier out of the rut and onto smoother ground. Keane got out and walked to the rear of the van where Thornton was storing the cable. Around the inside edges were piles of moving pads and a large toolbox. A clothesline rope lay coiled in a far corner.

"Sorry to cause you so much trouble," Keane said.

Thornton leaned back against the van and reached for his back pocket, yanking out a shiny flask. "Care for a sip?"

"Thanks, but I'd prefer a cold beer right now." He hitched up his trousers and glanced back at the Cavalier.

After a swig from his flask, Thornton said, "You travel much?" He screwed the top back on and returned the container to his hip pocket.

"Occasionally."

"Been out of the country?" Thornton asked.

"A few times."

"Ever been to Russia?"

If only he knew the many trips to Moscow and throughout the former Soviet Union, always by clients' requests to investigate sources of information. "I visited once. Are you thinking about it?"

"Just studying on it. Sounds like a strange place."

He was buying time. Keane searched the area, aware that a body disposed of there would never be found. It was crazy to have followed a homegrown killer all the way to the North Georgia woods. Little doubt Thornton had murdered his own father, a neighbor, his priest, and the four Latinos at the warehouse. And here Keane was treating a beast like a golfing buddy.

He had to get away fast. But what chance would he have racing into the woods with a madman hunting him down? He glanced at his watch—less than an hour before dark. He moved for the Cavalier. "I'd better be headed back. Getting late. You know how traffic is in Atlanta late in the day."

"Got another question for you," Thornton said. He didn't look up while he spoke but walked toward the back of the van. "You said you had a farm down around Cumming, but your license plate has Rabun County on it."

"It's a rental."

Thornton hopped onto the back bumper and reached inside.

Keane took off. He ran in among the trees and scrambled through a deep thicket then bolted for an open field before realizing that would make him an easy target. He circled back into the trees, ducking as limbs slapped at his head. Bristles and thorns whipped at him like barbed wire as he tunneled through the underbrush. Whenever he spotted a clearing, he avoided it and headed into deeper brush. At the crest of a hill he stopped to catch his breath. He held his head below his waist and grabbed onto the trunk of a pine. Spreading out his legs, he dry-heaved. He'd zigzagged so much he was no longer sure from what direction he'd come. He reached for his cell phone—gone. Somewhere it had fallen out of his pocket. Water rippled in the distance. He stumbled down the other side of the slope and plowed through heavier thicket as the ground dropped steeply toward a small creek.

Eventually the sun set behind a mountain peak, giving way to a violet afterglow. The idea of spending the night in the woods was inconceivable. But the fact that he was hopelessly lost was real. When he finally staggered back to the top of the hill, he collected dead pine limbs from the ground and ripped smaller ones from the trees. He stacked them all loosely into a pile and then slid beneath them.

The first stars of the night blinked through his crude shelter. His nerves raw, he refused to move a muscle and strained to read every sound—chirping bugs, the rasp of pine trunks rubbing together. He was alone, no connection with anyone, anywhere. Only one person had any kind of idea of his whereabouts and that was Felix Thornton. The only reason he was lying beneath a pile of pine limbs in the middle of a godforsaken wilderness after dark was stupidity on his part. The idiotic notion of chasing after Thornton.

He would've paid good money for a single sip of water. His only other consuming thought: in the heat of the night, he was shivering.

*   *   *

Damon!

The shout came in from the trees. Keane jerked up and slammed his face into pine needles stabbing his face. With a parched throat, he massaged his shoulders. The wrenching pain in his neck gave a feeling of having been hanging from a noose. He tossed the smothering limbs away and jumped up into an overwhelming darkness.

A billion stars shined in the cool night sky. The voice called out his name again. He jogged blindly through the dark in the direction of the calls before tripping and somersaulting into a shallow marsh. He lay there half submerged.

The churning ocean waves splashed his face. The salty water stung his throat as he gasped for air. He was going down, pulled farther from shore, far, far away.

He crawled on his belly into a dry bed of weeds and lay there until finally dozing off.

CHAPTER 20

Keane awoke to the sound of rumbling in the distance. He shook his head to clear it before realizing the noise came from above. A possible search-and-rescue operation? If he was going to be located by aircraft, he'd have to get onto higher ground. He jumped up and began to jog, searching for recognizable landmarks from the evening before. Instinctively, he moved in the direction of the rising sun.

Where was the Cavalier?

The thumping sound from overhead returned. He scurried into an opening among the trees and spotted a helicopter flying low. Frantically, he waved his arms as it began to circle. The chopper dropped into the clearing and he quickly recognized it.

When the door opened, Jessie Wiley jumped down. She yanked off her helmet and shook out her blonde ponytail. "You look like something out of a horror movie!" she shouted.

He tossed out his hands in a pretend look of surprise. They hugged, an extended squeeze as he rocked her back and forth, rubbing and patting her back.

"If Mr. J didn't keep constant tabs on you," she said, "you'd be scuttling all over these woods for God knows how long. I suppose there's some reason you're out here all alone. But I can't imagine one for the life of me."

"It's a long story."

She told him she'd received word from Mr. J, who'd worried that his boss hadn't called back. He told her that Keane was in the national forest near Dillard and added as much detail as he could remember. She then dropped everything and flew to Clayton to check out the terrain on the maps with the locals before beginning the search from the air. Once she spotted the Cavalier Mr. J had described, she assumed Keane couldn't be too far away. "I know the limits of your athletic ability, Damon."

He tried to explain why he'd taken on the job of staking out and following Thornton. But his utter frustration with Selsby didn't seem to justify his senseless actions as he listened to his own words.

"You don't owe me or anyone else an explanation," she said. "I'm coming to understand who we're dealing with. Let's get you home so you can clean up."

"I'm sure I smell pretty good. But you and I have to do some searching together—now."

"You're kidding me. Right?"

"There's got to be a reason Thornton was so interested in coming up here."

She shook her head in disbelief. "First let's get some fuel in your tummy. This ain't the Army. Besides, we still have plenty of daylight."

When they touched down on the helipad at the Clayton Airfield, he used Jessie's cell phone to call the car rental agency and explain that the Cavalier was stuck at the end of a forest-service road. He'd come after his Beamer later. He tried to reach Detective Selsby, but a recording said he was out of the office on assignment for the day. He left a quick message on his voice mail for him to get back to him quickly.

Jessie borrowed a car from the manager at the airfield and drove to Wal-Mart, where Keane could wash up, grab some fast food, and buy a shirt and jeans. While they shopped, Jessie briefed him on her visit with Thornton's ex-girlfriend in East Point.

"Krystal Cartwright wasn't educated," Jessie said, "but she's impressively smart and streetwise. I was surprised when I saw her. She's mixed race—black and white."

"Hard to put that one together with Thornton."

"Maybe, maybe not," Jessie replied. "He may have seen her as a window into the black world he hated. I suppose he lusted after black women. He saw a natural beauty in them that was more appealing."

"The very thought of that had to rip apart Thornton's soul."

Jessie nodded.

Before leaving, he also picked up a GPS unit off the shelf. "Let's go get the chopper," he said. "We're losing daylight."

*   *   *

After identifying the abandoned Cavalier from above again, Jessie flew in widening circles around the site. Passing above the vast expanse of the Chattahoochee National Forest, they hovered over streams, dry creek beds, and the maze of forest service roads.

"What exactly are we looking for?" she asked.

"I'm really not sure."

"Then how will we know when we find it, Dr. Keane?"

After thirty minutes, the situation seemed hopeless. They needed to explore on foot or horseback. Neither was an option. A million woodland acres spread out in all directions.

An open area came into view, an uncanny site in a dense forest. On the second pass, the bare field popped into sight. Scattered about it appeared to be freshly dug graves.

CHAPTER 21

Jessie flew lower to get a look at the cleared area among the native trees that carpeted the land for as far as they could see. Patches of bare soil stood out below them.

"I could find a place to land," she said, "if you want to hike back a ways."

"Let's do it. I've got to check out that field."

Hovering over the center of the open field, she turned a 360 to verify clearance. "Can't put down. Too tight."

She zoomed away and climbed to get a wider view, slowly rotating about while she rose. Then she pointed down to her left. "Look over here. There's a power-line pathway about a mile on the other side of that ridge. Not an easy hike. It's all uphill. But I can squeeze down between the trees and high-tension wires."

She hovered over the spot so Keane could store the coordinates in his new GPS unit. She headed directly to the power lines and curled back. Cautiously, she lowered the chopper to the ground on a steep slope.

"Lock this position into your GPS as well. I'm going back to load up on fuel. I'm giving you two hours to return to this spot."

He released his seat belt and shoulder harness then gathered from his Walmart cache a small backpack and canteen of water from behind his seat.

"Walk to the downhill side of me," she ordered. "And make damned sure I can see you until you clear the rotor."

He opened the door and held out his fist toward her. She gave him a firm knuckle-tap and they locked eyes. "Be careful, Damon."

He jumped out and ducked when he bolted. The chopper rose directly up and darted away. After checking the GPS display, he began to walk in a south-by-southwest direction, but as soon as he entered the wooded jungle he realized his mistake. Along with the underbrush, the trees—mostly second growth hemlock and hardwoods—were a hell of a lot more dense than he'd encountered the day before. He faced endless strands of blooming rhododendron and dog hobble. A machete would've come in handy. All he needed now was to run into a herd of wild boar.

The GPS arrow pointed dead ahead.

*   *   *

The woods opened into a small field, a square roughly thirty yards on a side. He counted more than a dozen tree stumps with the marks of an axe. Judging from the freshness of the cuts, the clearing was recent. He kept careful watch all about as he strode into the middle of it. Instead of graves, he found craters, most several feet in diameter and one at least three feet deep. A sludge with an acrid aroma lay at the bottom of another. He dropped to his hands and knees and crawled about to explore, picking up scattered pieces of wire and metal fragments that he stuffed into his pockets. He stood to look around.

Split bark on some trees showed traces of black soot. He approached a pine and found a two-inch rock embedded deep into the trunk. A creek ran by the field, and on its bank was a campsite with enough room for a tent and a fire pit. Stones from the creek formed a ring, each stone identical in size and shape and carefully positioned in a perfect circle. He squatted to rummage through the pit's ashes, when he heard the crack of rifle fire.

Dirt by his knees exploded. He jumped back and stumbled over a rock, hitting the ground. A second bullet ricocheted off a stone on the fire ring. His nerves reacted as if he'd been struck by lightning. He leaped for cover in the underbrush and smothered his face in the field grass. When he slowly rose to search for the shooter, another bullet whizzed overhead and a pine branch split open. Pressing his chest into the earth, he crawled through the high weeds and lay against a log and froze.

Where the hell was Jessie and the chopper?

The shots had come from across the creek behind him. He hugged the ground and listened for movement among the trees. When he shifted his glance toward the log, two vertical slits stared back. The pupils of a copperhead jutted out from the sides of a diamond-shaped head buried within a fat, spring-loaded coil beside the rotted log. The snake was three feet from his nose and a near-perfect camouflage nestled within the pine straw and bark. He was trapped—"a damned if you do, damned if you don't" situation. A drumming from above the trees interrupted the silence. The beating of rotor blades grew louder as a chopper descended into the open field. He took a deep breath then spooled away from the log just as the flash of fangs struck at his face. He leaped up and dashed for a tree, staying as low as possible.

When the chopper settled into the center of the field, a bullet tore through the windscreen. The pilot's door swung open and Jessie jumped onto the ground. She crisscrossed through the field before disappearing into the woods.

Two more shots rang out.

An automatic weapon burst out in a torrent of flashes from the grove of trees where Jessie had sheltered. Branches from the trees along the creek splintered.

Keane pinched his shoulder blades against the trunk of a tree and dug his fingernails into the bark. Ignoring a pair of mosquitoes buzzing around his cheeks and neck, he checked out the area surrounding the chopper. When he turned to his right, Jessie was crouched beneath a birch tree some twenty yards away. Strapped under her arm was an Uzi.

"Stay down!" she mouthed, using a free hand to signal the command. She dashed to a closer tree and patted the top of the Uzi's steel barrel. "Glad I keep her stashed in my chopper. We're going to have to make a run for it. You with me?"

"I damned sure don't want to be left here."

She motioned with one raised hand then sprinted low through the field toward the chopper while sweeping the air with the Uzi on all sides.

Running directly behind her, Keane dove into the helicopter's open door headfirst. Jessie jumped in and slammed the door, grabbed the controls, and took off. The field below quickly shrank away.

Glancing over at Keane, she smiled. "Improvise, adapt, and overcome."

It took only minutes to reach Clayton. After cutting off the engine on the airport's helipad, Jessie snatched off her helmet and tossed it onto the seat behind her. Keane was leaning back, legs and arms sprawled out, staring at the cabin ceiling with his chest still pumping for air.

"For crying out Jeezus Malloy!" she roared. "What was *that* all about? Are you okay?"

"I'm doing fine." He scratched the back of his neck. "Just another day in the world of consulting."

She threw an arm over her seat and reared back. "You really do need to spend more time in your office, Damon. You got an itch or what?"

"Nerves, I think."

"You didn't get into poison ivy, did you? I saw a few patches of it. They're three little leaves that—"

"I know what poison ivy looks like, thank you. What made you come back so early?"

"Had a hunch. You know how sometimes you're sitting around and a strange—"

"Spirit moves you? Please."

"Never mind. Next time I'll just ignore it and meditate. Now tell me straight. What was going on back there?"

"We've stumbled upon a lab setup, Jessie. Someone's been using that field for some heavy-duty chemistry experiments. The kind that go boom."

CHAPTER 22

The next morning Keane surprised Selsby by strolling into his cubicle. First things first. Keane apologized for the Waffle House scene, an atonement that was halfway sincere. Without question he needed to find a way to get through to Detective Sergeant Selsby, no matter what he thought of the man. Had to try a different tack. Use a little more finesse.

Looking bewildered, Selsby asked, "You're telling me you actually spent the night in the *woods*?"

"Not much choice." Keane sat scratching behind his right ear. The calamine lotion he'd applied after his morning shave was caked over one side of his neck and the top of his forehead. The back of his right hand was raw and bleeding.

"This guy was on your tail," Selsby said, "and because of your Olympic skills you managed to lose him?" He twisted away from his desk and crossed his legs. A yellow legal pad rested on his knee. He pressed his elbows into the arms of his chair and sat tapping his fingers together rather than taking notes. He seemed more occupied with the slipshod calamine makeup than with listening to Keane's dumbass adventure.

"I'm not sure he was chasing me, I mean—"

"What do you mean, you weren't *sure*?"

"I assumed he was chasing me."

Selsby sat up and swung his feet around. He leaned forward in his chair. "You were running through a fucking forest in the dark *assuming* someone was chasing you?"

"You had to be there."

Selsby drew back and stared at the ceiling, as if a message there might explain things better.

Keane asked, "What about the blood analysis on the victims. Did you follow up?"

Keeping his long body fixed in place, he turned only his head in Keane's direction. "They were sent to the Oak Ridge lab you recommended, Your Highness. Now will you do me a favor and stop the damned scratching?"

He smiled at Selsby, feeling the dried lotion on his cheeks wrinkling. "Did you ever have poison ivy?"

"Never. I learned in the Cub Scouts how to identify and avoid it. I was ten."

"I've got more for you."

"You haven't given me everything?" Selsby asked.

"I honestly don't know if this relates to Thornton, but when I woke up in the woods—"

"Listen to yourself, Keane. You sound like a Hans Christian . . . whatever the hell his name was."

"I woke up and discovered a clearing right in the middle of the forest. The place was full of pits blasted out of the field." He yanked a plastic bag out of his briefcase and tossed it onto the desk. "Look what was buried in the weeds."

The bag contained two feet of twisted, insulated wire and a blackened metal fragment resembling a nine-volt battery, together with the crushed circuit board. Reaching into his case again, he pulled a plastic sandwich bag with a scrap of the charred paper. Barely visible were the numbers *40-10-10*.

"Regular use-on-your-lawn fertilizer," Keane said. "High nitrogen content for greening up turfgrass."

"Classic ANFO," Selsby replied. "Ammonium nitrate and fuel oil. It was used in the Oklahoma City bombing. The recipes for it are all over the Internet. ANFO is popular worldwide. So what you found was probably a testing ground for kids trying to make an amateur bomb. But now you've contaminated the evidence."

Keane knew about evidence contamination. Everybody did. But it wasn't about that. It was all about one-upmanship. Selsby was blowing the whistle on a technical foul and that was all.

"I doubt if we're talking about kids," Keane said. "But whoever the nut was, he caught me snooping around his field lab. He fired shots at me from the woods across the creek from the field."

"You were fired on?"

"It was a close call."

"How the hell did you get out of that?" Selsby asked.

"Rescued by a friend."

"A friend? You got someone else into this mess?"

"It would be more precise to say, she got me out of that mess."

"*She*? How did a *woman* rescue you?"

"With a helicopter."

"She was riding in a chopper?" Selsby asked.

"Actually, she was flying it."

"God Almighty!" Selsby flipped his notepad onto the desk and covered his face with his hands. "She just happened to find you in the middle of a forest while she was flying over in a copter at the exact damned time someone was using you for target practice?"

"It's a long story."

"I would imagine it's another goddamned *War and Peace*."

"Have you heard of Jessie Wiley?" Keane asked.

"Sounds like a pole dancer from the Pink Pony. Are you sleeping with her?"

He let the question fall on its face. He didn't volunteer any more information and wasn't about to mention the Uzi. "It was Felix Thornton. He was doing the shooting."

"Did you *see* him?"

"No, but—"

"*Feel* him? *Taste* him?"

"Thornton had reason to be there. He wasn't up there for recreation. He has a single-minded purpose. He—"

"*He* has a single-minded purpose," Selsby said. "You're fixated on this guy like he was Judas reincarnated. You're not making any sense. When you get into those woods, God knows what you'll find. Leave what's happened up there with me for now, Keane. That's a different case altogether. I'll call in GBI. Just get out of the way of this one. There're a lot of nuts out there. Jesus, you should know that. Meth cooking. Weed farms. Dopers love it out there in the woods. Have you spent any time in the wild, Keane?"

"Not as much as you apparently," he replied, scratching the raw back of his hand. "I was never a Scout."

"Okay. You've made your case. We'll get a search warrant for this guy's place. I'll put out a precautionary APB as soon as I can take ten minutes. Forget about that shooting incident in the woods. I'll get that info to the Rabin County Sheriff's Office up there. Now get out of here so I can write all this up for my lieutenant."

Keane couldn't believe the sudden turnaround. Maybe what he needed during the whole ordeal was to let Selsby know he was the wise one, forced to work with fools like himself.

As he was leaving, Selsby called him back. "Listen to me, Keane. Every damn thing you've given me so far is guesswork. Pure speculation. Enough. If we're going to push this guy to the top of the list, we need hard evidence. Don't come back to me with anything less."

CHAPTER 23

The taxi driver grabbed the luggage from the trunk and carried it to the curb. The suitcase was vintage plaid with scuffed edges and a worn handle; the duffle bag, military green purchased from army surplus.

The international terminal of Atlanta's Hartsfield-Jackson Airport lay before Felix Thornton as he climbed from the taxi. The hullabaloo of traffic and the nauseating stench of jet fuel surrounded him. Planes taking off and landing roared overhead. Passengers rushed in waves to the terminal building, a concrete fortress with thick walls and monstrous windows running high. Lots of glass, he noted.

A shrill whistle blurted out as a cop motioned for cars to move away from the curb. Thornton studied the rest of the scene. Vehicles pulled off to the side and limos and taxis stopped to let out arrivals. In a free zone to his right, vehicles sat longer without any hassle. Across six lanes of traffic, cars and trucks crammed into acres of parking spaces and an open three-level garage. He picked up his bags and walked through the automatic doors toward the Delta Airlines ticket counter, where a board displayed Delta Flight 681 to Rome. He clutched his passport as the line snaked along to the counter.

"Is Rome your final destination, Mr. Thornton?" asked the agent checking passports.

"No. I'm flying on to Ekaterinburg," Thornton pronounced each syllable clearly, as though he knew the city well. He'd rehearsed.

The agent thumbed through his passport to check his tourist visa that had taken him five weeks to acquire.

"What business do you have in Russia?" the agent asked.

"It's only pleasure."

He stared back at Thornton, allowing his words to dangle. He flipped through the passport for the third time. "Did you pack all your luggage yourself?"

"Yes."

The agent continued his script before stamping his passport and handing it back. He looked over Thornton's shoulder toward the next in line.

Thornton checked his suitcase and moved through the TSA screening lines, glancing at the other agents and security guards as he maneuvered. Whenever anyone official caught his eye, he'd quickly turn his head. Along the concourse he entered a store with magazines and sundries and searched until he found a sewing pack that included travel scissors. Dull, but they would work. He quickly made the purchase.

When he arrived at the departure gate, he grabbed a seat near the boarding area and placed his passport back into the plastic holder that hung from his neck. He then opened his duffel bag to retrieve his US Army dog tags, now a part of his anatomy. He liked to keep them under his shirt and snuggled next to his breastbone. They had been silver-plated after he returned from the first Gulf War, his triumphant stint with the 24th Infantry Division in Operation Desert Storm.

The announcement to board burst out, and the throng collected their carry-on baggage and moved for the gate. He made his way to the back of the line, avoiding eye contact. Two female gate agents in dark blue uniforms worked the line from either side. He stayed to the left, drawn to the younger and less threatening woman who inserted his boarding pass into the scanner.

Red lights blinked and the scanner buzzed.

He backed away. Had to run. But where?

"Excuse me, sir," the gate agent said, smiling. "You're sitting in an exit row. Are you willing and able to provide assistance if called upon?"

He cleared his throat. "Of course, ma'am."

*   *   *

Cruising over the Atlantic, Thornton thumbed through his pocket Russian phrase guide, slowly mouthing the strange sounds. He'd forced himself the last two months to work exactly sixty minutes each day with the set of CDs from Rosetta Stone. But it was hard to focus. He yawned and shut off his overhead light then leaned back and closed his eyes. Fingering his dog tags, he considered his life, only one year from the half-century mark.

He reflected on all he'd accomplished in so short a time. Who would've ever thought he'd come so far? Thanks to Desert Storm, he'd learned firsthand strategies to overwhelm the enemy. In the first Gulf War, he was twenty-five and an explosive ordnance disposal tech attached to Naval Special Ops. He was taught all the right stuff in his training, working alongside the Navy SEALs: handling and disposal of every type of weapon—chemical, biological, nuclear. His feats so far even included side projects. Like the fitting job he'd pulled on his worthless dad, a goddamned disgrace to humanity. The man who watched the rape of his own wife while he stood shaking and pissing his pants. He was nothing but a drunken fool who spent his life roaming Piedmont Park, begging for food.

His pitiful dad had insisted that he become an altar boy. It would bring him a special place in heaven. The priest was Father O'Shannon—honored, respected, admired by so many for so long. Everyone thought him a role model in the lives of Catholic boys.

"You're a very special servant of the Lord, Felix Henry," Father O'Shannon had often said in those days. What was the good Father thinking now, burning eternally in his own special corner of hell? A place reserved for faggots with long fingers and soft hands. But

Thornton knew that what he'd accomplished so far was nothing more than child's play.

The dinner carts were stowed, the passengers blanketed and sleeping. Lights indicated a vacant restroom. He grabbed the plastic bag with his store purchase and unbuckled. Next to the restroom, three flight attendants sat in the rear, one gulping down pasta from a tray and another thumbing through the *New Yorker*.

Locking the restroom door behind him, he snipped at his beard with the travel scissors he'd purchased. Black and silver curls fell in clumps into the sink. He scraped at his face and neck with a plastic razor, using all the shaving cream in the microcanister. After rinsing, he slid his hand over his smooth cheeks and stared at his fresh image in the mirror. Red and raw, it was a new face to thwart off those who could be looking for him when he arrived.

CHAPTER 24

Keane paced along a path by the gardens on the temple grounds, pausing to observe a hummingbird feed at the bloom of a mimosa tree. California's Mount Shasta Abbey Monastery was an hour's drive from the Redding Municipal Airport where copilots Taylor and Roberto awaited his return.

Katherine—his ex—was devastated when she'd called the night before. Andy had left home without any warning three days before. When she finally received a call from their son, she found out he'd linked up with some kind of Buddhist order in California. They're monks and nuns who practice Soto Zen, "Whatever the hell that means," she'd told Keane.

Evidently, Andy wanted to wait for a while before telling anyone about his new adventure, especially his dad and sister. He didn't want to have to face the humiliation if it didn't work out.

A flock of monks moved in Keane's direction. Their heads shaved, each wore a cinnamon-brown robe with a lavender scarf around his neck. Keane stared as they walked by, examining each carefully. One straggler trailed behind. The young monk with the emerald eyes of his mother lifted his head and smiled hesitantly as he approached. "Hi, Dad."

Keane reached out with both arms to hug his son, who responded with a hollow squeeze. Holding on to Andy's shoulders, Keane stepped back for a better view. "You look different."

Andy passed a hand through his fine, bristling hair that was cut to a fraction of an inch. "I feel the same." He reached to grab the shoulder piece of his robe and pull it higher.

"You're a monk already?" Keane asked.

"That'll take time. I'm a postulant—sort of a monk in training. I was here for a retreat last summer. Remember? I told you about it."

"Sure . . . of course."

"I've been back twice since. I've learned the precepts and have an ordination teacher."

Andy spoke confidently, a trait new to him. Had he been that brainwashed so quickly? The pair sauntered down a path winding under a canopy of flowering crepe myrtle. "I wasn't aware you were so serious about this Buddhist thing."

"Buddhism isn't a thing, Dad. It's a way of life."

"But I just don't understand why you're walking away from all of us. I mean, your family and friends. How did we—"

"Go wrong?" Andy asked. "Do you think I've gone wrong?"

"I didn't mean it that way."

Andy turned away and began walking again, hands behind his back and his head down as Keane followed.

"This is an awfully big decision so soon out of high school. You're young, Andy. You have a lifetime ahead of you."

"That's all anyone has, isn't it?"

"I was hoping we could get together for a week. Just you and me. Go away to the Alaskan wilderness, take in the grizzlies and bald eagles. Get in a few days of salmon fishing."

"We used to talk about that a lot," Andy replied.

"Yeah. We just keep putting it off."

"That would've been fun. I think those opportunities are gone now, Dad." He dropped onto a park bench opposite the statue of a golden Buddha.

Keane sat beside him. A pair of blue jays fought above the Buddha's head. "Why are you putting college out of the question? You've always been so good in math—really, anything technical."

"Just like you?"

"You're far brighter than I was at your age, Son. Look, I pay Nicole's tuition. I'd pay yours too, if you—"

"School's the last thing on my mind."

"I know that. But it should be the first."

"My life is first. Can't you understand that?"

What he couldn't understand were most of the rash and ridiculous decisions his son had made of late. What did he know about life in only eighteen frigging years? He was putting his heart ahead of his head, a trait learned from his mother. "How will you support yourself?"

"The Order will take care of that now."

The Order will take care of you? "I just don't understand. Why can't—" He stopped.

"Why can't what?"

"It doesn't matter."

"Say it, Dad. Go ahead and say it."

Keane looked away.

"Why can't I be more like Nicole? Is that it? Isn't that what you flew all the way out here to ask me?" He jumped up from the bench.

Keane quickly followed. "Can you get away for a couple of hours so we can talk over dinner?"

Andy slowed to let his dad catch up, but spoke without looking at him. "It's against the rules. I can't leave the grounds for a few months." He said he had to rush off for evening prayers.

There was no parting hug. Andy rushed down the path, tugging again at the robe draped over that skinny, naked shoulder. Keane climbed onto the bench and watched his son turn the corner past the mimosa tree. Surely he would look back.

Carefully balancing himself, Keane rose on his toes, straining for one more glance. He stood staring for over a minute. Maybe Andy would think about what his own dad meant to him, all he had done for him over those eighteen years. Maybe it would all come to him in a flash. Maybe he would turn about, come running around the corner, rushing back past that damned mimosa tree.

CHAPTER 25

A miserably long line of drowsy passengers stretched across the tarmac from the Aeroflot jet at Russia's Ekaterinburg Airport, a thousand miles east of Moscow. Thornton had only napped in spurts during the nine-hour flight from Rome. He yawned and felt woozy but kept his aching eyes on alert as he pushed his way among the crowd along a dark passageway. The plane was three hours late because of a mechanical setback in Rome. At the terminal entrance, a group of passengers rushed ahead to the single line for foreigners that led to passport control.

Duffel bag in hand, Thornton moved cautiously, ready to take action at the slightest sign of recognition. He studied the face of the clerk where the line had formed. Dark skin, Arabic features, with a scarf over her head. She interrogated each passenger as if she was looking for recruits for jihad. When she motioned him forward, he handed over his passport. She studied it, glancing back and forth between his picture and face.

He smiled, folded his fingers and motioned as if shaving.

She looked back at the crowd as if paying him no attention, and he instinctively rubbed his dog tags beneath his cotton shirt. She scanned the passport under the black light and made an entry into her computer. He quickly surveyed the scene as she riffled through the pages again then glowered at him. "Why you to Russia?"

"Holiday," he replied, in the most pleasant voice he could muster.

She held up three fingers. "That be three hundred US dollar, please."

He'd watched the German ahead had put down eighty euros, no more than a hundred bucks. "I don't understand."

The clerk narrowed her eyes. "Visa. Three hundred dollar."

"I've already paid for my visa. I—"

The clerk bit into her lower lip. "Three hundred dollar. You know *dollar*, American?"

He wanted to grab her by the neck and pluck her out from her sheltered pit. Reaching into his jacket, he pulled out three one-hundred dollar bills, careful not to slam them down. She opened a drawer and stuffed the bills into a manila envelope then looked up as if surprised he was still there. With a frown and a thumb, she motioned for him to leave.

Thornton followed the signs to baggage claim, where at least four uniformed security guards roamed, one with a German shepherd on a leash. A black-billed hat smothered the head of each guard. Fancy decorations donned the narrow shoulders of their wrinkled brown uniforms. Near the end of the long corridor, two other guards strolled in his direction. He peeked ahead. To his right were three more official-looking SOBs who leaned on a food-stand bar. Both turned away when he caught their glance. The guards in the corridor quickened their pace directly toward him. His corner vision picked up others who approached from either side. He dropped the duffel bag and grabbed his chest, groaning as he fell to the floor on top of the bag. A woman in a long, drab dress walking beside him halted and screamed. One guard rushed to him, leaned down, and shouted.

He moaned louder.

Another guard bent down onto his knees and lifted his head. Thornton squeezed his eyes shut and clutched his chest with both hands. The guard jerked out his whistle and blew. Thornton glared out of one eye at a cluster of uniforms circled above him. He kept his right arm looped through the duffel bag's strap.

When the paramedics arrived, one checked him with a stethoscope and spoke in broken English near his ear. He ignored the questions. After two men lifted him onto a gurney, a third tugged at the duffel bag. He yanked it back. The crowd parted as they rolled him away, their stares fixed on him as if to get a delightful glimpse of a dying American. Loosely tied onto the gurney with one strap, he was maneuvered into the cool night and inside the waiting ambulance. A siren wailed as it the ambulance took off at half speed. He thought about the luggage piece he left behind and what might be in it that would be needed on the mission. Nothing he couldn't replace at a street market. No identifying info.

A paramedic massaged a vein on his arm in an attempt to get an IV into it. He arm-wrestled with him until the medic backed off. When a syringe moved toward Thornton's upper arm, he slapped at it and knocked it to the floor.

The ambulance jolted to a stop at the hospital entrance. The paramedics rolled him out and bounced him around on the gurney as if letting him fall onto the walkway would only be an inconvenience. He jerked up and snapped off a cloth strap that secured him. A paramedic grabbed at his arm, but he quickly broke loose, snatched his duffel bag and sprinted away. Shouting burst out from behind.

Thornton dashed around a corner and toward a dark street. When he scampered across, a car screeched to a halt, and the driver yelled at him with unknown words but unmistakable meaning. He trotted down the block and occasionally glanced over his shoulder while trying to avoid tripping. At the next intersection he slowed to a walk, turned the corner, and spotted what looked like a car for hire.

The driver, reading from a folded newspaper, stood next to the small rusted vehicle.

"Speak English?" Thornton asked, breathing heavily.

"Speak many language, my friend." No older than thirty, the Russian was a thin man with black hair and a mustache. He wore a woven blue-and-white cap and a yellowed smile that revealed a wide gap between his two front teeth.

"Is your car for hire?" Thornton asked.

"Amerikanish?"

"Yes."

"Where you go, my friend?"

"A quick tour of the city." Thornton lurched for the rear passenger door, thinking how wise a decision he'd made in Rome to convert seven hundred dollars to Russian rubles. He slid onto the rear seat and tossed his duffel bag across it.

The driver stayed outside and leaned into the open window. "It is dark for touring."

"Please, just take me around the city. Could we go? I'm in a rush."

The driver hopped in and cranked the engine then pulled away from the curb in nervous spurts. At the first intersection, the traffic light turned red. An anemic siren arose behind them. Thornton pretended to drop something onto the floorboard and bent down. When he rose up, a police car moved slowly past them before pulling away.

They traveled the deserted streets in a city that the guidebook said was the gateway to the Ural Mountains, a range that separated the center of Russia from Siberia. Rows of faded yellow and dingy-white apartment buildings emerged along the way. Other outdated buildings looked like remnants from another period of history. Lone pedestrians walked the streets, looking as gloomy as the shops they passed. Occasional restaurants and bars cropped up and brought signs of life to the sidewalks. A younger crowd had gathered around the outdoor tables, eating and drinking and chattering—and generally looking like the only people who wanted to be happy.

He desperately needed rest, but he knew he couldn't go to the Bolshoy Ural, the contact hotel he'd put on his visa application. He had no intention of staying in Ekaterinburg for any longer than it took to arrange transportation to his destination.

"Once, I in America," the driver said, smiling through the cavern between his front teeth.

Thornton didn't reply.

"New York," the driver added with even more enthusiasm.

"I need a place to stay tonight," Thornton said, ignoring the travel stories. "A place to stay and a driver for tomorrow." He was carrying more cash on him than ever in his life.

An impish grin crossed the driver's face. "You like to hire car to go around city?" He circled his dark index finger in the air.

"No. To go outside city. See the countryside."

"What means *kountrycide*?"

Thornton threw out his hands and swept them around. "To see your Russia. The Motherland."

"You very lucky. I know man with big American car. He can give you room to stay night."

"Tonight?"

"This night, yes. And with very big car. How you say, *Ulz-mow-bilt*?"

Thornton mouthed the word *ulzmowbilt*, thinking for a moment. "Yes, *Oldsmobile*. Nice big car."

"I that man. I am Osken. I have the Ulzmowbilt."

"Oscar?"

"Osken. My name given to me by my grandfather. Means I grow strong and healthy like ox." He displayed a biceps under a rolled-up sleeve and another gap-toothed grin.

Thornton smiled back. The mission would soon begin.

CHAPTER 26

On the way home from the West Coast, Keane kept repeating to himself what Andy had said about "the rules." He couldn't leave the monastery for a while to have dinner, to talk things out. Because it was against the *rules*? It was also against the rules to ignore family. It was against every rule in the book to just take off like you know what the hell you're doing when you're just out of high school. Andy wasn't thinking, he was rebelling because he was eighteen and he could. He was shaking his tail feathers for his dad and mom and the world to admire.

A string of messages had been coming in on Keane's phone during his flight, including the one from Oak Ridge National Laboratory he'd been waiting for. He told Taylor and Roberto to plan on a short trip for the next morning.

*   *   *

Keane's jet rolled into a private slot at the Oak Ridge Airstrip. He was met inside the terminal by a man in his sixties wearing a checkered shirt and sporting a hunting cap. They quickly departed in a Ford pickup with a gun rack and headed for the hill country of middle Tennessee. Keane sat silently listening to the driver's stories as he rode along the narrow highway across green rolling hills to a fortress atop

Chestnut Ridge: Oak Ridge National Laboratory, one of the world's leading nuclear research laboratories.

Colin Hickman, a thirty-year veteran of the facility, said that he was often called upon to pick up special visitors because of his knowledge of history. "The Oak Ridge nuclear reservation was an absolute key part of the Manhattan Project."

He spoke with a soft Appalachian twang. "An army of bulldozers began work in the fall of '42. Less than three years later, the scientists developed a large-scale method to separate the rare uranium-235 isotope from uranium ore. They delivered enough of it to Los Alamos during the spring and summer of '45 to make the critical assembly for Little Boy. You know that one, don't you?"

"You'll have to remind me," Keane replied.

"Code name for the bomb dropped over Hiroshima."

A chain-link fence topped with thick-gauged razor wire encircled the isolated facility. After receiving his visitor's ID badge—APD had called in advance—a security guard drove Keane into the depths of the complex. A jumbled array of buildings, they were both single-level and multistoried, and all of 1950s vintage.

The guard escorted him into a brick structure where they climbed two flights of stairs to reach the conference room. It sat next to a large lab area where a host of gadgets flashed lights and spewed paper graphs and digital readings on LED displays. Lab assistants in white lab coats and carrying clipboards roamed among the instruments. A large window loomed on one inside wall so that the laboratory could be viewed from the conference room. He was introduced to four scientists who were sitting around a rectangular table in government-issued hard-back chairs.

The introduction was delivered in staccato chunks by Dr. Denton Allenberry, a biochemist and a small man who wore his expertise and his years on hunched shoulders. "Our results are only preliminary at this point, Dr. Keane. But we expect the numbers to be in the ballpark of those in our final report. We'll provide that to the Atlanta PD and the Georgia Bureau of Investigation by next week."

The final report would be handled as a formality. What Keane needed on this trip was hard data, just as Selsby had demanded.

Dr. Allenberry continued. "We performed chromosome analysis on each blood sample, looking only for radiation damage stored in the white cells."

A scientist seated across the table, Dr. Irene Cassidy, spoke up. She was much younger than Dr. Allenberry. "We also used electron spin resonance to analyze molars extracted from what we were told were the warehouse victims. It's an alternative way to detect radiation exposure. We can locate the signals in tooth enamel. The teeth and blood samples matched well enough to give us confidence in our results."

"What data do you have for me?" Keane asked.

The scientists went carefully through the numbers for every sample, demonstrating with hard measurements the radiation exposure of each victim. Keane knew the alphanumeric code that had been agreed upon inside APD. When a coded sample was discussed, he knew who it was. The exposures were all in the lethal range—the Latinos in the warehouse received by far the highest radiation doses.

There was one exception. Blood sample RGD was at the lowest end of the dose range.

"Victim RGD has a chance of survival?" Keane asked.

"Our educated guess would be less than fifty-fifty," Dr. Allenberry replied.

The sample was blood from little Ronnie Davenport. That information alone was worth the trip.

On his way back to the airport, Keane wondered if Selsby might already have Thornton in jail, held on suspicion. While he waited in the hangar at the Oak Ridge Airstrip, he hit the speed dial on his cell phone.

Selsby answered after too many rings.

"Anything on Thornton yet?" Keane asked.

"I told you I'd call when I had something to follow up."

"I've just been briefed by the Oak Ridge lab. I'm landing at PDK in thirty minutes. I'll buy you lunch at the Fighter Group."

*   *   *

When Keane found Selsby, he was eating a grilled cheese sandwich at a corner table. Before Keane could speak, Selsby blurted out: "Who authorized you to go to Oak Ridge?"

"Suzanne Fowler," Keane replied. "She gave me a heads up that prelim results were ready."

"A forensic doesn't have that kind of authority. You know that."

"I do what anyone in APD tells me. Remember, I'm only a consultant. And don't forget what you told me. You said you wanted only hard evidence from now on."

Selsby's stare said that the detective wasn't buying his fake ignorance of protocol.

"Give me your bottom line from those geeks at Oak Ridge," Selsby said.

"They checked as many of the victims' blood samples as Grady could get their hands on. Even teeth. The results leave no doubt. Intense radiation exposures have killed at least eight people so far."

Selsby sat staring into the distance as if trying to determine what to do with the info, as if he'd have to pass on the case to someone more techie. Maybe one of the kid detectives. "Let me bring you up to speed on this guy Thornton," he finally said. "Chief Walters and the GBI lawyer took the request for a search warrant on his house to Judge McElfresh on the Superior Court. He turned the request down flat."

"You're pulling my leg," Keane said.

"The judge grilled both of them on all the details. They gave him the background on Thornton's employment, the missing radiation sources from the clinic, and the interview results. The chief was careful how he chose his words, but the judge wanted to know *who* conducted the interviews. He didn't like hearing that a consultant or his 'colleague'— anyone not on a specific, approved assignment—was a primary gatherer of info. Evidently he'd been burned by APD before. He refused to authorize the warrant."

"That's ridiculous!"

"The judge said that any evidence collected would never stand up in court. The whole process would be challenged. He was emphatic. He read the riot act to the chief for even bringing the request to him."

Keane shook his head, wondering if some conspiracy was working against him.

"Don't let it bother you," Selsby said. "We've started an all-out search for evidence anyway."

Keane dumped cream and extra sugar into the black coffee delivered to the table. "What about the sniper? The guy who took pot shots at me in the woods." He slowly stirred his coffee.

"GBI collected shell casings from the trees. Plaster casts on the tire tracks and footprints. These things take time to follow up. Everybody's got their priorities, Keane, not just you. Let 'em do their damn job. Whatever we do won't be much help at the moment anyway."

"Why not?"

"I just got some bad news before you called," Selsby replied. "Thornton fled the country."

"Thornton escaped the country?" Keane repeated. He sat back and grabbed the hair on the back of his head with both hands. That news was beyond ridiculous. All the frigging work he and Jessie did to pin down the evidence. And they let Thornton escape the country? Completely inexcusable by any standards of law enforcement. Damned incompetence of the highest order.

"It took us too long to locate the guy," Selsby said. "When we checked with all the air carriers, we found out he was on a Delta flight to Rome and transferred to a flight to Russia."

Keane remembered the chitchat with Thornton back in the North Georgia woods. He was looking for information on Russia. If you wanted to leave the US and the hand of American law as far behind as possible, that was a damned good choice.

"The FBI transmitted the photos and background to Interpol," Selsby continued. "We didn't get the word out in time to have them grab him in Rome. That's where he transferred to an Aeroflot flight. But Interpol will have local law enforcement waiting on him when he lands in Russia."

If anything, Interpol was efficient. Keane once had the opportunity to learn that firsthand. "Will the Russians return him?"

"They'll hold him. We're working on an international warrant. Don't worry. We've got him—he's sitting in the middle of a goddamn trap."

*   *   *

The three-man HAZMAT team from Georgia Environmental Protection jumped down from their van and approached the front stoop of Ronnie Davenport's home. The little boy's foster mother opened the door. She'd expected them.

The senior member of the team—Milton Johansson—led the way with a Geiger counter in hand. He walked the main floor of the brick Colonial, followed by trainee Gil McGrath and old man Peterson, who was only six months from retirement. Johansson held the radiation meter out in front of his wide girth as the team trailed him up the staircase to the bedrooms. At the top of the steps the meter's numbers began to rise. He paused and turned to face the main foyer below. "Which is Ronnie's bedroom?" he asked the anxious couple standing there, hand in hand and watching in silence.

"Turn left and go to the end of the hall," the woman called.

As Johansson stepped toward the bedroom, the meter response shot upward. By the time he entered the empty bedroom, the meter had jumped off scale.

CHAPTER 27

"A chunk of cobalt-60?" Keane asked Suzanne Fowler. He sat inside her forensics lab across from her corner desk.

"It wasn't much bigger than your thumbnail," she responded. "They detected gamma rays as soon as they got within ten feet of the boy's bedroom. It took a while, and they had to bring in special equipment. But they recovered the cobalt from his top dresser drawer."

Keane was dumbfounded trying to think of a way a fragment of radioactive metal could've been placed in Ronnie Davenport's home, much less in the very bedroom where he slept. Whatever the explanation for the other crimes, there couldn't possibly be a rational one for this one.

"You checked with the director of the clinic Thornton worked for?" Keane asked. "The one I told you about? William Titus?"

"Immediately. From the slug dimensions, intensity, and spectrum of its gamma ray emissions, there's no question it came from his missing source at the clinic."

Keane was stumped. "But how did the Davenport kid get hold of it?"

"One of Selsby's men questioned the boy in his hospital room. It took an hour, on and off, giving him a chance to recover between questions. His foster mother held his hand the whole time, reassuring him. The detective said it was one of the toughest assignments he ever

144

took on. He learned that the boy located the object in Piedmont Park. He played there a lot and said he found it taped under a park bench. You know how curious kids are. He slipped it into his pocket and took it home."

Keane quickly made the connection with Thornton's vagrant father, who made his home in the park. The hidden and deadly chunk of radioactivity that he'd used to kill his own father had fallen into the innocent hands of Ronnie Davenport. Thornton deserved the deepest chasm in the bottomless pits of hell.

"We've got techs with radiation detectors spread out over the city," Fowler said. "There're a total of six cobalt-60 slugs, each identical to the one they found in Ronnie's bedroom. All of them are small enough to hide anywhere easily. But radiation is a field I don't get into much. Seems like some victims got hit big-time with the radiation and some didn't."

"To have real harm," Keane said, "you have to be near the source for a long period. Like the priest who was within a couple of feet of one hidden cobalt slug for many hours. The parishioners were at the confessional with him for only a few minutes at a time. Their exposure wouldn't be enough to put them in any real danger. It's all about how close you are to the source and how much time you spend there. Just like heat from a fireplace. With gamma radiation though, spending long times at close distances can be fatal."

"But you'd think," she said, "that this Thornton guy would've gotten a deadly dose. I mean, considering how much he must have handled the stuff."

"He could have, easily. But if he kept the cobalt slugs contained inside thick steel or lead shielding, he could at least limit his exposure to something tolerable."

Keane knew the Georgia state environmental guys had the expertise and detection instruments to track down cobalt sources scattered around the city. "By the way, how helpful did you find Detective Selsby?"

She looked at him, puzzled. "I don't know what you mean."

"Sorry. A personal question."

Her bewildered look didn't surprise him. That was Suzanne Fowler—straight-laced, stick to protocol.

She removed her black-rim glasses. "Can we speak off the record?"

"Sure. Just between you and me." He blew it. Should've asked her if she wanted to go for lunch and talk it over.

She stood and strolled to the credenza where a coffee maker sat beside the window overlooking the city. "Coffee?"

He waved a polite *no*.

She poured the dark brew into a dirty-looking ceramic mug. "I'll admit I had more than a professional interest in Detective Selsby when we started working together."

"You were dating him?"

"That depends on what you mean by *dating*."

She returned to her chair with her coffee and settled in. "We had dinner more than once. Lots of getting-to-know-you conversations."

"I take it that you really got to know him?"

"I wouldn't say that. But we did talk about our outside interests. Mine's horses. He had other hobbies."

"I like horses, too," he piped up. "Love trail riding."

In fact he'd only been horseback riding twice in his life. The horses he'd ridden each stared him down with a suspicious eye, as if they knew a counterfeit cowboy when they saw one. They treated him accordingly on the trail.

"I do equestrian competition," she added.

Clearly out of his league—so much for looking for common ground.

"He belongs to a group that meets down in South Georgia," she said. "Spends a lot of his weekends there. I'm talking *every* weekend in the summer."

He recalled the conversation with Selsby at the Waffle House. "He did mention to me about his weekends. Something about shooting or a hunting club?"

"Oh, is that what he called it?"

"Did you have another name?"

She lifted the mug to her lips and emptied it. "I'd call it the Dawson Breakfast Club." She stood to take her mug to the sink. "I'm afraid I've got some lab work to finish up."

After an awkward silence, he asked, "Would you be interested in a quick lunch?"

"No, thanks. I normally work through lunch."

Of course. He should've guessed that before the question got out of his mouth. But the bottom line was clear—she was hinting at something about Selsby. For some strange reason, she didn't want to talk about it. That begged for follow-up.

CHAPTER 28

"Mr. Thornton! Mr. Thornton!" Osken's stale breath was six inches from Thornton's face. "We are here!"

Thornton rubbed his eyes. "Here? Where's here?"

"My dacha—our country home for all family. Where you will stay night."

Thornton had fallen asleep while Osken drove. Glaring over Osken's shoulder from behind was a man with a blue turban and a gray beard resting against Osken's left earlobe.

"Say hello to my Uncle Yerbol," Osken said.

Thornton reached through his open window and stuck out his hand. Uncle Yerbol grabbed onto his fingers and gave him a bloated grin.

With Osken proudly leading the way, the three men walked up to a tiny wood-framed house, painted lime green decades before and with a rusted tin roof. It was surrounded on all sides that he could see by a vegetable garden. Inside, he met Uncle Yerbol's wife. Her dark eyes inspected his with an expression as serious as it was cold. Anya was at least twenty years younger than lucky ol' Uncle Yerbol. Alien spices wafted from the kitchen. Osken explained that Anya was Khazak and a very good cook. "You must forgive my uncle," Osken said as Anya set out to fix a late evening meal. "He is old and sick. Took the Dag's baths many times. He speak only Russian and never meet Americans.

148

He says he hear Americans tall, but he not believe how tall. He says you are very big man."

Outside, kids stared through the parlor window, pointing and laughing. Osken jumped up to chase them away. Word had obviously spread in the village that an American walked among them.

Dinner that evening was a welcomed adventure. The food was hot, spicy, and plentiful. From Osken's explanation, Thornton caught only random words—roasted horse and cow offal, peppers, onions. He wasn't aware how famished he'd become over the last twenty-four hours. They washed down the meal with black tea mixed with mare's milk.

After dinner the men rose from their chairs and retired into a sitting area. Osken busied himself by preparing a hookah, loading it with a crude tobacco blended with dried fruit and unidentifiable shreds of something else. Thornton followed Osken's actions and grasped an embroidered hose sprouting from the bowl. Jamming the stem between his lips, he inhaled the sweet aroma. It felt good, relaxing, a much smoother drag than from his cigarettes. He could learn to like the custom.

While he sat sedated, quietly listening to the soft bubbling, Thornton thought it the perfect time to begin. "How far are we from Chelyabinsk?"

"Chelyabinsk?" Osken replied. "*Very* far!"

"How far would that be exactly?"

"Maybe three hours by Ulzmowbilt. Very, very far. Not good place." Osken looked to his uncle, repeating the city's name in his dialect. They both shook their heads from side to side, in sync.

"But I would like to go there," Thornton said.

Osken threw out his open palms and shrugged in disbelief. "We for certain do *not* go to Chelyabinsk. Many bad stories." He repeated the phrase to Uncle Yerbol, who added a wave of his finger and another serious shake of his head.

"What kind of stories?" Thornton asked.

"It was secret city after the war. Nobody allowed to go there unless you did secret work for Red Army." He turned to his uncle and spoke in rapid fire phrases. Uncle Yerbol gestured wildly, manipulating his eyebrows as if describing a tale of horror.

"All around Chelyabinsk," Osken said, "the Communists did their dirty work."

In stumbling English Osken explained that Stalin's chief monster, Beria—who ran the Soviet secret police—took charge of the slave workers. They were the hordes of people who built factories and secret laboratories and used army tanks to make roads. "My uncle say many young Russians die working there. The city closed to everybody for many years. Except secret workers and families."

Thornton didn't want to rush his response. He knew from how they talked that they had heard only tidbits and rumors—gossip over the decades. For the last six months he'd studied Chelyabinsk and its history, pouring through dozens of journal articles in the Georgia Tech Library. The world's most infamous nuclear weapons facility lay on the outskirts of Chelyabinsk. At that location the Soviets manufactured in the forties and fifties plutonium for their first atomic bombs. They'd planned to keep every operation involving nuclear weapons as far away from Moscow as possible—deep within the forests of the Ural Mountains.

The Chelyabinsk region, Thornton had learned, was the most promising place for hiding the massive weapons operations from high-altitude American spy planes. But thanks to the overwhelming success of these U-2 flights—with pilots like Francis Gary Powers who was shot down and captured—and their high-tech cameras aboard, the US discovered near Chelyabinsk the infamous Mayak plant where the Soviets built reactors to make plutonium for their nuclear weapons. It was a facility identical to the Hanford site in Washington State and yet another triumph of Soviet espionage.

What eventually followed was known in classified Soviet documents for decades as the *Kyshtym Incident*, named after the nearest town just outside of Chelyabinsk. An unbelievable story: the cause was the result of humongous amounts of radioactive waste from their weapons program stored in the underground tanks. The radiation emitted by the waste generated so much heat that extreme temperatures and pressures built up inside the tanks. Then in 1957 the tanks exploded with a force equivalent to one hundred tons of TNT. The nuclear waste and debris spread two hundred miles downwind, killing all the trees for ten square miles, contaminating over two hundred towns and villages, and exposing a quarter-million people to radiation. Hundreds of men, women and children who lived closest to the site received fatal or near-fatal radiation exposures.

Entire villages in the Ural Mountains were removed from the maps by authorities. Tens of thousands living farther away remained in the contaminated zone for years—without any knowledge of their radiation poisoning because the Soviets never revealed it. The air they breathed, the water they drank and bathed in, even the food they grew in their gardens, emitted deadly gamma rays.

The Russians never announced the death toll. Taken as a whole, the "Kyshtym Trace"—which originated on the outskirts of Chelyabinsk— had long been known as the most polluted place on the planet.

Thornton returned the mouthpiece to his lips and inhaled. "No doubt," he said, "that a visit to Chelyabinsk would impress my American friends."

Osken put down his hose and folded his arms across his chest. "Even God tried to send a message to the people of Chelyabinsk."

Thornton cocked his head, puzzled.

"The big rock flew in from the sky," Osken said. "It made much news over the world. Yes?"

Yes, indeed, Thornton remembered. Three years before, a gigantic meteor had struck the city, making international news. Amateur videos that caught the remarkable streaming flash of light and fire as it came crashing to earth in Chelyabinsk were all over the TV for at least a week following the event. It had injured over a thousand people.

Thornton nodded. "God moves in mysterious ways." He returned the hookah's mouthpiece to his lips, inhaled, and slowly blew smoke.

Osken looked up, shaking his head and apparently searching for the right words. "There is another big problem if we go there."

Thornton continued to smoke, giving Osken's remark a chance to settle in. He put down the hose. "Exactly what kind of big problem do you see?"

"Nasty police there may find something about us they do not like. They are stupid men."

"But not always, I'm sure."

"No, sometimes they are stupid women. But they are all stupid Communists from the old days. If they find something they do not like—or if they have unhappy day—they may arrest me. And you too. But that would be *your* problem."

"Do you know all of that for certain?" Thornton asked.

"It has happened to friends of mine, yes."

"I suppose this trip will cost me a little extra money?"

Osken glanced upward and stuck out his lower lip as if making a knotty calculation. Then he jerked his head down and fixed on Thornton. "Two thousand rubles. And we can stay there only one day."

"I'll pay you fifty US dollars. And we stay there two days."

Osken thought momentarily then smiled. He held up an index finger and waved it about. "We have deal. But remember, it is very dangerous place. Many foreigners find that a day in Chelyabinsk was their last day on earth."

Thornton grabbed the water-pipe hose again. He inhaled and unwound, feeling better, even more detached. When his puff of smoke faded, he spoke. "Danger is something Americans face every day in their cities, Osken. Tomorrow we head for Chelyabinsk."

CHAPTER 29

TWO days had gone by since Keane's meeting with Suzanne Fowler, and he'd followed media accounts as they developed. Interviews and updates played on the three local channels and on CNN. A reporter for the *Journal-Constitution* had written a detailed account of the murders of the Hispanics in the warehouse downtown.

The federal Nuclear Regulatory Commission—Region Two in Atlanta—confirmed that a cancer treatment center in Midtown had lost "a number of cobalt-60 slugs" from a radiation therapy clinic. The director of Georgia's Environmental Protection Division was interviewed and acknowledged that HAZMAT teams throughout the city were searching with highly specialized instruments, looking for radiation sources. The Nuclear Security Administration had called in a rapid-response team from the Department of Energy's Savannah River facility in bordering South Carolina. Their high-tech helicopter was one of a kind, equipped with instrumentation to detect and locate gamma-ray sources in a flyover of the city.

Mayor Stillwell had appeared daily in the media, reassuring Atlanta residents that every effort would be made to locate "any and all" stray radiation sources. Schools at all levels let out for a day to have their rooms scanned for radiation. Fire and police vehicles equipped with radiation detectors were called upon to search around city blocks, near Centennial Olympic Park, Turner Field, the Philips Arena. Protests were launched because the wealthier neighborhoods—Buckhead and Dunwoody—had priority, or so it seemed to many who wrote letters to the *Journal-Constitution* editors.

At 5:10 p.m. the cell call came in from Detective Selsby.

"You *lost* him?" Keane asked. It didn't make sense. He couldn't have heard him right.

"I don't understand it either," Selsby said. "How the hell do you lose someone de-boarding from an international flight? Damned Russians."

Keane held the phone away from his ear and listened in total disgust. Was Thornton really *that* clever?

"We'll go through channels to the State Department," Selsby said. "Give them everything we have on him. They'll put it into the data bank. We can only hope someone at a checkpoint over there can spot and hold him. Then contact the embassy."

"How serious will Russia take this?"

"You know the answer to that one."

"Looks to me like he may have gotten away for good," Keane said. Murder at will and disappear. End of filthy story. Perfect crime.

"Shit happens, Keane. They missed him by a lousy twenty minutes."

"Why didn't they get him at customs?"

"Chalk it up to miscommunication."

"A lot gets chalked up to that in bureaucracies," Keane replied. "Did he have a return ticket?"

"He wasn't stupid enough to buy one-way. He knew that would be a red flag. He doesn't intend to use it. Maybe the SOB's headed for Russia to collect a mail-order bride. Live the good life."

Not only did the Russians and Interpol slip up on Thornton's getaway. How aggressive had Selsby and APD been in seeing that Thornton got caught? Irrefutable evidence had piled up, linking him to the murders. And he got away with it. The whole affair stunk. *Miscommunication, hell.*

What had happened with his life, Keane asked himself, since the day Mayor Stillwell paraded back into it? He'd become a stalker after a killer and was lost like a fawn in the woods when he'd almost become a murder victim himself. The worst part was that he'd failed. Failed at his single goal of bringing about the capture of a heinous serial murderer when the beast was right at their fingertips.

But it wasn't the only area of his life where he'd failed miserably—and that awakening gnawed at his gut as if he'd swallowed a rat. He'd failed as a husband. And he had to come to grips with what he'd finally realized at the Buddhist Monastery two days before—he'd failed as a father too.

About to ring Mr. J to cancel dinner, he felt his cell phone vibrate. A text message from Jessie: "Dine at Rhett's tonight?"

Her favorite place to eat was Rhett's Parlor, a classic restaurant in downtown Atlanta established in the forties following the success of *Gone With the Wind.*

He texted back: "Sorry. Not in mood. Raincheck?"

Response: "U need to be in a MOOD to eat? Ur not tired, ur bored. Meet u there at 8."

*   *   *

"I still don't understand how Thornton selected his victims," Jessie said. She pushed aside the cheese grits and cut into a crisp golden brown chicken breast. Rhett's Parlor owed its reputation over the decades to serving true Southern cuisine in all its sweet and fried glory.

Keane put down his knife and fork. "The first ones were in Thornton's neighborhood. Both victims were black. Available prey. With success, he expanded his racial cleansing to any color that wasn't white."

"Revenge as well?" she asked.

"Yeah, like on his dad he hated. His first love, who rejected him. The priest at his church growing up—for reasons known only to Thornton."

"He's a demon," she replied, "who lives in the solitary confinement of his own private world, I suppose. But why didn't they grab him at customs?"

Keane picked up his fork and shoved the asparagus around on his plate, with every intention of eventually taking a bite of it. "Selsby called it a mix-up in communications." He rolled his eyes.

"It doesn't make sense that Thornton would choose Russia, does it?" she asked.

"He may plan on just hiding out there for a few months until everything blows over."

"Or maybe forever? Like the Nazis who fled to Argentina."

"Here's the problem with that line of thought," he said. "It's not the norm for serial killers. They're almost always lone wolves who want to return and revel silently in their glory. The fruit of their handiwork, the thrill of it all. Remember Eric Rudolph?"

"Of course. Atlanta's Olympic Park bomber," she replied. "Also suspected of bombing abortion clinics and gay bars."

"It took five years to track down and capture him," Keane said. "He'd holed up in the mountains of North Carolina while his face appeared on the Ten Most Wanted. He survived on lizards and wild boar until finally he was caught dumpster-diving for food outside a retail store in Murphy. Not far from where he grew up. Typical."

Jessie sipped her Chablis then gently set down the glass. "So, Felix Thornton's another one of your typical lone wolves? I've always been led to believe that these guys who join hate movements are 'belongers.' Like urban street gangs. It's important for them to be part of a brotherhood. Gives them a certain sense of fraternity they yearn for. The ancient tribal complex."

"You might think so," Keane said, "but everything I see in this case tells me we're dealing with the classic lone wolf. He hates blacks,

Hispanics, Asians, and God knows who else outside his pearl white universe. To him they're all parasites on the human race."

He explained that decades before, one of the pioneering Ku Klux Klan chieftains advocated a new way for the hate movement to operate, called "leaderless resistance." He preached the rise of the lone wolf because the government had succeeded at penetrating groups like the Klan. The lone wolf would make it even more challenging since he wouldn't have partners to make stupid mistakes and foil the plan. There'd be no accomplices to chicken out, or run, or take a bribe and spill the beans.

"But let's face it," Keane said, "only one in a million are skilled enough to pull off what he has. It doesn't take technical smarts only, it takes discipline. And the uncanny ability to adapt to anything, anywhere, anytime."

She raised her eyebrows. "You think Thornton's invincible?"

"Absolutely not. Everyone who tries to take on the lone wolf role lacks one key talent—knowing how to distinguish what he *can* do from what he *can't*. He might succeed at first, but sooner or later, he reaches too far. *That's* his Achilles heel."

"Isn't the case closed now?"

"Never, until Thornton's brought to justice. But there's no chance in hell that Selsby's going to pursue Thornton. These guys have their own club. I'm an outsider and have been from the get-go. They're not going to let someone like me—a damned consultant—into their world. Someone who just barges in out of the blue, like Willy Loman riding on a smile and a shoeshine."

"Then I guess Selsby's water under the bridge?"

"Maybe, maybe not. I asked Vinny to check him out."

"Now you're joshing me," she said. "He's a detective for the Atlanta PD, for Chrissakes."

"Vinny wasn't able to find anything on him. Other than his address in Peachtree City. Made for a convenient commute into headquarters. He was clean."

"Is that a surprise?" she asked.

"But there's something that Selsby told me when we first met. I can't get it out of my head. He'd admitted that his first love was getting far away from his job. 'That's why God made weekends,' he said. Told me it was a hunting or shooting club somewhere in South Georgia. Suzanne Fowler—the APD toxicologist—said it was in Dalton or Danville. Or something like that."

"Dawson, maybe?"

"That's it! She said he was part of the breakfast club there on Saturday mornings. She emphasized *every* Saturday morning in the summer."

"But why do you think she was telling you all this?"

"I asked myself the same question. It sounded like she thought it was something I should know. Just a gut feeling. Makes no sense, really."

"Trust your gut, Damon. That's where wisdom lives."

He finished off his wine. "You got any plans for Saturday morning?"

She swallowed a chunk of cornbread muffin and tipped her wine glass in his direction. "I bet I do now, partner."

CHAPTER 30

Osken drove the Oldsmobile to the side of the road and set the parking brake with the engine running. He pointed with a grimy fingernail on the map to M5, the highway south to Chelyabinsk. "Very lonely road, Boss."

Thornton leaned forward from the back seat where he'd been studying his Russian phrase book. "Just drive, Osken. Just drive." He lay back and tried to relax. Open country and one lane in each direction greeted them as Osken headed south. Vast areas of nothingness spread out toward the mountain peaks on the horizon, much like the Western US deserts Thornton remembered from his basic training at Fort Sill. Even the hot winds blasted through the open windows as if from a smelter—Oklahoma summers.

Osken kept his right hand on the steering wheel and rested his left arm out the open window. He dodged occasional bumps like a rabbit running through a meadow. To avoid a pothole he'd veer to the right shoulder or drift left directly into the path of an oncoming vehicle before jerking back into his lane. At no time did he let up on the accelerator, an action that would rob him of his manhood.

With everything going according to plan, Thornton tried to sleep. He fumbled with his dog tags and thought back twenty years. Basic Training and getting in shape . . . mercilessly hammering his buddies in hand-to-hand combat. The tense hours of Specialty Training in EOD—

explosive ordnance disposal. During Operation Desert Storm his Army reserve unit was called up. He found it ironic that on the eve of the Iraq invasion and each night during that one-hundred-hour battle, he'd slept like a baby. He never slept that soundly again.

*   *   *

When they arrived in Chelyabinsk, Osken slowly drove along the streets. Thornton's first thoughts were of Rahway, New Jersey, a place he'd once visited in his youth. Similar sights. Tall stacks belched smoke from Russia's World War II vintage factories. A haze heavy with nauseating fumes blanketed the city. A family of five strolled among the kiosks along the highway shoulders with sacks of meat and bread and packaged food. An old man dressed in rags and hunched over with a shovel scraped dirt along the curb. They passed a statue in a park and Osken spouted out the legendary tale of someone immortalized in bronze and drenched in bird shit.

They parked at a small restaurant squeezed between two higher structures that looked vacant. Osken ordered a soup and a meat plate for both. As they waited, Thornton said, "I need to explore on my own this evening."

"You need to find woman?" Osken asked.

"Perhaps."

"Ah, my friend, I can find good woman for you. One thing Russians do better than Americans—make beautiful women. Maybe I find one we share?"

"I don't share my women. I need to scout about on my own."

He'd made too many mistakes with women. Married his high school sweetheart, a hunk of a girl. Big tits. Big mistake. Big sham of a marriage that only lasted twenty-three months. Then lived with a thirty-something for a while. A black woman, but not your typical black. She was light brown, very light. Her nostrils flared a little, but you'd hardly notice. Only time he did was when they made love. It distracted the hell out of him. She moved out on him without even leaving a note. He never understood why.

Osken found a ramshackle hotel for the night near the city center. He negotiated a rate, and Thornton put down the cash for separate rooms.

*   *   *

That evening Thornton showered and slipped on wrinkled trousers from his duffle bag. He searched his wallet for the note he'd made on a torn fragment of paper: *56 ul Udakina.* After locating the general direction from the hotel clerk, he wandered the streets. No one claimed to speak English. Most just shrugged at his question and walked on.

Four younger men stood on a street corner ahead. One had a mustache and unbuttoned shirt, dark skin, and hardly more than five feet tall. The other two were smoking, surrounded by the aroma of Turkish tobacco.

When Thornton drew closer, the men ignored him until he passed. The short one called out. Thornton turned back. "Do you know *ul Udakina?*" he asked.

"*Da.* I will take you." The Russian motioned toward a small car parked on the other side of the street.

He shook his head. "I just need directions."

The man turned back to his buddies and continued chatting, while one tossed his lighted cigarette at Thornton's feet. Thornton hesitated for a moment, but moved on. For another hour he strolled the bleak streets. *Udakina?* he repeated to strangers, only getting back shrugs or turned heads.

He discovered the street sign on his own, barely making out the Cyrillic alphabet. It was no more than an alley. Walking down it, he stayed near the middle and searched above dark doorways. He almost whizzed past the number before he realized it—printed with stencil and white spray paint: *56.* Wrought-iron bars protected the freshly painted red door and windows. Flowerpots decorated the windowsills on the second story. He couldn't make out the letters on the sign over the door and hadn't the slightest hint of whether he was staring at a residence or a whorehouse. No lights shined through the windows. He stepped up to the door and tapped with his knuckles. In his peripheral vision, he spotted a man across the street who quickly vanished between houses.

No response.

He pounded with his fist. Rustling came from inside, and a light beamed through the window to the left. The door opened and a wrinkled lady squinted at him.

He pointed to himself. "I am from . . . At-lan-ta."

She spoke back in Russian and slammed the door.

He backed away to get a better view, when a light came on in another window. He approached the house and the front door opened again. A small man with big hair above his ears stood in the doorway. A splotch of black hair covered the peak of a baldhead. The bridge of his nose, built up as if by clay, formed a hump that commanded respect. "May I help you?"

His accent was hard, but his English flawless.

"I am Felix Thornton."

The stranger grasped Thornton's extended hand forcefully and shook it with the enthusiasm that seemed reserved for a long-time friend. "And I am Alfred Zuberman. Delighted you have finally made it."

CHAPTER 31

Jessie sat shotgun as Keane drove south out of Fort Benning and into the heart of Georgia and the Old South. She slapped playfully at his shoulder and handed him a long piece of a stringy purple plant. "Here, feel this. Just run your fingers through it, Damon. Smell it. Go ahead."

He leaned toward her, keeping his eye on the road while she twirled and brushed the weed under his nose. He jerked his head away and stifled a sneeze.

"It's lavender. Smell it! It'll relax you."

"I'm relaxed already. Look at me." He threw both hands into the air and only slowly lowered them back down to the steering wheel, scaring them both momentarily.

"You're as tense as a house cat in a dog pound, Damon. You need more things in your life that don't require so much thinking. You need to get more in touch with that inner animal." She poked her fingers into his ribcage and twisted them. "When are you going to Burning Man with me, anyway? You'll love the excitement and the scenery."

He lowered his chin and looked back at her. *Not anytime soon.* He knew enough about the annual gathering of free-thinkers in the Nevada desert. Her stories from previous visits were laced with "radical self-expression" and "actions that open the heart." All of it no doubt catalyzed by a few choice and freely shared drugs.

The land they passed along the highway was green and flat and the people a mix of white, black, and brown. The dominant features were the acres of pecan groves and peanut farms. Dusty pickup trucks and dented sedans were common on the highway. Many homes were the pillared white plantation style, but there were a lot more of wooden shacks on tiny lots.

Keane had never been to Dawson, which his odometer showed was sixty-five miles south of Atlanta. The feeling was that of stepping into an old film about a Southern town, a movie set complete with live oak, tulip poplars, and magnolias. The question was, where would you most likely meet on Saturday mornings for breakfast in Dawson?

A corps of young skinheads had collected in the town park. One held a US flag and another the flag of Dixie. Together they resembled fans of a Saturday night pro-wrestling bash. Similar-looking thugs with shades surrounded them.

"Let's stop for a second breakfast," he said, as he turned into the parking lot of a Shoney's restaurant packed with cars and pickups. From the back seat he grabbed a pair of discount-store sunglasses and then donned a ball cap with *Martin and Sons Lumberyard* printed above the bill. They walked past two dozen Harleys parked near the entrance and into the restaurant filled with what looked like regulars. A waitress with a short skirt and a hard look marched them to a booth ten feet from a table surrounded by a passionate group of hungry bikers piling plates high with scrambled eggs, bacon, grits, and biscuits submerged in gravy.

He spotted another booth in the corner with a view of the buffet table and asked to be switched. The hostess sighed as if she'd have to pack a lunch to walk that far and then led them to it.

"Coffee for both, please," he said. When she handed them menus, he added, "We'll just have the buffet."

"Farther to the food from *here*," the waitress snapped.

"I like dark corners." He looked around at the men and boys who occupied the table in the area they'd come from. Camouflage fatigues, scarlet bandannas tied around foreheads, tattooed biceps. It was a showcase of denim, ponytails, gold chains, and shaved heads. Weekend warriors of a different ilk. He scooted the scrambled eggs around on his plate while staying fixed on the line at the buffet, and he tried to recognize faces beneath the ball caps. One man, a good bit taller than the others, stood out. He wore dark wraparound sunglasses, a hunting cap with its bill pulled down over his forehead, and combat fatigues. He moved with a familiar gait.

Jessie returned to the buffet while he sat sipping coffee and keeping watch. When the tall one and the rest of his table finished eating, they rose to leave. Keane quickly swallowed the last drop of coffee and tossed cash on the table to cover the tab, plus a more than generous tip, and they moved for the exit.

A biker, shirtless and with a leather vest decorated in medallions, held the door for Jessie to walk through and Keane followed. The biker smiled at him when he passed and gave a thumbs-up. Outside and across the street in the park the music of Black Sabbath roared over loudspeakers mounted on two trees. Scrawled on a large cardboard sign and nailed to a separate tree were the words *Remember when Heavy Metal was for Whites only?* Men Keane recognized from the buffet had gathered at the back end of a Ford pickup next to the skinheads. He drifted toward a law officer who stood leaning back on his boot against the restaurant wall. "What's this all about, Deputy?"

"Nazi assholes." The lawman lowered his head and spat a thick brown juice toward a shrub. "I served two tours in Afghanistan for these pieces of shit? They have to strut around acting important before they head out onto the Fitzwater property."

"Where?"

"You're not from around here?"

"Only passing through."

More spitting. "It's a couple mile south from here. Big-time quail hunting plantation. Maybe a thousand acres. That's where they camp out for the weekend."

"What goes on?" Keane asked.

"Who knows or cares. Private property and a free country, I suppose."

"How do they draw recruits?" Keane asked.

"Mostly teenagers. Every once in a while they hold a demonstration in town, wearing armbands with swastikas. They rant about blacks and Jews and pump their fists like they was real men. Throw in some *Sieg Heils*. That's when we move in and they take off in a caravan for the Fitzwater place. Cowards, all of 'em."

"How many would you guess?"

"Maybe fifty. Could be double that, easy. Not everyone comes every Saturday. Sort of like church on Sundays. And many don't never show their face. Respectable citizens and all. Men and women. You'd be surprised the judges and preachers you'd find among them. Hell, I even know of—" He stopped himself and spat on the ground again.

Jessie gave a head flip toward the restaurant. "I suppose they bring in business like this place does."

"Shoney's loves having them for breakfast on weekend mornings. And Gerardo's Pizza is probably getting their dough and boxes ready. Most Saturday evenings they deliver pizza out to the plantation. I think the weekend campouts there alone keep them in business."

Interesting, Keane thought. "This place—Gerardo's—where could we find it?"

Jessie shot him a surprised look. He winked back and smiled.

CHAPTER 32

Alfred Zuberman's smile at the door settled quickly into a business-like scowl. Thornton followed him through a musty hallway and into a parlor, dark except for a lone lamp that rested on a table in one corner. He sank into a sofa as Zuberman barked orders for tea toward a back room. His demeanor was of someone who made a living growling at peasants.

"I trust your trip from Atlanta was satisfying?" Zuberman asked.

"Tolerable. Didn't mean to arrive so soon, of course. Had a last-minute change of plans."

"Your timing is excellent."

He'd found Zuberman through Athena, the network that functioned totally detached from the Internet. Painstaking research had uncovered a secret network that used the highest levels of encryption and security. It allowed smart operators to remain anonymous, at least for a while—usually all that was needed. Thornton knew that the site on Athena that Zuberman ran was a spinoff from the old Silk Road—a global black market that the feds had discovered and shut down a few years back.

"You took a train from Moscow?" Zuberman asked. One eye meandered with a lazy motion and was obviously made of glass. Although it was dark blue, his other eye—brown as a chestnut—carefully probed the world.

"I had a discounted fare and flew into Ekaterinburg from Rome," Thornton replied.

"Ah, interesting city. Quite historical you know. It was the place where the Bolsheviks assassinated the Romanov family."

"I'd rather talk business," Thornton said. Last on his list of things he wanted to learn before he died was Russian history.

Zuberman wrinkled his forehead over the bulge between his haunting eyes. "Such haste. Why are Americans always rushing?"

Thornton smiled for the first time since they greeted. "We want to get things done, Mr. Zuberman."

An older lady shuffled into the parlor with a silver tray holding a ceramic pot of tea. Zuberman poured for himself and Thornton, and then continued. "We must discuss mutual interests, yes?"

"I understand that you have many treasures in this historic city of yours. Treasures from your past."

"Not that distant," Zuberman replied. "They are only tokens of our twentieth century. Postwar artifacts, you might say."

"Collectibles?"

Zuberman waved a hand above his head. The glass eye aimed in one direction while the other converged on Thornton like a hawk after prey. "Most definitely. I have access to some of exceptional quality."

"I'm prepared to pay for quality, Mr. Zuberman."

"The higher priced items are—how do you say in English—more radiant?"

"I like radiance."

"You are aware of the barriers customs may present in transport back to America?"

"I can pay for special arrangements. But my time here is short, Mr. Zuberman."

The Russian shoved his head back and again looked down his nose with his good brown eye that carefully tracked Thornton's movements.

"Then I believe we can do business. I planned for a small conference only a short drive from here. You will enjoy meeting my associates."

*   *   *

When they began the trip, "Viktor" walked to the silver Mercedes with the bearing of a Sumo wrestler. Carefully stuffing his belly in behind the steering wheel with both hands, he showed no sign of speaking or understanding English. Zuberman sat in a commanding position in the front seat beside him. Thornton sat uneasily in the back.

As they rode about the city, Zuberman pointed out special places, but Thornton was paying more attention to the driver.

"I saw an interesting statue at the entrance to a park," Thornton said.

Zuberman leaned over his shoulder and looked back at Thornton with his good brown eye. "We have many statues dedicated to our heroes."

"It was one of your prized scientists, I believe."

Viktor steered off the highway and onto an unpaved road winding through grass-covered foothills. Thornton kept his arm pressed against the car door.

"Ah, yes. Igor Kurchatov," Zuberman replied. "In America you had Robert Oppenheimer. But we had Doctor Kurchatov, the greatest nuclear scientist of all, the Father of our atomic bomb. Born in our very own oblast."

The car approached a log house surrounded by birch trees. The three of them were met at the door by another of Zuberman's goons, this one as stout as Viktor but six inches taller. His plush eyebrows spilled over the lids like shrubbery.

Zuberman headed straight for a cupboard and brought out four small glasses while "Semyon" fetched an unopened fifth of Green Mark vodka. After pouring drinks, Zuberman toasted his guest, first in Russian and then adding, "Cheers to our American comrade." Thornton only sipped while the others swallowed their drinks in one tip of the glass. Zuberman quickly refilled them. He pointed at Thornton's and babbled in Russian. The three men hooted.

"We often hear," Zuberman said, "that Americans mix their liquor with water."

"Sometimes. But in Atlanta we mix it with Coca-Cola."

Zuberman guffawed and repeated his remark in Russian. The bellies of the goons spasmed with laughter again.

When Zuberman recovered from the coughing fit his laughter brought on, he said, "We do not make fun of you, of course, Mr. Thornton. We laugh at American ways."

"I can toast to that." He tossed back his head and finished off the last of his drink. Zuberman quickly replenished it and then patted him on the back. "I would like very much to have you join us for a *banya.* It's our custom. It will give us opportunity to relax before . . . how you say? . . . getting down to business."

At the back of the house the men undressed in a locker room and grabbed white cotton robes from wall hooks. By the time Thornton had donned the robe and entered the steam room, Zuberman was sitting back on a cedar bench, sipping a beer and stoking a fire that heated a stack of rocks. He poured the beer into a water bucket by his side and then scooped the mix onto the scorching stones. Steam sizzled to the ceiling.

Viktor planted himself like a walrus onto a bench along the other wall. He lay naked, massaging his chest above his heart where Thornton spotted a patch of reddened skin the size of a cigarette pack.

"His new pacemaker," Zuberman said, when he saw Thornton's stare. "He's quite proud of it. His doctor planted it there three weeks ago. Saved his life, he claims. He only paid two thousand rubles."

Semyon bolted into the room, hauling a bundle of slender tree branches and grunting. When he hurled them onto the floor, Keane noticed stubs for two of his fingers. The goon then stripped off his robe and lay down on his belly on one bench. He flaunted a polar bear ass that contrasted with the black hair coiled in briar patches over his back and shoulders. Zuberman stood and snatched a leafy branch from the pile and began to beat Semyon's back as if swatting at spiders. Viktor grabbed a branch and joined in. The stench of body odor and beer wafted through the sweltering room.

Zuberman turned to Thornton. "The juniper leaves rid the body of poisons. Yes?" He waved the branch at him, teasing in a daring manner, but Thornton ignored it. Zuberman jumped up and ran out the door into a walled garden covered with flowering vines. The two goons followed, and all three belly-flopped into a swimming pool with floating blocks of ice. Thornton paused at the concrete edge. When Viktor reached for his ankles, Thornton plunged in and reeled underwater to the other side. He broke through the surface, coughing and sputtering, and grabbed for the wall. The others had already made a dash for the steam room. When Thornton jogged to the side door and opened it, steam swirled out. The goons sat on benches, sharing a flask that Zuberman then offered him. The sweet-and-spicy brew warmed his gullet as it traveled and he took another sip before handing it back.

Wrapped in towels the two sat together on the bench opposite from Viktor and Semyon. Zuberman motioned toward the pair and whispered. "They are my trusted partners. We all worked at Mayak in our military program." He pointed to Viktor on the left, who sat massaging his cherished pacemaker just beneath his skin. "He worked there for seventeen years." He then pointed to the right. "Semyon worked at the super facility at Ozersk for nineteen years. I was there for twenty-two as a supervisor. My team designed everything. Should I dwell any more on our impeccable qualifications?"

"My only interest is in obtaining the perfect substance."

"You hinted at something with a long active life."

"I want a source of gamma rays that will last many years."

"I suppose you have a precise use in mind?" Zuberman asked.

"My client and I want to keep it confidential. We'll be doing a good deal of business with it."

"There is one concern I have. Western spies work among us—a special vigilante group. We know them well. It's a secret international force, sponsored not only by your CIA, but by England's MI6 and Israel's Mossad. The group is charged with following closely our private nuclear activities. Not a particularly nice bunch of gentlemen. I suppose the rest of the world doesn't trust Mr. Putin and his new-style security services to take care of our country's obligations and legal duties. We're always on the lookout for these spying swine. But as Americans say, Mr. Thornton, the 'bottom line' is that we can meet what you require. It only depends upon how much of our treasure you desire."

Thornton held steady and glared back at Zuberman. He spoke slowly so that he'd be understood perfectly. "Access to your inventory is why I traveled six thousand miles."

Zuberman nodded, smiling. "You know that prized material like this doesn't come cheap."

"I'm prepared to pay. Up to a reasonable limit."

"We are reasonable people, Mr. Thornton. We'll be at your hotel tomorrow evening. Seven-thirty."

CHAPTER 33

Jessie sat chewing spearmint gum in the passenger seat beside Harland Wingfield. His aging blue Datsun displayed a *Gerardo's Pizza* sign on the roof. Her ponytail protruded through the loop in the back of the *Martin and Sons Lumberyard* ball cap.

After she and Keane had approached Harland in the strip-mall parking lot, he told them he'd been making pizza deliveries for Gerardo's the last three months. He was saving money for his first year at Georgia Southern and planning to major in environmental engineering. In exchange for help, Keane had offered Harland two crisp one-hundred-dollar bills to buy a new pair of tires for the balding ones on the Datsun's rear.

Keane's story was that his good friend "Julie"—he nodded toward Jessie—was in terrible straits over a boyfriend who'd recently got her pregnant. He'd broken up with her before she had a chance to give him the news. If only he knew her condition. He was a good man and Julie was sure he'd have her back. They got word that he'd joined the weekend group at the Fitzwater plantation. She sorely wanted a chance to ride in with Harland to help him with the delivery of all the pizzas. She just wanted to get a glimpse of this handsome brute and find out once and for all if the father of her baby was there.

Harland was firm. "Now, ma'am, I can't get into any kind of conflict between you and him, if you know what I mean. My boss wouldn't take kindly to that. I really need the work."

"Julie" promised that there was no chance of nasty words or anything of the sort. She'd wait patiently for him no matter how long it took that weekend. If she couldn't find him, she'd just head back to Atlanta and keep on searching. Her tears and wet eyes did the trick.

When the Datsun moved up to the gate of the Fitzwater plantation, Harland and Jessie waved at the two lollygagging warriors dressed in camouflage. They raised the crossbar for the Datsun with the pizza sign on top to pass through. The pair wended their way over a makeshift road through the pines and broom sedge for a half-mile until they came upon a cluster of three wooden buildings. Groups of men stood about or sat on benches around an outdoor kitchen area. Harland jumped out and Jessie followed. Stares greeted her as she meandered toward them with a grin as big as Texas. The troupe from the buffet was holding court by a tree next to the outdoor grill.

She made it a point to aim her path near the tall one whom Keane had targeted. Her phone was set to camera mode—no flash—and she held it beneath the stack of boxes she clumsily carried. When she got near the target, she stopped. "Sir, do you mind grabbing a couple of these boxes? I'm 'fraid I'm about to drop them."

He snatched the top three and lead her to a picnic table where they stacked the boxes. She took off the sunglasses and stabbed them above the bill of her cap. "Ahhh, get a whiff of this!" she said, lifting the lid on one greasy box.

He shoved back his ball cap and removed his shades. When he peered in to sniff, she did a subtle tap on the phone. Suddenly she turned her head and stifled a sneeze. Holding a hand to her nose, she apologized and blamed her allergies as she softly tapped the phone twice more. Harland thanked everybody for the privilege of serving them, and she quickly followed him back to the Datsun. After they exited the plantation, he dropped her off where Keane waited. She slipped into the front seat and held up the pictures captured on her cell phone—the perfect likeness of Detective Crawford Selsby.

"Do you think he recognized you?" Keane asked.

"Not a chance."

CHAPTER 34

Thornton squatted on his knees and hugged the toilet bowl as he threw up the contents of his stomach. He'd slept until noon. The curtains that hung like rags from the clouded windows couldn't block out the damned light. With a pounding head he staggered into the hallway and knocked on Osken's door.

No answer.

He stood still for a moment, then tested his balance and tried to make sense of the fluttering wall. Back in his room, he jammed his head under the bathroom spigot and washed his face and hair with the foul water. After peeling off his clothes, he twisted a sock into a band and tied it around his head as tightly as he could manage, then threw himself onto the bed.

*   *   *

At 7:33 p.m. Zuberman and his two goons arrived in the hotel lobby. Thornton's head had stopped throbbing but his gut grumbled. He'd only eaten stale crackers and small chunks of hard cheese for dinner. Everyone crowded into an ancient Russian-made sedan. Instead of using the key for the ignition, Viktor hot-wired under the dash.

Thornton noted the highway and road signs as they departed Chelyabinsk city limits and passed through barren forest. The others gabbed while he sat as still as possible, trying to prevent any movement of his head. When they arrived at an abandoned industrial facility, a chained gate stood ten feet high, with razor wire running along the top. Zuberman pulled a silver key ring from his pocket and tilted his head slightly back so that his good eye could search for the right key. He handed it to Semyon, who waddled to the gate to unlock it.

Broken windows checkered the five-story structure baking in the afternoon sun. The goons followed Zuberman inside, their march echoing within the concrete cave. Thornton lagged behind. At a dark stairwell Zuberman led the way up. His goons trailed, puffing and clutching the handrail. At the second level Semyon stopped and yanked a dirty handkerchief to wipe sweat from his forehead. Panting, Viktor bent low beside him. Zuberman turned and threw his hands into the air. He waved them about and harangued the two overweight pansies who couldn't climb three lousy flights of stairs. The gist of his words was clear. They were lazy, sorry-ass excuses for partners.

On the third floor they entered a massive concrete hall, empty except for a row of odd-looking devices and metallic containers stashed along one wall. Zuberman stopped beside one canister that resembled a military relic. "This contains strontium-90, recovered from one of our lighthouses in Siberia."

"A lighthouse?" Thornton asked.

Radiation within the strontium source, Zuberman explained, was so intense that it produced enough heat to make electricity—a self-contained generator. Devices using strontium-90 were ideal for supplying power to searchlights so that airplane pilots and ship captains could spot the jagged coastline in remote areas.

Thornton stooped and tugged on the canister. "How much does it weigh?"

"About thirty-five kilos."

Eighty pounds. "I need something more portable."

Zuberman strolled along the floor as if inspecting meat in a slaughterhouse, keeping his head tilted to favor the good eye. He stopped at one smaller container and mumbled at Semyon, who held a meter resembling a Geiger counter. A cigar-shaped probe was attached to the meter by a two-foot cord. Semyon brought the probe along the outside wall of the device, and a rapid ticking burst forth.

"Not well shielded," Zuberman said. "It holds cobalt-60. If you want intense gamma rays—"

"No, thanks." He had access to a sufficient supply of cobalt-60 in Atlanta. But it wouldn't do for the planned Big One. Cobalt was a heavy metal and in an explosion would splinter into fragments like shrapnel. It would only spread at most a few hundred yards from the site. An amateur operation.

Zuberman continued looking until he found another canister half the size of the one with a cobalt source. He nodded at Semyon, who held the probe of the Geiger counter up to the canister wall. The needle beneath the glass face of the meter flickered.

"This source may meet your requirements best." A cylinder with a dull military gray finish, about two feet long and six inches in diameter, lay on its side.

"Not very well shielded," Thornton said.

"It has enough. You just wouldn't want to sleep with it."

"What isotope?"

"Cesium-137," Zuberman announced.

At the top of Thornton's list, it was one of the primary radioactive isotopes released from the Chernobyl disaster and carried hundreds of miles by the winds. Its fallout still covered the region around Chernobyl—the reason that land wouldn't be inhabitable for decades. The cesium-137 in the dirt and the weeds and the rooftops and playgrounds continued to emit gamma rays, even after three decades.

He lifted the cylinder. Maybe thirty-five or forty pounds.

"A little more portable for you, perhaps?" Zuberman asked.

"Manageable." He knew there was always a trade-off between ability to lug it around and heavy shielding for protection from the gamma rays. The shielding was hardened steel, maybe lined with lead, but would it escape radiation detection from the most sophisticated systems at harbors and airports?

"The chemical form is cesium chloride," Zuberman said. "Looks like sodium chloride—table salt. And it weighs less than a hummingbird."

The more Zuberman talked the more beautiful it all looked. When placed inside a bomb and detonated, cesium-137—the devil's fairy dust—would spread like baby powder in the wind. He stifled his enthusiasm. Zuberman had come through.

"How do you open the canister?" Thornton asked.

Zuberman motioned to Viktor, who turned the canister upright. A painted arrow pointed upward along the side. Viktor stood at arm's length and rotated a wheel with a matching arrow on top of the device.

As the arrows approached alignment, Viktor slowed the rotation. Semyon stood back but kept the Geiger probe in front of a slot on the side. Zuberman backed away and pushed Thornton with him. With the final, barely perceptible twist, the needle on the Geiger counter shot upward and pegged against the stop.

An iridescent halo of blue emerged. The counter's clicking became a ranting buzz.

Viktor quickly twisted the wheel back, and the ticking halted.

Zuberman turned to Thornton. "How's that for hot?"

Thornton smiled.

"The operator must be especially careful," Zuberman said. "When the slot is full open, five minutes of the gamma-ray exposure is enough to cause a slow, painful death over many weeks. Make it ten minutes and death is quicker—perhaps in days."

"I suppose you've confirmed this?"

"There are plenty of rats and stray dogs around. But Semyon has been careless at times." He pointed toward the goon, who rolled up the sleeve of his right arm as if on cue. The skin below his elbow had eroded away, exposing a cavity as raw as an open wound.

"He's been acting funny since the accident."

The three stared at Thornton, looking troubled. Then Zuberman slapped Semyon upside his head and they let out another of their collective belly laughs.

Thornton smiled nervously and drew a deep breath. Everything to that point in the game had been too easy. He'd waited long enough. "How much do you want?"

"Thirty thousand US dollars," Zuberman replied, without blinking his working eye.

Fucking outrageous—a lifetime of salaries and pensions for all three combined, plus their families. "I don't have that kind of money."

"It's exactly what you requested—an isotope with a long life. It will emit intense gamma rays for years to come."

"Why do you keep it here?" Thornton asked.

"We guard and protect all these treasures. They're grand prizes for terrorists throughout the world to steal. We are paid to safeguard everything you see."

Lucky world.

Zuberman placed a hand on Thornton's shoulder. "I know that any of my devices would be in good hands with you. You will put it to good capitalist use. Yes?"

"I can offer you half that price at most."

Zuberman pulled his hand back as if he'd touched a hot stove. "That's crazy."

"I can give you ten thousand today," Thornton replied, "and have the rest wired from my bank by tomorrow."

"But you cannot wire such large sums to Chelyabinsk. Not without alerting officials here and in the US. You know that."

"I'm willing to take that risk."

"Don't speak like a fool," Zuberman said. "*We* cannot take that risk."

Viktor moved toward Thornton. He backed up and pressed his spine into the wall.

"Show me your cash," Zuberman demanded.

"I don't have it with me."

He whacked Thornton across the face and he collapsed to the floor. "Take off your clothes, *zhopa!*"

Thornton struggled to sit up, but the room gyrated around him. He flopped backward and wiped at his mouth, spitting blood before gradually pushing his way into a sitting position. He mopped at the blood with his sleeve.

Viktor gripped the front of his shirt and ripped it open, exposing the two money belts crossing his bare chest. Semyon moved in with the five-inch blade of a folding knife. He seized both belts with one hand and with the other sliced them off. He tossed the bounty to his boss. Zuberman unzipped each and flipped through the crisp green bills while Semyon stood over Thornton with the blade pricking his right earlobe. Zuberman counted out $12,000 in hundreds and slapped Thornton across his bloodied face with an empty belt. "This is part payment for insulting me. And after all the hospitality I have shown you."

Semyon grabbed Thornton's hair, yanked back his head, and held the knife to his throat.

"*Nyet!*" Zuberman shouted, adding a verbal salvo.

Semyon threw Thornton's head forward, and Viktor's steel-toed boot smashed into his temple.

He crumpled to the floor.

Viktor slung a rag around Thornton's mouth while Semyon bound his hands and feet with rope. The pair dragged him across the floor and down the stairs, his spine bouncing off each concrete step. When they reached the sedan outside, they picked him up by his shoulders and ankles and hurled him like a bag of manure into the trunk. The open wound on the side of his head hit a steel jack inside.

The last thing he saw as the trunk lid slammed shut were the smiling faces of his executioners.

CHAPTER 35

AS the mayor's guest on a sixteen-foot Tracker bass boat, Keane straddled a raised swivel chair while they sped across Lake Oconee beneath a cloudless sky. But rather than tussling with a native largemouth bass, he fought a wave of nausea caused by a rocking boat in choppy water. He'd left a message on Mayor Stillwell's private line on his way home from Dawson. The response was the mayor's invitation to join him and his son in their favorite pastime on Sundays.

As they drifted and cast their lures, Keane shared with him the recent news about Ronnie Davenport's improving condition. His ecstatic foster mom had said they'd moved him into a regular patient room at Grady Memorial. His bone marrow had recovered for the most part, and he was free of infection and getting stronger by the day.

The mayor was delighted by the news and smiled down at his own son, ten-year-old Josh, who sat low in a seat by his dad.

"Tell me," the mayor said, "what is it about this detective that we needed to get together so quickly?"

Keane carefully shifted around to face him as the boat wandered slowly under the power of the trolling motor. "I'll be straight with you. Detective Crawford Selsby has been dragging his feet on the case from day one."

The mayor kept an eye on his son working a black plastic worm through the weed bed along the shoreline. "When a criminal suspect escapes the country, Damon, you do realize his capture moves pretty dang far down APD's list of priorities. And if he's found in a place like Russia, what kind of resources do you think we have to follow up with? At that point, we got to rely completely on the Feds. I don't like being put in that position any more than you or anybody else. But that's a fact of life in this business."

"But my point is," Keane replied, "going after Felix Thornton was *never* a priority for Selsby."

"But Chief Walters told me it was his number one job!"

"On the other hand, Selsby was always telling me he had a lot of irons in the fire. He said he couldn't *possibly* be on Thornton's case all the time."

The mayor paused to help Josh cast out his lure again then turned back to Keane. "I'll be frank with you, Damon, the chief said that Selsby thinks you've been more a problem than a help."

"You believe that?"

"Not for a minute, but I can see how he might think it. He's spent thirty years in APD working his way up from a beat cop. He believes there's no knowledge—"

"Like field knowledge."

"You've heard that one before?"

"He made it clear that all my degrees aren't worth—he paused to mouth the word *crap*—when it comes to investigating crime."

"Whoa! Hold on!" the mayor shouted. He grabbed Josh's rod as both reared back to fight a bass splashing across the surface. When they reeled the fish into the boat, the mayor quickly handed Keane the camera out of his shirt pocket. "Get a picture of this rowdy monster. Hold on tight, Josh!" He clutched at his son's shoulders and held the flapping bass by its lower lip at arm's length, closer to the camera than his face.

Keane smiled at the boy's beaming eyes. When Andy was that age, he'd caught his first catfish, and his face showed the same glow. How many times had he and Andy gone fishing since that day? He didn't want to think about the answer.

After the snapshot the mayor slid the bass into the live well behind him.

"I did a lot of background on Thornton before he got out of the country," Keane said. "I had to find out what was driving him."

"We hired you as a consultant. Someone who gives advice. Sits in an office analyzing, thinking, and sipping sweet tea. What were you trying to prove?"

"I already got that lecture from Selsby."

"Well, bells of Hades, did it take?"

"There's only so much info you can dig up from an armchair. Even in the Reinauer case, I—"

"Now you're trying to tell me there's no knowledge like field knowledge."

Keane looked away and drew the fresh lake air into his lungs.

"You're a smart guy, Damon. That's why I wanted you on the case. You've got remarkable talent to offer. We got plenty of beat cops who can chase down bad guys. What we'll never have enough of is smarts. Real honest-to-God smarts. People to put together the big picture from the scattered torn pieces of a puzzle when half of 'em are missing and the other half are as jumbled as my tackle box. That's the role we planned for you."

The mayor was right on. Keane couldn't explain to anyone why he'd drifted into his own little gumshoe-detective fantasyland. Maybe a detective was what he'd always wanted to be. Who knows why boys grow into men who only want to be boys again? It beat growing up to be old men. He glanced over at little Josh's radiant face.

"What'd you learn about Thornton," the mayor asked, "that we couldn't already guess? For whatever good it would do us now?"

"Thornton saw himself as a guerrilla in a holy jihad. In his dreams he wanted to rid Atlanta of a malignancy eating at the white race—the black man, the brown man, the yellow man, the immigrant of a different color. As if skin pigment determines your rightful place in the animal kingdom."

The mayor made another cast and handed the rod to Josh. He then drew close to Keane and whispered. "And may his soul rot in a Russian grave."

"Would it surprise you, Mayor, to know that Detective Selsby is also a died-in-the-wool racist?"

The mayor recoiled. "What kind of talk is that?"

"Crawford Selsby is as active in the neo-Nazi cause as you are in Atlanta politics."

"He's a *what*?"

"A neo-Nazi sympathizer. Member of a paramilitary unit—a racist hate group."

The mayor reeled in his lure and dropped the rod at his feet. "That's one"—he looked down at Josh and lowered his voice—"hell of an accusation, Damon. Talk like that is just an ugly rumor. I'm downright disappointed you'd even pass it along."

"But I saw proof of it with my own eyes, Mayor. He was down south in Dawson this weekend. I spotted him yesterday going to one of their gatherings. Evidently he's a regular."

"Did you *talk* to him?"

"No, but it was him."

"Why were you all the way down in Dawson?"

"A tip from a source at APD," Keane answered.

"Someone like who?"

He paused. "I forgot."

They stared at each other without blinking.

"I've got pictures," Keane finally said.

The mayor picked up his rod again and cast out another plastic worm. He slowly cranked the handle of the reel while twitching the rod. "I don't want to see any pictures. If it's true, he does that kind of stuff on his own time. I can't control what city employees do outside their jobs."

Keane leaned forward in his seat. "My point is that we were hunting a killer who hates most anyone who doesn't have lily-white skin. Of all people, the lead detective on the case has the same warped ideology. It's no wonder Selsby's dragged his feet from the beginning. He doesn't have a problem with the Felix Thorntons of the world."

The mayor reeled the worm back in and unsnapped it from his line, tossing it into his tackle box and slamming it shut. "Okay, Damon. I'll look into it. But if what you're saying is true, it's our problem. You hear me? It's *our* problem, not yours."

"But the point is—"

"The point is what? Tell me your point, now that Thornton has escaped the country for good."

"Selsby should never have been put on the case."

"So I should've been doing Chief Walter's job too? Micromanaging the police department?"

There were similarities, Keane thought, between the mayor's reaction and that of Thornton's former boss at the clinic. No one—absolutely nobody—wants to believe that one of his own had gone astray and totally misread a fellow human.

"Face reality here," the mayor said. "Felix Thornton got clean away. The fact is that he's disappeared—and I'm sorry you didn't catch any bass today, either."

CHAPTER 36

When Thornton awoke in the suffocating oven of a trunk, he had no idea how far the car had traveled. They were still moving, but without sounds of traffic. He took deeper breaths through the gag cutting into the corners of his mouth and struggled to draw in air. He wrestled with his hands and wrists, attempting to loosen the rope that bound them behind his back.

The car turned off the road and jolted to a stop. Muffled voices. Doors slammed shut.

When the trunk lid opened, he peered into the dark moonless night. Semyon and Viktor wrenched him out while he squirmed and tried to fight back, but he was too weak to resist. With Semyon's gigantic hands wrapped around his feet and Viktor gripping his shoulders like a vise, they swung him back toward the car and then tossed him forward into the night over the embankment of a river.

He flew through the air, unable to flail out with his bound arms and legs. When he hit the river's surface, he felt the cold hard sting of the water as if his face had slammed into a wall. He sank like a stone.

He opened his eyes but couldn't see because of the murky water. He jerked his arms bound behind him up along his spine again and again, not caring if he threw his shoulder out of its socket as he sank. His throat filled with water that tasted of kerosene and piss. His lungs on fire, he battled to free his wrists until his right hand slipped from the rope. He waved his arms upward and pumped his legs like a dolphin.

Pump! The word screamed inside his skull. *Pump!* His lungs had filled with the filthy water. *Pump! Pump!*

His head exploded through the surface. He grabbed at the greasy rag around his mouth and yanked it away. Coughing, sputtering, fighting to breathe, to keep his head above water, he finally reached the shallows, where he grabbed onto the weeds and snaked through the swampy muck. His feet still bound together, he wallowed through the quagmire on his stomach to reach the rocks along the shore. Near the road he worked his legs as if riding a bicycle, rubbing his ankles raw until he could slide one foot and then the other from the tangled mass of rope. After resting his back in the mud, he gave in to exhaustion.

*   *   *

At dawn a man and woman hovered over Thornton where he lay along the roadside. They argued as if trying to determine if he were dead or alive.

Shaky and weak, Thornton mumbled the name of his hotel in town.

The man, who looked to be in his seventies, dragged him panting into the back seat of a compact car. They drove away, but Thornton sensed from their babbling that they were still uncertain what to do with him. It seemed like an hour before they arrived at a hospital where a husky orderly lifted him onto a gurney and wheeled him inside.

He passed out again.

When he awoke, a group draped in green scrubs had gathered around him. Two wore white hats as tall as stovepipes. Apparently they were doctors. One spoke in broken English and prodded him with questions.

Yes, he was an American, the victim of a robbery while hitchhiking. Someone stole his money and kicked him in the face and ribs and dumped him along the highway. He couldn't describe the bastard. Yes, he understood that he was injured badly and that they needed to watch him for a day or two. But he had to leave. He had important business.

As if out of a page of scripture, the prodigal partner returned. Osken rushed into the ER and threw his hands to his head, acting as if he'd found his beloved brother who he'd given up for dead. If Osken knew nothing else, he knew drama. Later he explained to Thornton that he'd assured the doctors the victim was a visiting American, an idiot who'd decided to take off on his own. He added that he'd searched everywhere for him and was worried sick. He was about to call the police when the hotel contacted him and told him about the hospital's call. He rushed right over.

After they drove back to the hotel, Osken became his faithful nurse. They rested in his ungodly hot room while Thornton kept a towel dipped in cold water on his cheek and mouth. His ribs were taped so tight by an emergency room doc that he could barely breathe. A purple bruise covered the left side of his face. Three ice cubes were all the hotel barkeep could manage to provide.

Thornton swished the liquor around and spat it out into a large ceramic bowl. He turned to Osken. "We have a mission."

"*Mission*? You mean, church?" Osken asked.

"No, dammit. A charge. A duty."

"What kind of duty, Boss?"

"There's a vacant factory on the outskirts of town. I have to find it. I lost a rare treasure there and need your help to get it back."

"You must rest. You need heal."

Thornton rinsed his mouth with another guzzle of vodka and then wiped the spit and blood from his chin. "You will help me, won't you, Osken?" He could now only plead.

"Of course, Boss. I am your friend."

"I don't feel good about traveling without protection," Thornton said. He used a ragged piece of a towel to apply over the wound.

"I am your friend *and* your guard."

"I want extra security, Osken."

"You want me find guard man for hire?"

"No, I want a gun. I know how to use it."

*   *   *

Outside the hotel the streets had grown busier. People rushed about, some walking dogs or shopping around sidewalk kiosks to buy cigarettes and produce. Midget-sized European and Russian cars honked and fought at intersections. A light breeze carried the odor of diesel fuel and ancient cooking.

Occasionally Osken would stop a stranger for directions. When he turned into an alleyway, he picked up his pace until they came to a ramshackle storefront with the look of a pawnshop. Inside, a slew of knives lay neatly placed on open tables. Antique swords and daggers hung from the walls. The clerk, a man with lean features and a sad face, led the way into a back room where handguns were spread out within glass cases like a museum collection. He unlocked a corner case and brought out a pistol that he carefully offered to Thornton with both hands.

"Beautiful Makarov," the clerk said. He turned it over to show it off at all angles, like a diamond bracelet. Thornton lifted the weapon. It was heavier than it looked but a perfect fit to his palm and fingers. He brought the pistol to a small lamp at the end of the glass casement and sighted down the open end of the four-inch barrel. The rifling within the bore was smooth, clean.

"Blowback design," the clerk said. "Accurate to fifty meter." He added that it was safe to operate—the extra weight delayed opening of the breach. The price was quickly negotiated without hassle. After all the months of planning, there was no way in hell he was leaving Chelyabinsk without getting what he'd come after.

CHAPTER 37

Exhausted from a day with the mayor on a lake under a ruthless sun, Keane walked toward the music room, his secure sanctuary from the world. His cell phone rang on his way up the winding staircase.

"I thought I'd let you hear directly from me, Dr. Keane," Chief Dallas Walters snarled. "Detective Selsby's no longer with APD."

Unbelievable. "He was fired?"

"You might say that. He resigned. The mayor shared with me what you'd told him about the Nazi skinhead gathering down in Dawson. Our internal affairs people took little time to find out what you already guessed: he's a classic ghost skin."

"You've got me on that one, Chief."

"Ghost skins are white supremacists who act like ordinary citizens. They don't shave their heads and wear combat boots or anything else to give themselves away. But they all have an agenda."

Chief Walters paused and Keane heard a long sigh.

"Sorry to say," the chief continued, "they sometimes even get into law enforcement to advance their cause. I confronted Selsby and gave him the option to resign or face a board of inquiry for conduct unbecoming an officer. He handed over his gun and badge on the spot."

Keane paused and sat down on a step, stunned.

"I wished him well," the chief continued. "But he's a bitter man. Feels he got a bum deal. I reminded him that the oath he took with APD included a pledge. A promise to keep his personal life beyond reproach. He held a position of public trust and he was damned well aware of that."

"What's he going to do now?" Keane asked.

"No idea. He's had a whopping comedown. All he knows is police work."

After clicking off, Keane continued up the steps toward the music room. Images played out inside his head of conversations with Selsby over coffee and scrambled eggs. All the rugged volleys of a doomed relationship.

A storm had moved in and brought with it a jarring downpour. Occasional lightning strikes lit up the entire house. He'd heard from Mr. J that a weather front had crossed over from Alabama, where the day before a tornado had touched down north of Montgomery. The local news had reported that a mother of three, an Auburn graduate, was killed when a century-old oak crashed through the roof and into her bedroom.

When Keane approached the music room door, a feeble noise arose.

He stopped.

The strange sound seemed to come from within. He couldn't be sure, but it was a definite rustling as if someone were moving quietly across the carpet. He stood in the hallway and planted an ear to the door for a full minute.

Nothing.

Stepping back, he called out for Mr. J—not loudly, more as an automatic reaction to something out of kilter. He only half-expected him to answer.

A soft rumble of thunder rolled in like a midnight train. He inched open the door and peered into the darkness. Rain blown by a sporadic wind from the east pelted the window on the far wall. He moved guardedly inside and switched on a lamp that cast a faint yellow glow over the room. After sinking into a wingback chair, he gazed at the sheets of rain battering the windowpane. A Steinway Grand stood near the room's center. He often found enjoyment just sitting there, focused on absolutely nothing, while listening to a talented visitor playing the keys—sometimes, for hours.

A suspicion overcame him again, an inkling that someone else shared the room. It was an absurd feeling that went far beyond normal senses, and he tried to dismiss it. He stood and strolled across the floor. The curtain on the right of the window twitched, only a slight swishing that was barely perceptible. He studied the heavy drapery to see if he could spot a bulge or a tremor in the fabric.

The window was closed; it hadn't been opened in years. He walked to it and paused. Reaching out, he yanked the drapery to the side and stared into the blank wall behind it.

He jerked around and rushed to the room's double-doors, wrenched them open, and barged into the hall. He searched both ways before scrambling down the staircase, yelling for Mr. J and shouting, "Where did she go?"

At the bottom of the stairs Mr. J placed a gentle hand on his shoulder. "I didn't see her, sir. I swear, she's not here. I *never* see her." He motioned toward a hallway chair. "You're quite flushed. Please, sit down. Relax for a moment. Shall I get you a drink?"

"No . . . thanks. I'm fine, really."

Both stood quietly for a moment, neither looking at the other.

Then Keane walked away in the direction of his bedroom.

CHAPTER 38

It was already dark when Thornton and Osken crept along a path toward the razor-wire fence that surrounded the run-down complex. Thornton rubbed his fingers across the thin leather holster holding the Makarov strapped beneath his trouser pocket. A fanny pack positioned over it hid the chunk of steel plastered to the point of his hip.

No lights shined through the windows of the deserted factory within the gate. He'd explained to Osken that the guard inside was the bastard who stole his money and beat him up. Their mission was to recover what rightfully belonged to him, a matter of justice. He didn't give Osken time to ask questions.

When they reached the padlocked gate, Thornton could picture again the fat goon Viktor opening it again. The fence hugged close to the building and a tall birch tree stood just outside it at the corner. He motioned toward the tree, and Osken hustled to it.

Clinging to the lower branches, Osken scampered up the trunk. He clutched a sturdy limb above him with both hands and feet. Hanging upside down, he moved like a chimp along it until he cleared the razor wire on top. He then let go and dropped into the weeds with a dull thud.

As Thornton climbed, he attempted to mimic Osken's acrobatics. But every time he reached with his arm, pain shot through his tender ribcage. When his trouser leg caught on the wire, he wrestled to jerk it free, losing his grip. As he fell, his hand grazed the razor wire and ripped open his palm.

They headed to the corner of the building, wading through a puddle of water from a recent rain. Thornton yanked out a handkerchief and squeezed it to stop the bleeding of his palm. He spotted a window with broken panes. Grasping the sole of Osken's foot with both hands linked, he held him up to it.

Osken pounded glass out of the window with the butt of a flashlight and cleared away the glass shards. He crawled in, then turned and helped Thornton wedge through. With Osken standing guard, Thornton grabbed the flashlight and moved for the stairwell at the end of the corridor. On the third level he entered the large open area and beamed the light slowly along the wall. A rusted lamp lay on the floor by an electrical outlet. Tempted to plug it in, he noticed the frayed cord at the neck by the prongs. Touching a Russian 240-volt power system while wearing wet boots was a bad idea.

His light landed on a small canister that matched what he'd remembered: a galvanized-metal cylinder, between two and three feet long. He stuffed the flashlight into his back pocket and stooped to lift it and gauge its weight—roughly forty pounds, a typical bag of fertilizer.

The door on the opposite wall creaked open.

A bright shaft of light shot at him from across the room. He dropped the canister. It hit the concrete floor with a clang. Behind the blinding beam, a massive figure mumbled in Russian. Thornton cautiously rose up, and the beam moved with him. He then recognized Semyon the goon, who stood there bewildered as if staring at a corpse.

Thornton jerked away from the light and reached for his pistol as he snatched the flashlight from his back pocket with the other hand. He aimed his light and weapon at the goon's face and motioned for him to squat with the wave of his gun.

Thornton approached his victim and crouched down. He stared into his pleading eyes and carefully buried the pistol's muzzle into the folds of fat just shy of his breastbone and in the direction of the spleen and liver. He'd learned anatomy well at the clinic. When he squeezed the trigger, the goon's mouth opened wide and he labored to scream. Three more rapid shots pierced the glob of flesh. Semyon's panicked expression turned wooden.

Before Thornton could react to a commotion in the hallway, the ceiling lights flashed on. Viktor stood at the door with a long barreled revolver in one hand and Osken's throat firmly locked in the grip of the other.

Disregarding Osken's fate, Thornton took aim at Viktor's head and pulled the trigger. The pistol only clicked; the magazine was stupidly empty.

Viktor smiled.

Thornton slowly bent down and carefully slid the weapon across the floor toward Viktor then raised his hands in surrender.

"He's going to kill us!" Osken yelled.

Thornton turned to his partner. "Tell him I'll pay him well to let us go."

Osken and Viktor exchanged quick words.

"He doesn't want your money," Osken said. "He wants to see you die. He says move to the wall. He's going to—"

"Tell him that I am a faithful Christian," Thornton said. "I must kneel to pray before he kills us."

Viktor pointed at the wall and shoved Osken by the nape of his neck toward it.

Thornton turned and moved for the electrical outlet by the rusted lamp. Although his feet were wet and his shoes soaked, the concrete floor was dry. The only question was how much current he might draw. The odds of surviving electrocution were a helluva lot better than Victor's gun missing its target at the base of his skull. Either way, it didn't matter. He hadn't planned to be a martyr, but he'd be dying for a noble cause. Maybe Atlanta wasn't worth saving anyway.

He knelt and bowed his head, his eyes fixed on the frayed electrical cord with the plug directly beneath the outlet. He raised his bloodied palm. "Join me, Osken. Pray with me. Come hold my hand, my friend. God is our salvation."

"*Nyet! Nyet!*" Osken shouted.

Thornton closed his eyes and chanted. "Our Father who art in Heaven . . ."

Sobbing, Osken shuffled toward Thornton's outstretched hand.

Viktor followed, one hand on the revolver and the other still clamped around Osken's skinny neck.

"Hallowed be thy name . . . thy Kingdom come . . ."

Thornton waited until Osken reached out and touched his hand and then he grabbed Osken's and jammed the plug of the frayed cord into the wall socket. He wrapped his fingers around the bare wires of the torn insulation.

A blinding light flashed with an ear-piercing crackle.

Knocked backward by the jolt, Thornton felt the blow of a locomotive as the current surged through his body. Osken hit the floor. Viktor's gun flew from his hand and he grabbed for his chest. He wheezed as he fell to the floor, kicking his feet and gasping for air.

Thornton jumped up, two of his fingers scorched and stinging. Viktor struggled on the floor, mashing his hands into the pacemaker above his heart. He massaged and clawed at it until he collapsed and his limbs spread out on the floor like a rag doll.

Thornton scooped up the revolver and delivered the coup de grace with a single bullet to the forehead.

While Osken lay still, Thornton squatted beside him. He grabbed his head and shook it, shouting his name. "You did well, Osken! You are a hero—my friend for life!"

As he slowly came to, Osken stared back at him with a timid smile. Thornton gave him time to recuperate. In the meantime, he ruffled inside Viktor's pockets and found keys for the outside gate.

With Osken staggering beside him, Thornton carried the prized cylinder down the steps and outside, grunting and panting all the way. A torrent of sweat drenched his face and arms as he plopped the cylinder into the trunk of the Oldsmobile. He then held his good palm high toward Osken, who sheepishly slapped it in mock celebration.

CHAPTER 39

Thornton and Osken arrived near midnight back at Osken's family home on the outskirts of Ekaterinburg. Thornton awoke early and showered under an overhead pipe that was minus a showerhead. The water draining from it was tinged brown.

Later, he stood at the mirror over the sink and stared for a long minute at the makeshift bandage on the side of his head. He peeled away the tape and gingerly pulled off the piece of hand towel he'd wrapped around the wound. Dried blood covered the open gash delivered by the goon's steel-toed boot. He threw the bloodied scrap into the trash and picked up a sewing needle from the sink. Bending his neck at an angle, he repeatedly stabbed the needle into the crusted areas while squeezing out the brown-and-yellow pus. He poured vodka down the side of his head and face as he cringed.

After slipping on jeans from his duffle bag, he put on a cotton shirt and trudged downstairs. Osken sat in the kitchen's center at a round table covered with a white cloth stitched at the edges in colors of the rainbow.

"Good morning!" Osken bellowed.

He was flanked by two women, each with a man beside her. Nervously twitching, Osken likely considered himself a fugitive from the law. He looked as if he felt lucky to be alive. Undoubtedly, he'd gathered the family around to share his adventures in Chelyabinsk and confirm the rumors of terror surrounding the city. The sight of Thornton's wounded head and face along with the scarred hand would lend credibility to his story.

Osken introduced each family member. One man was a cousin, who smiled at Thornton and shook hands, unmercifully squeezing his scorched fingers. The other, stocky-framed, was an older brother of Osken's. A chain of tattoos streamed down both arms like ink spills. He bore all the features of a carnival barker and looked skeptical at the presence of an American. Thornton stared back at him to let him know he was aware of his suspicions. Carnival man blinked first.

The women were shy and withdrawn, with the exception of a bubbly one who was married to carnival man. Thornton acknowledged her polite attempt to speak in broken English. He said that she looked like someone he knew in Atlanta who also had beautiful dimpled cheeks.

Osken translated for him, using a hell of a lot more words. When he dimpled his cheeks with a finger, everyone laughed—but not carnival man. Osken then nodded toward the woman on his right. A dark green veil drooped down her slender milky neck and looped around her stunning face. She sat square and silent, wearing a shawl around her narrow shoulders to match the veil. Osken spoke in softer tones when he introduced the young woman as Yelena, a name that carried a soft melody. Osken said she was his lovely sister, the artist. He pointed to her paintings that lined the walls.

Thornton was paying no attention to Osken. He focused on Yelena. She kept her eyes aimed downward, only occasionally looking up as if to make certain he was still staring at her. It was a delightful game that gave him a boner.

After a breakfast of mush and surprisingly tasty sausages, Thornton motioned at Osken, and they moved away from the table. Osken followed him outside where they sat on a step while Thornton smoked.

"I've got another challenge for you," Thornton said.

Osken grinned. "I like challenge, Boss."

"I need to ship my prized artifact back to America."

Osken had to think for a moment on that one, but Thornton guessed his response before the words got out. "Not a problem! I have friend who can handle it."

No doubt he could. "I was also thinking about your sister."

"My *sister*?"

"Her paintings are beautiful. I'd like your sister to paint a scene of Russia for me. A scene upon the artifact."

"My sister would be most willing to do anything for my fine American friend."

That single thought preyed on Thornton's mind as they moved to the Oldsmobile to fetch the canister. When they carried it into the parlor, everyone gathered about to stare at the spooky hunk of metal. After Yelena and Osken spoke, she suggested painting a scene of the snow-capped Ural Mountains. Disappearing into a back room, she glanced over her shoulder and smiled at Thornton.

Returning a few minutes later, she wore an apron and carried artist brushes and paints contained in an open wooden kit decorated with red-and-white flowers and birds hovering over treetops. She squeezed paint from each tube onto a palette. The sun beaming in from a window gave a Jesus-like glow to her face.

*   *   *

Inside the cluttered office, Thornton immediately caught sight of a faded framed picture of Lenin hanging on one shabby wall. Osken introduced Thornton to his friend the exporter, Sergey Kabdechev. Matching the image on the wall, he looked like a communist chieftain under the old Soviet regime. His shiny head matched the globe of lights that stood on the credenza behind his desk. He gave Thornton a measured look as if smelling the likes of a capitalist. Thornton showed no hint of a smile. He didn't want to suggest he was to be taken casually.

"I have been your country many times," Kabdechev croaked. His words spewed out with a thick accent from the back of his throat. The way he said *country* sounded condescending, as if the US was some podunk place north of Cuba.

"New York, Chicago—I know America well," Kabdechev said. "Tell me more about this object of art you own."

"It's a souvenir I wish to send to my mother in Atlanta. She and I collect artifacts from all over the world. Now that I have a better idea of what Russia has to offer, I hope to return soon." *Treat me well. There may be more business ahead.*

"We always like foreigners spending money." He glanced at Osken and winked. "But, I still do not have good picture in my mind of what you wish to ship."

"It looks like an antique milk churn," Thornton replied, "but without handles. A dull metal cylinder, less than a meter long, and it weighs fifteen, maybe twenty kilos. It has a beautiful scene of the Urals painted on it."

Kabdechev sat nodding as he listened, as if contemplating a strategy. "Too bad it's not an antique," he said. "Then we could ship it crated with other cultural artifacts. Much easier to pass through customs in batch inspections. In any case, antiquities are getting closer look these days. You perhaps know about the statue of Aphrodite from the Getty Museum in Los Angeles? It was returned to Sicily." He shook his head in disbelief, as if the event were the equivalent of the fall of the Berlin Wall.

"Yes, I've heard," Thornton said. He had no idea in hell what he was talking about. "So, customs clearance here can be difficult?"

"Not so much *our* customs. I'm more concerned about *your* country. It is more challenging to reach out to our contacts in this business on your West Coast. Going by sea is safest way to get by our customs officials on both sides of the Pacific."

"How long would it take by sea?"

"Thirty days out of Hong Kong."

"Not an option. My mother's birthday is in two weeks. I'd like to surprise her."

"Of course we can do air freight." He glanced at Osken. "I believe we can move your shipment by air from Ekaterinburg to Atlanta without problems. We have contacts, all part of a worldwide trusted network. We can ship to Hong Kong by air cargo tomorrow."

"You still have Los Angeles or Seattle to go through," Thornton said. "I assume inspections happen at every port?"

Kabdechev broke into a soft laugh. He pulled open a bottom desk drawer, brought out a bottle of vodka, reached for three shot glasses, and poured. Thornton only sipped.

"You don't like vodka, my friend?" Kabdechev asked.

"I don't drink."

"We find that a fine beverage helps to make for good business." He tipped his glass. "Both your UPS and Federal Express make daily flights into and out of Ekaterinburg. But we have our own fleet of a dozen Ilyushin cargo jets. They deliver each morning to Hong Kong, Singapore, Seoul. The customs authorities we routinely work with know our reputation. They take our papers at face value. It's called good working relations."

"But I'm still trying, Mr. Kabdechev—"

"Please call me Sergey. Isn't such informality your American way?"

"I'm still trying to understand, Sergey, how you can guarantee that my shipment six thousand miles around the globe won't fall into the hands of customs officials somewhere. It could be confiscated. Or lost."

"Guarantees? If you want guarantees, seek the love of your mother. You think air cargo from all over the world into your country is inspected? Do you know that a thousand aircraft fly cargo into New York City every day? That your Federal Express hub in your state of Tennessee handles thousands of tons of goods from all over the world daily? Do you know how many shipments coming into the US get hands-on inspection? One or two in every hundred . . . maybe. Our contacts have determined that it couldn't possibly be more often because of the impact on your precious American delivery times. Most inspections are mainly looking at paperwork, not even opening a container. What is it that you Americans say? We want it all and we want it now."

Thornton had enough of the goddamned lecture from a blowhard Commie who'd just discovered free enterprise yesterday and thought he could now sell his shit on the free market. "I'll need to pick up the package in Atlanta within five days."

"I can make that happen," Kabdechev said, smiling. "Bring it to me. We will crate it and get it out on a Il-96T tomorrow, headed for Hong Kong. A Boeing 747 will take over from there. You can relax. Your treasure will arrive safely. But of course the price of such requests must take into account our very special expertise."

*   *   *

When they returned to Osken's home, the family had gathered in the kitchen to watch the artist Yelena work. Like a red-tailed hawk focused on a kitten, Thornton studied her movements, how her long fingers firmly grasped the brushes, how she tipped the bristles on her tongue when painting detailed features. At times she would lean forward, exposing her soft breasts. Then a glance at him. The flutter of an eyelash, the swaying of inviting hips as she hummed and stroked.

He grew harder and more excited as darkness approached.

In the early evening, carnival man's wife brought in a jug of wine and fruit with crackers, horsemeat sandwiches with the crust cut off, and a hot broth that smelled of ginger. When Yelena finally finished the mountain scene, she had transformed the repulsive chunk of metal into a work of art. He couldn't believe the vivid colors, with mountain peaks leaping high into a blur of blue and white.

He hustled upstairs where he showered, scrubbing far more thoroughly than usual. After he shaved, he patted the swollen side of his head and carefully fixed locks of hair above his ears. Despite the cold shower, he felt warm. He sat on the bed and struggled to pull on a fresh pair of jeans over his erection.

*   *   *

After an agonizing hour, Thornton slipped along the dark narrow hallway toward Yelena's room where a crack of light shined from underneath her door. He rapped with one knuckle. A voice responded, a tender voice. He gently pushed open the door. Countless framed paintings of different sizes and scenes hung from the low walls beneath a slanted ceiling.

Lying in bed, she hopped up and tossed aside a paperback book before grabbing at the bed sheet and pulling it up over her shoulders.

"Hello," he whispered.

She stared back without speaking, acting surprised.

He smiled. He hadn't planned what to do or say if she didn't smile back. He advanced to the foot of her bed and gently lowered himself onto it. Quickly jerking her legs out from under the sheet, she jumped to her feet and stood in a pink-and-blue nightgown with her arms folded over her breasts.

He rose up and reached for her delicate waist with both hands. She withdrew. He surged forward and lightly brushed his fingers across her neck, then around her chin. He tilted it upward and smiled. "Please, Yelena . . . ."

She stiffened in fright. When he brought a hand to her shoulder, she snapped her head to one side and chomped down deep into his arm, drawing blood.

He yelled out and grabbed his wrist. "I didn't mean to scare you. I thought—"

She rushed for the door. He leaped up to follow when the door sprung open. The carnival man burst in, snatched his bloodied arm, and began to twist.

Shocked by his surprising strength, Thornton kowtowed to his knees and struggled to unwind his body. The beast continued twisting until his arm was ready to unscrew from its socket. He could only cry out and beg for mercy.

Yelena stood smiling as carnival man led Thornton back into his room and slammed him to the floor. The husky Russian then shoved his foot into Thornton's crotch and mashed the heel of his boot into his balls until he blacked out.

CHAPTER 40

Lying half-naked across his bed, Thornton opened his eyes to a blurred vision of a bantamweight Russian grabbing his shoulders and shaking him.

"Everybody's gone! Everybody!" Osken shouted.

"What are you talking about?" Thornton rolled out of bed and immediately recoiled, groaning from the strain he'd placed on his swollen balls.

"What about my canister? Where is it?" Thornton asked.

"I don't see it anywhere. What happened last night?"

"We've got to get the canister back, Osken. Call your brother."

"But why my brother? What he know—"

"Shut up. Tell him I'll pay him for it. Just bring it back."

After they rushed downstairs to the kitchen, Osken tapped on his cell phone. He paced the floor as he spoke, waving his arm above his head. When he flipped the phone closed, he looked at Thornton. "My brother says he will think about it."

"Let's go to his home. I want to drive there. Now."

"That is not possible."

He thrust his face into Osken's. "Why not?"

"I know my brother. He is very upset what you did to Yelena."

"I did *nothing* to your sister. I just wanted to talk. I didn't lay a hand on her."

"I will wait until you and my brother calm down. We will visit him later today."

He grabbed Osken by his jawbone with the hand of his good arm and lifted him off his feet. "I want the goddamn canister. I want it now or—"

"Put me the fuck down and get your filthy hands off me, Amerikos!" He pronounced each word in startlingly good English. Thornton released his grip. Osken sank to the floor, then jumped up and rushed to a drawer and whipped out a steak knife.

Bad mistake.

Thornton had grown to trust the little Russian. He backed away, waving his palms high. "Sorry, Osken. Really sorry, man. I got carried away."

"Let me make one thing clear," Osken said, now panting. "You do *not* put your pig American hands on me again."

"I was only—"

"Do you understand me?"

"I understand," Thornton replied softly.

Osken tossed the knife back into the drawer and slammed it shut. "You pack your clothes. I tell you what my brother decides."

When Thornton returned to his room, he closed the door and quickly unzipped the duffle bag to rummage through his belongings. The pistol was gone.

He dove onto the bed and beat at the pillow with both fists. He was at the utter mercy of two sewer rats taking him for a ride. They thought he was nothing but slime on their hands. He rolled onto his back and mashed the pillow into his face. They had made a very big mistake.

*   *   *

Hearing loud footsteps on the stairs, Thornton jerked up. Osken burst through the bedroom door without knocking. "My brother says I bring you to his home to talk."

"I'm not going to be surrounded by your family while we negotiate. Tell him I'll pay him five hundred dollars for what rightfully belongs to me. And tell him to meet us at the small park by the bell tower downtown. We can do the exchange quietly, as gentlemen. After that, you can drop me off at the airport, and I'll be gone from here for good."

He followed Osken back upstairs and sat outside on a step leading to the entryway. He lit a cigarette with a shaky hand. Osken had been a good friend, a faithful companion. Thornton could never have accomplished what he'd set out to do so soon if it hadn't been for the little Russian. In a strange way, he'd miss him. But his one regret before leaving was Yelena. He never intended to hurt her, not Yelena. Someday he would return.

While he was taking the last drag of his cigarette, Osken walked out the door and squatted beside him. "My brother ready to make change. He says he will take one thousand dollars. He will meet you here."

"Call him back. The deal is five hundred dollars, and we'll meet at the bell tower. Otherwise, I'll leave for the airport now, and he can keep the goddamned canister in memory of me. I will even show him how to open it for the surprise inside."

Osken sat for a moment, then turned to him. "It is deal."

When Osken stood, Thornton noticed a bulge in his shirt above his belt. He smiled to himself.

*   *   *

The Oldsmobile approached the park by the bell tower. Osken drove until he spotted a dilapidated pick-up at the roadside near a grove of trees. He pulled behind the truck and looked at Thornton. "You be kind to my brother. Very bad temper."

"Tell him to drive deeper into the trees. We don't want to look like some black-market deal."

Osken stuck his head out of the window and yelled. Carnival man brought the truck farther off the road, sliding in under the leafy branches. Thornton directed Osken to back the Oldsmobile in beside the truck to make an easy transfer from the bed of the pickup to the car trunk. Both hopped out and moved slowly toward the truck. Carnival man stood with the tailgate down. He rolled back a tattered blanket, revealing the canister. Thornton rolled it over to locate the mountain scene then pulled ten fifty-dollar bills from his trouser pocket. Carnival man snatched them from his hand. Osken motioned for his brother to grab the canister and follow him to the Oldsmobile.

Thornton surveyed the highway. While carnival man lowered the canister into the trunk, Thornton gently slipped beside him as if to help. Then he reached for the tire iron that was secured behind the spare wheel. Squeezing both hands around the bar, he leaned back, lifted it high, and rammed the notched end deep into carnival man's skull where it lodged.

Osken yanked the Makarov from underneath his shirt. Thornton wrenched the bar out of the dead man and reeled about. He swung it back over his head and heaved it downward like an axe into Osken's face, spraying blood into Thornton's eyes as the little Russian flew backward into the grass. He speared the weapon's chiseled end into Osken's chest until he felt the crunch of his breastbone, and then he leaned into the bar with all of his weight and impaled his former partner into solid earth. He held on firmly until the jerking stopped and Osken's pathetically weak screams faded away. After recovering his money, he stuffed both bodies into the Oldsmobile's trunk and wiped his hands and face with an oily rag before slamming the trunk lid shut.

Keeping watch over his shoulder for passing cars, he then walked behind a birch tree and took a leak.

*   *   *

Thornton exited his car parked by the small office building and stood on his tiptoes to stretch his lower back. While straightening his shirt collar, he spotted Mr. Kabdechev peeking at him through the blinds from his ground-floor office.

The door was already open when Thornton lugged the canister inside and gently lowered it onto the floor. Kabdechev ran a finger across the painted scene and studied it with interest. "A beautiful object indeed. We can have it flown into Atlanta for you within one week. The cost will be twelve hundred dollars."

"That's rather high."

"In fact, it's cheap. No other delivery service would even accept this"—he waved at the canister—"this hunk of metal, at any cost."

Thornton doled out the cash and gave him all the details, including the phone number of the business hub nearest his home in Atlanta with package delivery service. Before leaving Atlanta, he'd alerted the owner of Midtown Business Center to expect a special shipment to him in the coming weeks.

Thornton held out his hand to shake. "Osken and I have a long road ahead."

He'd left the Oldsmobile parked along the outer boundary of the city's Koltsovo International Airport, jammed in between an oversized truck and a recreational van of 1970s vintage. He strolled toward the airport's entrance, toting his duffle bag and wondering how many days before the stink of decaying flesh in the trunk would attract attention. Time was on his side now.

Passengers stood by the departure display overhead to look for gate numbers. One Western face stuck out. He'd noticed the man standing near the airport entrance when he arrived and again when he stopped to buy three bars of candy for breakfast.

The stranger appeared to stare at the board, checking out flights. He looked to be European or American. His clothing was neat and properly tailored—a debonair gentleman who wore thick glasses with black rims. He had the look of an academic. Keeping a safe distance, Thornton meandered behind him. Then he picked up his pace and passed the guy to get a better look at his face. After a few yards

Thornton slowed to a stop. When he looked back over his shoulder, the stranger was gone.

CHAPTER 41

One week later . . .

Wilbur barked as he jumped up on all fours and snapped at a crumb of buttered rye toast fluttering through the air. Keane sat wrapped in a robe at the kitchen bar. He was finishing off a bowl of cream-of-tomato soup with his toast and doing his best to return to a normal routine.

Mr. J strolled into the kitchen. "Sorry to disturb you, sir, but I wanted to make certain you didn't miss the mail that came yesterday." He handed his boss a letter. Keane immediately guessed from the small pastel envelope and handwritten address who had sent it. And he knew why it had arrived today. The card inside displayed a picture of a dove on a cream background. The scribbled note from his loving sister read:

> *Thinking of you. Hope you are doing okay.*
> *Margot*

It was the anniversary of Danielle's death. Margot knew his twin would be on Keane's mind. It always was as the Fourth of July holiday approached each summer. He thought about giving Margot a call but dismissed it. They had learned over the years that there was little either could say. Both would try too hard to come up with the right words, as they had so many times before. He knew she meant well.

His thoughts turned to Felix Thornton, as they did most nights since his nightmare experience in the North Georgia woods. And there was little doubt that the monster was responsible for Ronnie Davenport's life-threatening condition.

Would Thornton ever be brought to justice?

He should revisit some of his old contacts, like his longtime friend from FBI's Special Intelligence Unit in the Atlanta regional office. James Kessel Jr. was known to those who knew him well as Kessel Jim, to distinguish him from his eminent father who served four terms in the Georgia State Senate.

Kessel Jim was a curmudgeon who'd reeled Keane into a consulting role on three cases in five years. The last one involved a Maryland mental hospital for the criminally insane. Someone had knocked off three of the inmates. As it turned out, it was a psychiatrist who was the crazed killer. Keane grabbed the cell phone to search his contact list but was interrupted by Mr. J rushing into the room. "The cameras have picked up the same car passing in front of the gates, sir. Much too frequently, I'm afraid. A black Cadillac Seville."

"Just keep watch," Keane replied. Likely another reporter who'd learned about his background role in Atlanta's "great nuclear scare," as one *Journal-Constitution* reporter had coined it. APD had assured the public that all but one of the six missing cobalt-60 slugs had been found and an exhaustive search was still underway throughout the metropolitan area and beyond. Investigative journalists then set out to resurrect all the old serial-murder types and legends. They were playing the role of amateur psychologists, interviewing the physicians and staff at Grady Memorial to get the gruesome details of each victim's death. Chief Dallas Walters was repeatedly pressed in interviews to explain APD's tardiness in determining the MO of the killer or killers.

The cell phone rang in Keane's hand. The name *Carl Stillwell* popped up on the screen. "Good morning, Mr. Mayor."

"Got great news, Damon. We can cross the godforsaken Felix Thornton off our list of worries."

Keane paused a beat. "Because?"

"He's dead."

Keane sat dumbfounded. He had to repeat the words in his head.

"We don't know all the particulars yet," the mayor continued. "The State Department contacted us just a short time ago. He was discovered in a Russian airport—inside a restroom toilet, strangled. They've got positive ID. Just wanted you to know that we're all aware of the role you played in hastening his fate. And I wanted to give you my personal thanks for that."

Keane still hadn't fully recovered from the news. "Will you be sure to fill me in on details as they come in?"

"Of course. You've got my word on it."

As soon as the mayor hung up, Mr. J burst into the kitchen, out of breath. "Excuse me, sir. We have a visitor at the front gate. The driver of that black Cadillac. Says his name is Selsby."

Keane looked up. "Detective Selsby?"

"He just said Crawford Selsby."

Wilbur jumped and wagged his tail as Keane slid from the stool. He was always careful to leave his address out of the public record. He'd certainly never mentioned to Selsby where he lived. His first thought was to have Mr. J tell him he wasn't there, but there was no use kicking the can down the road. "Open the gate, but let him know our firearms rule."

As Mr. J turned to leave, Keane called out, "And turn on full surveillance."

"Certainly, sir."

He followed Mr. J through the hallway with Wilbur in a fast trot to keep up. Keane charged into the drawing room and Mr. J dashed to the closet next to the butler's pantry. The closet door opened onto a panel of video screens monitoring the entrance. Keane peeked through a slot in the shutters to survey the driveway. When Selsby's car pulled near the front door, he rushed to the monitoring station.

A stone archway and alcove surrounded the outside entrance. Four microvideo cameras were embedded within the stone around the massive oak doors. All were disguised by a combination of real and fake vines of English ivy.

The doorbell rang.

Keane studied the color images on four eight-inch screens, all focused on the visitor. Mr. J turned a control to bring one camera into closer range. As it zoomed in, the face of Selsby was unmistakable. To the right of the video screens a larger one displayed a 3-D image of his entire body using a system of reflected sub-millimeter electromagnetic pulses. Mini-transmitters were mounted next to the video cameras as well as at three camouflaged positions along the alcove roof and within the half-ton ceramic flower pots and faux pillars. The images revealed a cigarette lighter, car keys, and coins scattered in his trouser pockets.

"Should I answer the door, sir?"

"I'll get it. Just keep a close watch."

With a twinkle in his eye Mr. J patted beneath the breast pocket to remind Keane of his trusty Derringer.

Keane moved cautiously to the front door and opened it with a guarded smile. "This is a surprise, Detective."

"Sorry. I know it's early."

"Please, come in."

They sat in leather chairs facing each other in the drawing room. Selsby looked bedraggled—unshaven, deeper lines in the recesses of his cheeks. He'd aged ten years since Keane saw him last.

Selsby checked out the room with rapid glances. "Nice home. All these square feet for only one guy?"

Keane nodded. "Seems like a waste, huh?"

An uneasy silence followed.

"I'm sorry it all came to this, Detective."

Selsby glowered back at him with narrow eyes. "It's not 'Detective' anymore."

Keane squirmed. Selsby knew damn well who had initiated the probe that took him down. "That wasn't my intention."

"Like unintended consequences?" Selsby asked.

"You could say that."

"What exactly *was* your intention? To seek truth, justice, and the American way?"

Letting Selsby through the gate was a mistake. But it was too late for second-guessing.

"There's a thing called freedom of expression," Selsby said. "I thought any American citizen had the right to belong to any organization he wants on his own time."

"You took an oath when you joined the APD. You—"

"I know the line."

Mr. J entered the room with a nervous smile. "May I get either of you gentlemen a cold beverage?"

Both declined. Keane held contact with Mr. J's eyes longer than usual before turning to Selsby. "Have you heard the news about Felix Thornton?"

"Why should I give a damn about him?" Selsby asked.

"I guess it makes no difference now."

Selsby lowered his head and cuddled his face with both hands. He then lifted his chin and looked directly at Keane. "I'm outta here. I've had twenty-four years with the department. It's no pension to write home about, but I can get by. My brother has eight hundred acres he farms over in South Carolina, down near Gaston. The cotton-and-tobacco business is booming and he can use the help. He's giving me a hundred acres to till for myself and a small house on the property. Should have looked into it years ago. You did me a favor, Keane. I got no hard feelings. Wanted to tell you that face-to-face."

Curious with new smells about, Wilbur drifted lazily into the room. Selsby reached for him. "Hey, boy . . . good dog." He let him sniff the back of his hand before gently petting him behind his floppy ears. The dog then moseyed over to Keane and lay at his feet.

The two men sat gazing at each other for a long moment.

"We had others doing deep background," Selsby said. "I never told you about the psych profiler. She took a quick look at all the suspects and put the finger on Thornton immediately. Stupid of me, but I didn't want to give you the satisfaction of knowing that a professional in the business came to exactly the same conclusion you did."

Confession time? "Good to know, but doesn't mean much now," Keane said. "I never understood how Thornton escaped the country so easily."

"He was long gone before we could nail the stolen cobalt slugs on him. You know that."

You knew days before that, dammit. I put you onto him early. "Why didn't you ever go back to his field site up in the mountains?" Keane asked.

"We did. We searched the entire area. Collected evidence and sent it to the GBI labs. We even found another Thornton hideaway a couple miles north of where your car bit the dust. It was just off the power-line right-of-way. Made an easy path for Thornton to get back and forth. Face it, Keane. He was a damn smart guy. Worth writing a book about. But it's all water under the bridge, as far as I'm concerned." He stood to leave.

Keane rose from his chair. Selsby extended his hand to shake.

"Just curious," Keane said. "Why didn't you mention that hideaway before?"

"You know the answer. I didn't want you to know more than me."

"You didn't search it?"

Selsby stopped and shrugged. "I'll let you in on a little secret. After Thornton fled the country, APD didn't give a shit. He might as well have been dead."

Keane stared through the shutters as Selsby's car disappeared between the rows of live oaks along the winding driveway. He walked upstairs to the master bedroom where he showered and dressed, and then he lay on the bedroom chaise and tried to put it all together. He'd report to Chief Walters about the visit and conversation right after the holiday. Looking back, he should have figured Selsby out a lot quicker. But sizing up strangers had always been a problem. His approach of trying to analyze people contrasted with that of every cop he knew. Each possessed an instinct implanted like a chip in his central nervous system. If there wasn't something right about a stranger they met, they could immediately smell it.

But Keane didn't have it. He lacked the skill to fathom what lurked beneath. He had no talent for gauging people with his gut. That was an acquired skill, honed over a lifetime.

Screw it. He pulled up the news on his cell phone. The president was going to speak at the UN. The Braves had won the night before, sweeping a three-game series with the Mets. The next day the city headed for another sweltering one in the nineties, but the mountains to the north would be ten degrees cooler.

Before he reported it to Chief Walters, maybe he should verify Selsby's story that he'd mentioned only in passing—some kind of hideaway that Thornton had used.

Was it possible that the one still missing colbalt-60 slug could be there? Plausible. If so, he could put to use the mini-instrument for detecting radiation he'd acquired the week before.

The whole thing was a crazy idea, but crazy ideas had a way of trumping boredom. It was a little above and beyond, a good way to close out his final consulting report to APD and the mayor. Something that would leave a *Damon Keane* trademark.

CHAPTER 42

The road that Keane remembered wended through the Chattahoochee National Forest. Mr. J had packed him a ham-and-cheese sandwich on whole wheat, a red delicious apple, and three bottles of water. All of it was stashed inside a backpack on the passenger seat of the Land Rover that Mr. J had hastily rented for him.

He stopped at the same general store as before—the Pure Oil station with one gas pump. The owner he remembered didn't recognize him. He was too busy whittling. After hitting the restroom, Keane found the graveled forest-service road and headed up it. When the road eventually disintegrated into nothing more than a path, he parked in a flattened area. Squatting on the Land Rover's back bumper, he donned a pair of hiking boots and grabbed his backpack where he'd stuffed his new RadEye detector, not much larger than a cigarette pack. The convenient device would alarm as soon as it detected any intense source of gamma rays.

He sauntered through the cool mountain air, recalling that Selsby said the cabin was roughly two miles north of the site, following the direction of the power lines limping above the tall pines. Hiking came easier than before. In addition to proper boots, he'd worn the right clothes this time—khaki shorts and a T-shirt. When he finally reached the power lines, the sun was high. A wide swath of field grass rose above his knees. An uphill climb faced him in the heat of the day.

During the hike he quickly learned not to take on the steep slope straightaway. It was much easier to zigzag along the open corridor. He followed grasshoppers splaying out ahead, bringing back the days when he and Danielle ran barefoot through mountain meadows chasing locusts and katydids. Teenagers, not fixed on any particular goal, they only wandered and watched and dreamed.

He made a mental note to check out the trout streams after the hike. He'd then invite Andy out for a fly-fishing trip. Maybe take the opportunity to teach Nicole that fine art. He thought about the mayor's son—how he'd lit up when he caught the little bass. The mayor wasn't fishing, he was loving, bonding. An incredibly busy man, but he knew his priorities.

Keane kept a close lookout for ankle-twisting rocks and creatures that slithered. The sun burned his neck where the sweat beaded, drawing mosquitoes that mostly dodged his slaps. Occasionally he'd lift his sticky arms to allow his armpits to breathe. When he came to a narrow plateau, the pines opened into a natural gap. Glancing back from where he'd hiked, the ground fell away sharply. He moved into the shade to take a break. With one foot upon a boulder, he took off his backpack to grab his second bottle of water and gulp half of it down. When he stood, he spotted a deer darting across the open space, its white tail wagging high. He followed it with his eyes through the brush until he fixed on a structure beneath a thick grove of trees. A pine-log cabin squatted below the low limbs as if hiding from hunters. Crude, but crude in a grand style with a green-shingled roof.

Since he was approaching the cabin from the rear, he made a wider circle and moved to the front. The structure was set on pillars of stone. A rusted iron handle on the narrow door served as a doorknob. As soon as he reached for it, a hornet dive-bombed his ear.

He jumped back and swatted at it. A small paper-like nest decorated one corner of the doorjamb. Stepping forward again, he grabbed the handle and jiggled.

"Raise your hands!"

The words ambushed him from behind like a rifle shot. He froze.

"Are you fucking deaf, Keane?"

He threw his hands above his head and prayed that the voice came from an undercover cop stationed as a lookout.

"Take off the backpack and turn around."

He put a thumb under a shoulder strap and repeated the move with the other. The backpack fell to the ground. Holding onto his weapon, Felix Thornton reached forward with his free hand and patted him down.

"Glad you made it," Thornton said.

Keane's mind whirled like a tornado. Had Thornton risen from the dead?

"If you put your gun away, we can talk about it."

"I screwed up before," Thornton said. "That won't happen again. Turn around and open the door."

"I already tried. It won't—"

"I said, *push in* the goddamn door!"

But Keane knew that if he entered the cabin, he wouldn't come out alive.

*   *   *

Jessie sat behind the wheel of her Porsche, headed for the North Georgia mountains. She'd called Keane twice, but his phone rolled over to voice mail each time. She finally called Mr. J, who told her that Keane was going back to the Chattahoochee Forest. He was still complaining about the last time Keane had rented a pint-sized car to navigate the old logging roads.

She couldn't believe that Keane was going back to where both were fired on by a psychopath before. What was this obsession he had with Thornton? It was an overwhelming fixation that refused to quit. What drove such mania in men? Of course, Keane would be pissed off when he found out what she did—driving all this way to chase him down like some kind of mother hen. Were her emotions taking her overboard?

She called his cell one more time without luck then shoved down hard on the accelerator.

CHAPTER 43

Thornton thrust the barrel of his pistol toward Keane then turned and grabbed the cabin door's latch with both hands. When he rammed his left shoulder against the door, it broke open.

Keane stumbled inside to a musty smell of mold. A bunk bed hugged one corner and a handmade workbench of used two-by-fours lined the far wall. Neatly arranged buckets and cans, stacked rolls of electrical wire, and a scattering of tools lined the bench: screwdrivers, drill bits, assorted hammers. Two broad axes hung on the wall and a long shovel leaned against a corner. Isolated in the middle of the room was a black wrought-iron bed frame with a box spring but no mattress.

While he kept his head steady, Keane shifted his eyes about to search for other doors and windows. "I was told you were dead," he said. It was better to talk than shut up.

"Then your advice came from incompetent idiots, didn't it? You have to be clever in my line of work."

In fact, Thornton thought, getting out of Russia and back to Atlanta turned out to be a cakewalk. He had watched with great interest the stranger in the Ekaterinburg airport that day. A few inches shorter, he was close to his own age, and his hair was a little lighter and thinner. Thornton could recall the details. He had followed the stranger's glances as he stood checking out the flights on the overhead electronic board. Thornton walked down the corridor a short distance. When he stopped and looked back, the stranger had departed. Thornton was strolling back, looking for him, when he spotted him at the wall, speaking on his cell phone.

Thornton moseyed to the flight board and pretended to study it while watching for him to return. When he did Thornton shuffled up beside him. "Pardon me, do you speak English?"

The stranger hesitated, as if it required too much effort to speak. "Yes."

"I was wondering about the Frankfurt flight. By chance are you going on that one?"

"I'm flying to Dubai."

One of the world's major hubs. "Never been there."

"I'm only changing planes there to New York."

"You're an American too?"

The stranger nodded and turned back to the board.

Thornton made his way to an empty seat on a bench by the wall. The American stood near the flight board, still focused on it. His face wasn't pockmarked like Thornton's. And his thick glasses could possibly present a problem.

The American walked away from the board. Thornton quickly followed along the hall, weaving through the crowd. When the American darted into the men's room, Thornton waited for a moment then entered. One man stood at a urinal and another stooped over a long sink, combing his hair in the mirror. Burgundy shoes under a stall against the wall belonged to the American. Thornton opened the stall door next to his, closing it behind him. He crammed his duffle bag down by the door, removed his belt, squatted on the toilet seat, and waited.

The American flushed.

Thornton jumped up and hopped over the duffle bag. He kept his belt looped in one hand while he cracked open the door. No one else was around. When the American opened his stall, Thornton barged out and shoved him back onto the toilet as the surprised victim yelled. In the same motion, Thornton threw the loop over his head while pushing the door closed with a foot. Grasping the two belt ends, Thornton wrenched the leather loop tightly around his neck.

The American reached for his throat as he gasped for air. His face turned scarlet as his eyes bulged beneath his thick lenses, the look of a goldfish nestled against the side of his bowl. When Thornton jerked harder, the American's hands finally dropped to his sides. His cheeks puffed out and his guppy eyes stayed open.

He found the passport and plane tickets in the stranger's coat pocket. Etihad Flight 5897 departed at 7:20 p.m. from Ekaterinburg to Dubai. At 10:35 the next morning, Flight 101 departed for New York, landing at JFK at 4:42 p.m. The passport picture was a problem because of the damned thick glasses. Fortunately, James Alexander Martin's birthdate—18 July 1968—put him only three years younger.

He wrenched the wallet from a back pocket and riffled through it, counting out $400 in fifties and twenties. Leaving two twenties in the wallet, he pulled out all the cards with his name on them, including two credit cards and his New York driver's license. He switched the license with his own issued in Georgia and tucked his MasterCard into the wallet.

Many hours would likely pass before the body would be discovered. Who was going to suspect that somebody had died on the toilet? Their tracking would find that Felix Henry Thornton had escaped US law enforcement. Not a big surprise that he was found murdered in a bathroom stall. It would take another few hours before they found out that the body wasn't his.

Thornton walked with caution, barely making out images through the Coke-bottle lenses. He passed through customs without incident and later boarded the Etihad flights, eventually reaching New York. Although weak, exhausted and starved, he had the pleasure of hitching rides on eighteen-wheelers from JFK to Atlanta, allowing plenty of time for sleep. And plenty of time to plan, which brought him to where he now stood, eyeballing Damon Keane.

"Lay down on the bedsprings," Thornton commanded.

"You know, Felix—"

"I said, lay down!"

Keane rolled onto the rusted box spring, his heart battering the walls of his chest. While staring into the barrel of the pistol, he scooted onto his stomach to position his head at the end of the bed. Thornton cut off two pieces of rope with a switchblade. He tied Keane's hands to each side of the iron railing and looped the remaining rope around his neck to yank his head off the springs. He wrapped and tied the other end to Keane's feet with his legs bent at his knees behind him.

Keane lay hog-tied on his belly with his head suspended in the air. He could only relieve the pressure on his throat by arching his back to bring his head closer to his feet.

Thornton scooted a wooden chair over and flipped it around. Throwing his leg over one side, he squatted and held the tip of the barrel's pistol level with Keane's forehead. "Here we are again, Dr. Keane. *Mano-a-mano*."

The vertebrae in Keane's neck were wrenched to the verge of cracking.

Talk to him. Stretching his neck muscles, he struggled to speak. "Nobody knows you've returned to Atlanta, Felix." He swallowed hard. "APD has dropped the case. You got away scot-free. You could—"

"Where you fucked up was in turning on my companion—my brother in the cause, you might call him. You never even guessed that mine and Selsby's paths crossed at more than one crusade around the state. You didn't even question why he volunteered on the Piedmont Park cases." His sneer gradually shifted into a smile. "And everyone thought you were so damned smart."

He stuffed the pistol into his waistband and walked toward a back corner.

Keane heard rolling across the wood-planked floor. When he strained to look, Thornton was pushing a metal box on a two-wheeled hand truck. He scooted the object off at the foot of the bed directly below Keane's head.

Thornton sat back down, pulled his pistol from his waistband, and laid it on the floor. He then rested his forearms on the top of his chair and stared into Keane's face. "This little container hides the last one of the charming cobalt sources I've planted around Atlanta."

Keane arched against the relentless tug of the rope and stretched his abdominals to the point of snapping like a rubber band. He focused all his attention on his chin—he had to keep it rock-solid, absolutely still, so Thornton wouldn't notice the trembling of his head.

Thornton leaned toward him. His dog tags swung from a thin chain as if to hypnotize. "We knew you would come," he said. "Selsby put a tracker on your fancy car. He could call up the software on his laptop and follow you like it was a computer game. He kept me informed. You're not very bright are you, Keane? Selsby told me all about you and your family. They've deserted you. I'll bet you don't even have any real friends."

He's a madman talking nonsense.

"You're the crazy one here, aren't you, Keane? And you thought you were chasing one. Big hero, gonna track down the psycho. Gonna save the world."

Thornton was right. Keane had been outsmarted by two scumbag cowards. He held his head still—perfectly still—as sweat trickled along one cheek, collected at the tip of his chin, and dripped to the floor.

"You're not afraid to die, are you?" Thornton asked. He spoke softly now, as if lying back in an easy chair and sipping a brew.

Keane swallowed hard. "Why do you need to kill?"

"It's a laxative. Cleansing my life from those who hated me. Purging the city of human sewage."

"But you killed your own father, Felix."

Thornton lunged forward and slapped him across the face with the back of his hand. "He made me what I am!"

A blow from the opposite direction drew a stream of blood from the corner of Keane's mouth. "I hated every minute I knew him."

"But why did you *hate* him?"

He stuck his pockmarked face into Keane's. "Because he killed my mother."

"Your mother was murdered by a criminal gang on Christmas Eve."

"He was a goddamn coward. He hid in the basement while they took turns at her. His life and everything he stood for was a lie." He paused and stared at Keane, the whites of his eyes filled with blood. "You've never hated. Right? Never wanted to take revenge on anyone?"

"I don't have that much hate inside me."

"Everybody does. You just don't want to admit it."

As he spoke, Keane's eyes drifted. He'd now tuned out the barrage of words.

"Such a true Southern gentleman, aren't you, Keane?"

Thornton's features began to melt into a fog, a blur of confusion.

"I kill because I hate. I kill again because it feels so good the first time and even better the next. And I'm not just another killer . . . I've been called to a higher duty. That raises me above the others."

Keane peeked over Thornton's shoulder through the small window by the workbench.

"But you, you're willing to just give up and die. You're the sad fool here, aren't you, Keane?"

She seemed to be stretching herself tall to search inside through a lower windowpane. A soft, beautiful face.

CHAPTER 44

Keane wanted to reach out to his twin, Danielle, stretch toward the window to tell her he was sorry. He was ashamed that their dad had chosen him instead of her that day, destined to be the worst day of his life. Not today. Not the day he would die.

Their dad, a strong swimmer, could have rescued either in the swirling riptide off North Carolina's Outer Banks that fateful day, their fourteenth birthday. The riptide emerged quickly, whipped them in the face and dragged both away from shore like a tornado at sea. Their dad stood terrified on the beach as the twins struggled and shouted for help in the raging whirlpool. He had to make a Sophie's choice—he swam for Damon, not Danielle. His only son, in place of his younger daughter. Keane's life was saved that day, that tormenting day, that day he'd reenact in his mind over and over, waking in the middle of the night, reaching out to her, screaming for her. At age fourteen, he'd been cursed with a burden too crippling to carry for a lifetime.

Look at me now, Danielle. Now would Dad be proud of the one he saved?

Her face dissolved and drifted away, replaced by Thornton's sharp features pressed into his.

"Tell me, Keane, who have you hated? Who have you hated even more than me right now?" He slapped him across the face. "Answer me, goddammit!"

He whacked him again with a flying palm. "I asked you a question."

"Myself," Keane whispered through bloodied lips. "I hate myself."

He'd finally said it. After all these years, he'd said it out loud. Not just a thought that popped into his head that he could quickly toss away. From the minute he'd arrived on shore that day, safe in the arms of his dad, and looked back at the swollen waters, he could only cry out and beat his father on the chest with his fists.

Why should he live and Danielle die? Her body had washed ashore the next day.

"Why, Dad?" he'd asked years later as his father sucked in his last air from a mechanical ventilator. He'd never found the nerve to ask his dad before that day. But then he stared into his dad's pale eyes, repeating the question until he heard him murmur the words with his final breath. "I . . . already had a daughter."

He already had a daughter—Margot, his older sister. The Atlantic swallowed Danielle, but he survived. He lived only because he was born with a Y chromosome in place of an X. Through a torrent of tears, he watched his father take his last breath, but they were not tears for his dad.

Everything he'd ever set out to explore, to conquer, to master, to love—all that and more were to prove that his dad had made the right choice that day. The fatal decision that rescued him, but stole his soul. All his days since were filled with the same hatred that raged within Felix Thornton. But instead of being directed out at the world, his own hate had spread inward like a malignant tumor.

Thornton grabbed Keane's hair and wrenched back his head. "Don't give me that blank stare, those teary eyes. You're just trying to save your neck. This chunk of cobalt is especially for you. Kept it safely right here in the cabin."

He pointed at the metal box. "Tell me, have you heard of the Xinjiang procedure?"

Keane no longer nodded or spoke.

"I'll take that as a *no*. You should be interested. There was a time when prisoners in China were executed by firing squads while doctors just like you waited with scalpels. They rushed in to harvest their organs after the prisoners were shot. Those docs who confessed years later said the worst part was listening to a dying man gurgling blood and trying to scream while they carved out a kidney or a liver. Are you following me?"

Keane's eyes were inflamed from the salty sweat. He squeezed them shut.

"I have a fate like that in store for you," Thornton said. "When I open this little contraption, the gamma rays will beam at you like a thousand suns. But that's when I'll be leaving. Sorry you'll miss the Big One I've got ready for Atlanta." He reached out a hand and cuddled Keane's chin. "It'll be a while before you'll feel your head heat up. Then your sweat will flow like a stream instead of a trickle."

He mashed Keane's jaw back with a force that nearly snapped his neck.

"After a while, you'll puke away your guts. You'll be worried about gagging in your own vomit. In a few hours the spasms will start, and your throat will swell and burn like you're eating fire. Your bowels will let go and the seizures will start. That's when you'll try to swallow your tongue and choke yourself to death."

Keane focused on the dog tags.

"So, tell me," Thornton said, "I'm curious. Where will they bury you?"

Keane imagined a thick carpet of emerald-green grass surrounding a small headstone isolated high on a hill in the Blue Ridge Mountains. But he could tell that Thornton was growing tired. He'd likely had little sleep since returning from Russia. He couldn't possibly operate at full strength. He just wanted to get it all over with, to carry out a grand scheme he'd cooked up inside his own decaying mind. He wasn't thinking straight; otherwise, he'd use the pistol to end it all now. Like a puppet on strings, he was manipulated from within by a coward who had nothing to live for.

The phone in Keane's pocket rang. He stretched his head back toward his feet to relieve the pressure on his throat and blurted out, "It's my security guy. He's waiting for me to return back to the main road."

"Let it ring," Thornton said.

"If I don't answer, he'll follow my trail. The locators on our phones are networked."

Thornton lunged for Keane's pocket and yanked out the phone. The screen was blank, but the phone kept ringing.

"It won't work for you," Keane said with a sudden coolness that even surprised himself.

The ringing stopped.

"It's biometric," Keane said. "The phone uses my fingerprint for ID to unlock it."

Thornton pulled out a switchblade, snapped it open and moved toward him.

Keane gritted his teeth.

Thornton slipped the blade between the rope and Keane's wrist and cut the binding to free his right hand. He then slashed the rope between his feet and neck, leaving his left wrist still tied to the railing.

"Call him back. Tell him to wait." He tossed the phone on the bed and held the blade to Keane's throat. Thornton's dog tags reflected a flash of sunlight from a lone window on the far wall.

Keane sat on his knees and reached for the phone. He had only one chance.

CHAPTER 45

K̲eane knew he had to strike the base of Thornton's nose with a blow that called upon all of his strength for a fraction of a second. The nasal bones would slam like a spear into the frontal lobes of his brain and cause massive hemorrhage. Death on the spot—knowledge shared by those skilled in combat jujitsu and neurosurgery.

In one swift move he hurled the phone at Thornton's head and seized the chain around his neck. He jerked back with every muscle of his upper torso and smashed his face into the wrought-iron railing of the bed.

Thornton recoiled. Dazed, he clutched his face then peered at the blood that smeared the palm of his hand. With one hand still tied to the bed, Keane swept down toward the pistol, wrenching his rib cage as he stretched. He caught the tip of his index finger on the trigger guard and tossed the weapon onto the bed.

Thornton swung at him with his knife.

Keane ducked and snatched the gun. He aimed it at Thornton's head. "Drop the knife! Drop it or I swear I'll—"

"How do you know it's loaded, shithead?" Thornton flipped the switchblade in the air and caught it by the handle with his other hand. Staring down the barrel, he stepped toward Keane. A blood-splattered smile crossed his face.

Thornton stopped when Keane released the safety. Keane motioned to the binding on his arm. "Cut it off."

Thornton glared back, bewildered. "You want *me* to cut it off?"

"I trust you."

"What if I slip and slice your wrist?"

"I'll blow your head off."

Thornton moved cautiously to the bed and leaned down, still following the barrel pointed between his eyes. He slid the switchblade under the rope on Keane's wrist and sawed upward without looking away from the weapon.

The rope split open and both of Keane's hands were free. Thornton held the knife at waist level, the blade tip pointing at Keane.

"Stick it into the bedsprings," Keane commanded.

Thornton lowered the knife and slipped it between the rusted springs. Blood dribbled from his chin onto the railing.

"Back away," Keane said.

Thornton did exactly as he was told. Keane grabbed the knife and cut the ropes that bound each ankle. As soon as he threw his legs over the edge, Thornton lunged for the bed and shoved it upward. Keane fell to the floor, and the switchblade flew across the room. The bed frame rolled overtop of him. He fired blindly through the bedsprings then at the ceiling.

Thornton ran for the door and raced outside. Keane shot in his direction. He shot again before realizing he had no idea how may rounds the clip had left. He kicked the bed away and jumped up. His fingers wrapped tightly around the pistol's grip as he sprinted to the opposite window and mashed his back against the wall.

After holding steady for one minute, he jumped to the other side of the doorway and peered out. He crept outside, the pistol held high, and tried his damnedest to see in both directions at once.

A barking squirrel chased a robin onto a branch. Then an engine fired up in the distance, the noise muffled by the trees.

He lowered the weapon to relieve the ache in his muscles and began to walk in shock but now acting on instinct and autopilot. When the overhead power lines appeared, he quickened his pace and jogged. There was at least a mile to go.

*   *   *

Jessie bounced about and her teeth chattered while she navigated the low-riding Porsche over the washboard road. She'd stopped on the highway at a Pure Oil station and grocery mart, the only place for gas and a restroom for several miles. An older gentleman with red-white-and-blue suspenders and a black patch over one lens of his glasses sat behind the cash register, whittling. The cedar shavings had formed a tidy heap on the wooden floor that creaked with each step. In answer to her question, he did recall a guy who'd stopped in earlier and who fit the description she gave.

She already had an idea where to find Keane from that hectic day she'd rescued him. Studying the county map the clerk provided, she assumed that Forest Service Road 57 was the road Keane would've taken. There was no other option. She tried calling him on his cell one more time. No answer.

But it was a glorious sunny day, a good time to pull over and put down the top.

A Jeep Wrangler zoomed toward her, raising dust.

Dammit!

She punched the air recirculate button and slowed to the right shoulder to stay clear as the vehicle passed. The driver looked like a hunter in his camouflaged Jeep and matching hat pulled low over his eyes. She drove back onto the road and into his swirl of dust, forgetting the idea of the top coming down. Her plan was to go as far as possible and then hike for a while, hoping to spot Keane's vehicle. The longer she drove, the more she realized she should've thought through the whole damn thing before taking off like a cat on the prowl.

A dust cloud appeared in her rearview mirror. Someone was closing in from behind. She recognized the Jeep that had just passed her from the other direction. He was close enough to her bumper that if she braked, he would ram into her rear end. She stretched for the glove compartment and pressed it open. Reaching inside for the Glock G31, she placed the weapon on the passenger seat and pulled to a stop.

The Jeep did the same.

She watched in the mirror as he reached for the roll bar and hauled himself out. He waddled toward her. In one motion she shoved open the door and jumped out with the Glock pointed at his chest.

He stopped midstride and held up his hands. "Oh, I'm sorry, ma'am. I thought you was the real estate agent I worked with yesterday."

"Do I look like a realtor?" She kept the weapon aimed straight ahead. His swelling nose had been battered plum purple.

"I've been looking for property in the area but I lost her card like a fool. I didn't know how to contact her. Hope you didn't take me as some kind of pervert." He pointed to his face. "I accidently hit my nose chopping wood this morning."

Blood was caked in one of his nostrils. She carefully lowered the gun, keeping the weapon pointed at his midriff.

"Sorry for the mistake, ma'am. I didn't mean to frighten you."

"You'll be driving back down to the highway?"

"Got a cabin a few miles north. I remembered after I'd passed you that I left my fly rod there. If it's just the same with you, ma'am, I'll just move on ahead and get up to the cabin. Can't tell you how much I'm sorry for giving you such a scare."

"Not a problem," she said. "A woman traveling alone in the woods these days can't be too careful." The weapon was heavy in her hand.

He tipped his cap and hopped back into the Jeep. Revving his engine, he slowly took off in a light cloud of dust. Twenty yards up the road, he accelerated.

She returned to the Porsche and sat for a moment to think about what had happened, to make sense of it all. She didn't have a good feeling about moving forward—the guy looked too damn suspicious and the forest ahead looked too damn dense. No doubt that turning back was the better option. Then she glanced down at the piece resting on the seat beside her. A Glock G31 with 357 caliber, double-action, and sixteen-round capacity had a way of easing anxiety.

As she continued driving, the road eventually became rougher and narrower, more dirt than gravel. The tree branches above arched across like interlaced fingers. Flashes of blue sky alternated with green limbs until there was a dark awning with no sun peeking through—a long tunnel of pine.

A large limb that was likely from a recent storm blocked the road. To maneuver around it required driving into a monster rut, so she pulled to the side and got out. It would take a little work to push the limb away. Feeling uneasy, she walked back to the car and reached inside to retrieve the Glock.

A sound erupted from the weeds behind her.

She quickly backed out and stood up. The last thing she remembered was the excruciating pain that exploded from the rear of her skull to her forehead in a shockwave.

CHAPTER 46

Thornton stood gripping a fat hickory branch and gawking at the most luscious female body he'd ever seen up close. He wiped blood from his broken nose with his sleeve and bent down to examine the bump that was swelling on the back of her head. Then he checked her pulse. Breathing rapidly, he slid his callused hand into her warm bra and squeezed, then withdrew his hand and moved it along her smooth skin. A knife was holstered at the small of her back. Clever woman. Or so she thought.

He yanked out the knife and tossed it into the weeds and slipped off her swanky belt. After tying her hands behind her back with the belt, he took off his own and gagged her, pulling it tightly through the corners of her exquisitely shaped mouth. When he picked her up, she was unconscious and dead weight. He delicately placed her on the floor behind the Jeep's front seat and threw a plastic tarp over her.

The fire-engine-red Porsche Boxster convertible was no surprise. He'd spotted it entering and leaving Keane's place. Selsby had filled him in on the woman but he'd forgotten her name. He hopped inside the Porsche, started it up, and rammed it through the trees as far as it would go before getting stuck between two trees out of sight from the road.

Keane had lied, of course. His only "personal security" was that beautiful piece of ass. She would be delightful bait. The operation had to get under way earlier than planned. He'd carefully plotted it out in stages. Although he hated to rush—he had to move cautiously—the timing couldn't be better. The most celebrated weekend of the summer had begun.

*   *   *

Keane ran his fingers around his rope-burned throat as he drove. He lowered both front windows to let in fresh hot air and tried taking deeper breaths, but his chest was too tight. Selsby had set him up, and the two criminal bastards were plotting and working together. Thornton had referred to the "Big One" coming. The two of them were in cahoots.

He'd had no luck in getting Chief Walters by cell. He had to rely on Dallas Walters more than ever, but it would likely be impossible to reach him on a holiday weekend. When he finally got through to his office, he was told the chief was on "urgent business." Sure he was. They'd get a message to him.

What might he hear from the chief? Had he cried wolf too often? *Are you certain you're talking about Thornton? Interpol made it absolutely clear he was dead.*

Then he'd tell him about Selsby.

You followed a tip from Crawford Selsby after he was fired? Were you high on something?

Maybe he should contact GBI, convince them to send a forensics team to the cabin, sweep the place, and put out an APB on Thornton.

It wouldn't work. He knew he wasn't recognized in any official way with GBI. Protocol was clear. He had to talk directly with the chief or be ignored.

He hit the speed dial for Mr. J and asked him to check the perimeter surveillance system. There wasn't time to get into all that was going on inside his head. "Make sure everything is working, Mr. J."

"Right away, sir."

"Would you do the alarm tests too?"

"Is there a problem?"

"Someone could be coming for me. We can't be too careful right now."

"Should I call the sheriff's office, sir?"

"Good idea. Tell 'em we've received a threat. They should keep watch on the estate. Try to talk to Captain Brett Fisher. He'll do us a favor."

Brett Fisher had been a Rockdale County deputy sheriff for over twenty years. Keane had gotten to know him recently at the Roadhouse where they both enjoyed the Friday night fish fry. He only wished he had someone like Brett at APD.

"One more thing before you go, sir. Jessie Wiley called. Said she wasn't able to reach your cell. I told her where you were headed when she asked. I hope you don't mind. She seemed terribly concerned."

"If she calls back, put her onto me pronto."

"Will do, sir."

Jessie may have been worried, but she certainly wouldn't have tried a fool thing like driving all the way up there after him. He took out his cell phone and called her. It rang three times before rolling over to her voice mail, just as it had been doing for the last two hours.

CHAPTER 47

Thornton raced south from Dillard to pick up I-85. He had to drive with care—no time to be pulled over by a cop. Occasionally he'd reach behind his seat and check out Keane's woman under the tarp.

He ramped off the interstate toward Chamblee. The dirt road into his mobile-home park passed a row of mailboxes attached to posts. Phone and electrical lines ran down to the trailers in jerry-rigged fashion behind garbage bins and propane tanks. Satellite dishes decorated roofs. Concrete steps led to each front door. Fans or air-conditioning units jutted from windows. He gave a polite wave to the old lady who sat hunched over in a wheelchair under an oak tree in her bare front yard.

Everything is fine, honey. He shot her out a candy sweet grin for reassurance. His rented trailer balanced upon crumbling cinder blocks at the end of the road. He'd chosen the thirty-year-old junk heap because it bordered woods rising onto a hillside, and the back door opened into a gravel parking area between the door and the woods. The trailers on either side were vacant. The landlord had told him that he didn't expect any renters during the scorching summer.

The woman had come to but didn't try to fight when he carried her from the car and dumped her onto the back bedroom floor. He tied her against a bedpost then grabbed her chin and gazed into her tightly drawn face. She stared back, her pleading eyes wide-open and round. When he walked away, he smiled at the thought that her pretty head was crammed with nothing but the single thought of what he could do to her.

After locking up, he drove the Jeep out of the park to the storage facility on the edge of town where he kept the van, with Alabama tags he'd stolen from a pickup abandoned along a country road. For only a seventy-five dollar charge he had a sign painted on each side of the van:

ANNISTON COURIER SERVICE
"We pick up and deliver"

When he returned to the trailer, he found the woman propped up with her back against the bedpost and cringing in pain. Sweat ringed her forehead and neck.

Since his return to Georgia, he'd worked in the ungodly heat to prepare the one-ton van with everything needed for the big day. Forty bags of ammonium nitrate fertilizer—purchased over two weeks in April—filled most of the back of the van. Precisely stacked in tidy columns, the bags surrounded the center except for a small passageway from the side door. To avoid raising red flags, he'd used three separate farm-supply stores to buy all forty bags, staying within a fifteen-mile radius. A fifty-five-gallon drum, half-full of nitromethane, sat next to the "hallelujah hole," that exclusive holy spot reserved for the cesium-137 powder. He'd pilfered the high-energy fuel from the drag-racing track in nearby Commerce during the Southern Nationals in the spring. Luckily, the event included the Top Fuel competition.

He got lucky with the ANFO. Through his contacts with a paramilitary unit near Butler, he bought four fifty-five-pound bags of the solid ammonium-nitrate fertilizer and number two fuel-oil mix. He'd picked them up from a storage facility on a private quail-hunting preserve.

The van's front cabin needed to be shielded for protection from the cesium-137 gamma rays. For that, he built a thick wall of lead ingots on one side of the hallelujah hole. He'd stolen the ingots from the clinic one at a time over seven months. The vehicle's suspension had been modified twice to carry the full load, but there was still a noticeable sag. Too late to do anything about it. Inside the van he'd set up the electronics with the cell-phone receiver connected to a firing circuit. It had taken hours to verify the signaling trigger.

An LED light had been linked into the firing circuit for the critical test. He left the van's rear door open and walked back into the woods where he could keep a line-of-sight view then hit speed dial number three on his cell.

The light flashed red.

Bingo!

He moved back to the van and carefully attached the switch to the detonation cord. It snaked from under the lid of the nitromethane drum. That part was down pat, thanks to all of the small-scale blasting tests in the middle of the North Georgia woods. The only thing left was to place into the hallelujah hole the treasured cesium-137—the trophy he'd come close to paying for with his life. The fleeting thought made him wonder if Osken and the carnival man were still rotting in the Oldsmobile trunk.

The delivery from Ekaterinburg of the disguised canister holding the radioactive cesium had gone like clockwork. The small crate arrived Wednesday, eight days after the promised shipment. The paperwork showed that it had come by jet into Hong Kong, from there on China Air to Nashville, and then it was trucked to the Midtown Business Center in Atlanta—a delivery for F. Henry Thornton.

All the necessary details had been arranged two months before. After the shipment arrived, he'd retrieved it from the office manager Betty Beebe, a young lady who had family in Savannah. By the most "remarkable coincidence," he did as well. The conversation was warm, lively and extended. No surprise that Betty remembered him when he came in for his latest shipment. Her only comment was on the weight of the crate for its size.

After he dragged the canister from behind the couch in the trailer's main room, he carried it into the kitchen to the tabletop and flipped on the window fan. The wall thermometer read ninety-eight degrees. He rolled the canister over a half turn to the scene of the Urals, picturing Yelena's soft hands painting the image. The cesium powder had to be recovered from the canister fast. He'd get a whopping dose of gamma rays while he worked, but not enough to cause any real harm in the short run. His long run was fucked up anyway.

He walked outside and sat on the top step. Sweat dotted his forehead as he squeezed out his pack of Camels from his shirt pocket. There was absolutely no room for error. Only someone who knew what he was doing could pull it all off.

He smoked calmly for several minutes and after taking the last drag, he flipped the cigarette into the road and returned inside. A Cold War vintage Geiger counter, purchased online, rested on the table. He switched on its battery power to keep track of the radiation level during transfer of the cesium to an empty jam jar with a screw-top lid. With the canister in one hand he placed the other around the valve at the top. He paused, remembering Zuberman's warning from his experiments with stray dogs and rats. He had to limit his exposure to three minutes tops.

The crash of breaking glass erupted in the back of the trailer.

CHAPTER 48

The last thing Keane wanted was to wait on a call from Chief Dallas Walters. But he had absolutely no leads as to the whereabouts of Thornton. Locating Selsby could be a different story, if Suzanne Fowler would cooperate. She worked a compressed schedule and always had Fridays off. A long shot, but the only shot he had. Her home address had come up with an easy directory search on his phone.

In the parking lot at Fowler's condo, Keane adjusted the rearview mirror to take another look at his face. He'd already stopped at a Shell gas station to wash up. He straightened out his sweaty shirt and glanced again into the Land Rover's mirror. No doubt about it, he looked like hell.

The Oakmont Estates appeared to be a modestly priced condo complex in Roswell, just outside the perimeter freeway. The doorman, a burly guy wearing what was supposed to resemble a guard uniform, gave Keane a once-over as he rang Fowler from the lobby.

"A Mr. Damian Keeeen here for you, ma'am." He listened momentarily and then handed Keane the phone.

"It's Damon Keane. Sorry, I know this is—"

"I'm a little indisposed at the moment. This is certainly a—"

"It's important."

"I understand. But—"

"Suzanne, please. It's more than urgent."

She buzzed him through the entry and he took the elevator to the fifth floor.

As soon as she opened her door, he blurted out, "I need to find Crawford Selsby. I need to find him now."

"You're a total mess! Where on earth—"

"I need your help."

She likely read the determination on his face. "Come on in."

He followed her into a sitting area by a bay window overlooking a pool. She looked like she'd thrown on the jeans and a green blouse while he was in the elevator.

"Crawford Selsby's gone," Fowler said. She sank into a sofa with loose pillows. "We both know why. So I'm really not getting what this is all about."

"Selsby's working with Felix Thornton. And Thornton just tried to kill me."

She stared back at him as if he'd escaped from an asylum. "That's not possible!"

"Forget what you've been told. Thornton's alive and back in Atlanta. He's working with Selsby on something big."

She hugged a pillow tightly to her chest. "Why didn't you go to the chief?" she asked.

"I'm waiting on a call from him. But he'll want APD to investigate. There's no time for all that. Look, my partner Jessie Wiley's in big trouble. I found her car abandoned near where I got away from Thornton. She's gone, Suzanne. She's either dead or still in the hands of one or the other."

"Slow down, Damon and listen to me. How can you be sure that—"

"I don't want your frigging questions right now. I'm the one who's been through this. I know what's going on."

She held up a palm to signal she didn't need any more drama and stood. "You need a drink. I only have bourbon." She moved for the kitchen area.

"I don't want a drink," he fired back. "I know you can help me find Selsby. The two of you were more than colleagues."

"We were only friends, goddammit. I've told you that. He's long gone from here. Why can't you get that through your skull?"

"You're lying."

"Why would I lie about it?" she screamed. She stood with her hands on her hips and glared back at him, as if ready to slug it out.

Neither spoke.

She turned and reached into a cabinet above the counter and pulled down a bottle of Jim Beam and two glasses.

"Over ice," he said.

He took a deep breath and let it out slowly. He couldn't lose it right now. Fowler's help was all he had. He checked his phone to make sure it still had charge and then leaned forward with his hands folded between his open legs. He surveyed her digs—sparse furniture, a group of framed photos on one wall and a large print of a sandy beach with sea oats on another. It was the type of condo you'd expect for a professional early in her career and on an APD salary. But this was a different woman from the one he'd first met. Less confident and more careful in how she chose her words. Why?

When she brought in his bourbon, he quickly took a swallow— bigger than usual. She seemed to do the same. They sat in silence. With her legs crossed she was shaking her foot as if she were high—or damned nervous.

"You haven't heard from Selsby since he supposedly left town?" he asked.

"Nothing. And he never stopped here to tell me good-bye either, if that's what you're wondering."

"No calls?"

"No nothing, Damon."

It wasn't working. She wouldn't give him any info even if she knew something. Yet if he left now, he'd leave with absolute zilch. He'd have nowhere to go but home, there to sit and wait on a call from Chief

Walters or Jessie or God only knows who. His insides gurgled as if he were ready to puke all over her fancy ivory carpet.

He glanced at the walls. "Interesting pictures."

"Just memories." Her answer was cold, detached.

He placed his drink on the coffee-table coaster then stood and walked over for a closer look at the photography while he bought time to think. One picture was of a younger Fowler on skis with what looked like the peaks of the Swiss Alps in the background. Another showed her next to a gate at Buckingham Palace with three friends, two of them male. The next photo was of a large grassy park with a small group sunning in front of a building with tall columns resembling a war memorial. A scribbled word was in the bottom left: *Luitpold.*

Keane had to think when or where he'd seen the word. "Where was this photo taken?"

She shrugged and took a drink. "Germany, I believe."

"Nuremburg?"

"Not sure. The other is in the Alps. My favorite place for skiing."

He knew about the Luitpold Arena. It was a military parade ground, a rallying spot for the Nazi Party and the SS . . . and a popular area in wartime Germany for speeches by *der Führer.*

Before she had time to react, he grabbed her blouse at the shoulder and yanked at it, ripping off a button and knocking her glass to the floor.

She wrenched away and jumped back. "Get away from me!" She rushed for her cell phone on the bench by the window.

He chased her down and snatched her wrist. "You've been lying to me, Suzanne. All along you've lied, haven't you?" He pointed to her naked shoulder.

The tattoo of a purple iron cross almost glowed against her porcelain skin. Her shifting eyes and everything about her demeanor from the moment he'd met her should've warned him.

"I'll have you arrested, dammit."

"Where did that tattoo come from, Suzanne?"

"Get out of here *now!*"

"Go ahead, page the cops. Tell 'em I tried to rape you. But understand one thing: it'll be the end of your career. I swear I'll make sure that APD finds out about your connection with Selsby. You'll have to find another way to make a living. No law enforcement agency in the country will hire you."

She wrapped her arms around her bare shoulders and drifted to the bay window. She spoke softly, a sudden transformation. "I've tried to leave the whole goddamn group. I never knew for certain, but I sensed Selsby was tied in with the radiation killing. What happened to the little Davenport kid was the final straw for me. That's why I gave you that hint about his weekends. I wanted the SOB caught. He found out I was responsible for sending you there."

She spun about and faced him with the look of a frightened puppy. "I'm afraid he's going to kill me when he gets the chance, Damon. Make it look like an accident. Do you have any idea what it's like to live like this?" She wiped away tears from the corner of her eye with the back of her hand.

"Where is he?" Keane pleaded. "Just tell me where he is."

"I don't know."

"You're lying to me again."

She held a tissue to her nose. "He told me he has an appointment."

"Where?"

"How should *I* know?"

"Was he going to meet Felix Thornton?"

"I don't have any idea . . . I mean, maybe."

"When did you speak to him?"

"An hour ago. Now get out of here. I've got a gun and I'll use it. Self-defense is an easy reason to kill somebody."

He moved for the doorway. Gripping the knob, he stopped and looked back. "Leave APD, Suzanne. Move away from forensics and Atlanta for good."

She glared back at him, mascara tracking her tears. "You know something, Keane. You're really no better than any other fucking man on the planet."

He slammed the door behind him and ran down the steps to the parking lot as his cell phone rang.

CHAPTER 49

When he heard the crash, Thornton hustled to the trailer's back bedroom and burst through the door. The bitch had torn away a bedpost and slipped from the rope. She'd used the post to shatter the room's window facing the back of the trailer toward the woods. She was halfway out and screaming for help when he grabbed her ankles and jerked her back in through the broken glass.

Tying her hands behind her again, he no longer cared whether he was cutting off her circulation. He headed out of the bedroom to grab more rope and a knife from the kitchen. When he returned, he shoved her head back and rammed the tip of the knife within a hair of her taut, slender neck.

Thanks to Selsby, Keane's cell number was stored in Thornton's contact list. He yanked his phone from his pocket and told her what to say, forcing her to repeat the script twice as he carved ever so gently along her throat, drawing thin scarlet ribbons of blood.

As soon as Keane answered, he held the phone to her mouth, keeping the knife in place.

"I'll meet you at the . . . airport, Damon—HELP!"

Thornton snatched the phone away and raised his fist high behind him. His head was filled with drums, a constant barrage of banging, banging, banging . . .

He started to swing his fist into her face, but stopped. She did okay. That would work.

Her skin had been ripped by the glass shards from around the window and blood soaked through her blouse. He gagged her again then tossed her over his shoulder and carried her to the van, where he crammed her down onto the front passenger floor.

It was already 4:35. The schedule was shot to hell.

He ran back to the kitchen table, tediously arranged the screwdriver, teaspoon and glass jar, and then checked the Geiger counter.

It ticked slowly, randomly.

Taking deep breaths, he rubbed his hands together and stared at the top of the canister. He wiped his forehead, grasped the valve, and twisted it while he gazed at the slot on the side. The slot creaked open.

A soft aqua glow flooded the room. The Geiger counter needle jumped across the meter's face and machine-gun ticks fired off.

4:37

When he cranked the valve full open, the ticking from the Geiger counter fused into a constant hum. He grabbed the screwdriver and stuck it through the slot, breaking the thin glass window of the chamber holding the cesium. He scooped the powder into the jar.

4:39

He paused to wipe at the perspiration creeping down his cheek. Holding the canister with his other hand, he quickly dug into the far corner, causing the canister to slip, roll over the edge of the table, and slam to the linoleum floor. He drew his crushed foot up to his knee and groaned.

4:41

Then he discovered the disaster. The powder had spread like flour over the floor.

He dove to his knees and swept the white dust into a pile with the spoon. Careful to capture each beloved granule, he raked all of it into the jar and screwed on the lid.

4:43

He rushed outside with his treasure, aware that the glass container provided zero shielding from the deadly gamma rays. After yanking open the van's side door, he shoved the jar into the hallelujah hole and stuffed it between the fertilizer bags and the drum of nitromethane. He carefully jostled the last of the bags inside the van to close the gap.

4:46

Grabbing the expansion band on his Timex, he tore it from his wrist and slung it against the trailer wall. He ran back into the bedroom, ripped off his T-shirt, and put on the blue short-sleeved shirt with a red-and-white *Anniston Courier* patch sewn on the back.

When he finally slid into the driver's seat, he flipped on the ignition and glanced down beside him at the woman. She'd folded into a ball on the floor.

He drove off slowly, using extra caution to avoid the potholes along the road.

CHAPTER 50

Keane jerked the ringing phone from his pocket. "Unknown number" flashed on the screen. The voice was Jessie's, crying out for help.

"Airport!" she'd shouted before she hung up. She'd been searching for him in the North Georgia woods. God forbid if Thornton ran into her after he'd escaped. But at least she was alive!

Suzanne Fowler had mentioned Selsby's appointment. Was he going to meet Thornton at the airport? Could all this have something to do with the Big One that Thornton had boasted about?

Atlanta's Hartsfield-Jackson airport was the world's busiest—vast, spread out, with underground trains connecting concourses. Dozens of restaurants. Without more details, how would it be possible to find *anyone* there? It was Friday afternoon before the celebration of the Fourth on Sunday. In the traffic it would take an hour or more to get there.

After he sped away from Fowler's condo, he pushed the phone connection on the steering column and pulled up the number for APD. "Damon Keane here. Listen up. I've got to speak to Chief Walters."

The dispatcher responded in an I-don't-give-a-damn monotone. "I have a message here from you earlier. The chief's been notified."

"It's an emergency. I need him now!"

Pause. "One moment."

Keane swerved around a corner and rammed the curb. *Pick up the call, Chief. Pick up!*

"I'm sorry, but Chief Walters is out on assignment. I can give you one of his assistants."

"I'm begging you, ma'am. Please page Chief Walters. Tell him it's Damon Keane. There's an emergency at the airport. I've got to get to him directly."

He slowed enough to look both ways then ran through a red light.

"I can try to page him, but—"

"You're not hearing me. I don't want you to *try* anything. I want you to page him now."

She exhaled into the phone. "Hold a moment, please."

He slowed at a stop sign then accelerated through it as a Mack truck barreled down the highway, blaring its horn.

Chief Dallas Walters answered. "We've got an armed robbery at Five Points, Keane—with hostages. We can talk later. Understand?"

"Felix Thornton is alive and well," Keane replied between breaths. "He's back in town."

"You're talking like you're running a marathon. Slow down. Where are you?"

"In my car, headed for the airport."

After a momentary silence, the chief replied, "Didn't you get the report we got from State? Thornton was murdered."

"I came face-to-face with him, Chief. He tried to kill me. I escaped within an inch of my life." He swerved to avoid a car heading at him from a side street. "You've got to send a SWAT team to Hartsfield-Jackson. This is your chance to grab him. He's looking to pull off something big."

"How the hell do you know that, Keane?"

There was no time to explain. "You've got to trust me on this one, Chief." Another long silence passed while he weaved in and out of traffic with horns blowing all around him.

"Nothing personal," the chief said, "but all I can do right now is put APD at the airport on alert. I hope you know what you're doing. Or we're both in a goddamn heap of trouble."

The connection cut off. He sped up to pass a bus.

                    *   *   *

Thornton's van crept along in airport traffic. His hands had turned scarlet and two blisters had formed on the fingers of one hand. The tint of his red face matched that of his hands, and his cheeks and jowls had begun to swell. Nauseated like never before in his life, he wanted to barf out the window. He glanced into the rearview mirror at his bloodshot eyes, their lids on fire and stinging as if covered with wasps.

The woman was still curled up on the passenger-side floor, the mat beneath soaked in blood. He couldn't tell if she was alive or dead. Traffic inched along, each bumper sniffing the one ahead. Flags of the world flying above the highway signaled a breeze to the northeast toward the city.

Pure luck.

He drew nearer to the road in front of the international terminal and stayed in the middle lanes, keeping away from curbside. Whenever he reached a speed bump, he slowed to a stop and sneaked over it, gently lowering the tires back onto the pavement. Staring out at all the concrete above him, he wished he'd replaced a few fertilizer bags with another drum of nitromethane. Fortunately, the fifty-foot-high walls were more glass than cement. He looked through the tall windows. Inside the great hall at the terminal's center, soft violet lights lined the ceiling. How ironic, he thought.

He pictured the blast crumbling the high struts of concrete and shattering the colossal windows. The plume of smoke bathing the entire airport with radiation. The cloud rising a hundred feet, the winds taking gamma rays directly downtown. Everyone in the path of the cloud inhaling fine radioactive particles that would lodge deep within their lungs. Their bloodstreams spreading cesium-137 to livers and spleens and kidneys. Penetrating gamma rays bombarding them from the inside out for the rest of their lives.

Mamma! the kids will cry out.

But they would learn in time how to dull their pain, erase their fear. Gradually over the years, they'll grow to accept their burden of poison—"Thornton's Poison," they will name it, trapped in the marrow of their feeble bones.

Eventually, everyone will understand. His achievement will be viewed as a perfectly rational act of a desperate man who had tried to save Atlanta from decay. What had *they* done to save the city?

Men don't walk, they run through life. Scared, searching.

He counted himself among the lucky few who owned his destiny. A man who recognized his God-given duty and carried it out without fail. The city will be the better for it. Valuable lessons of history were like that. Rome burned. Berlin crumbled. Hiroshima melted.

Moving into the curb lane, he found a vacant spot behind a catering van. Sandpaper lined the pit of his stomach. He reached down and ran his bloated red fingers through the lovely bitch's thick blonde hair. Ever so gently, he patted her head.

He opened the door and stepped onto the curb to search the walkway for his partner.

CHAPTER 51

Keane circled the airport's South Terminal then drifted to the curb and waited while the engine idled. Travelers crossed the busy street toward arrival entrances—families on vacation, business people returning home for the long weekend. Teenage girls dressed in maroon gym clothes with silver stripes down their legs piled into a bus that had windows painted with *Go Wolverines.* Airport police waved threatening gestures at the cars to keep them on the move. One determined cop blew his whistle and pointed at Keane. He drove around the loop road one last time and into hourly parking.

When he dashed inside the main building, he headed for the atrium between the terminals. Hordes of holiday passengers huddled in small groups or spread out on benches. He strolled about the area twice, each time glancing into the open restaurants and fast-food joints—the Rib Shack, TGI Fridays, Burger King, Atlanta Chop Shop. He crossed over from the south to the north terminal and repeated his search then walked outside to pace among the smokers lining the wall by the curb.

A bus marked *International Terminal* pulled up.

A flash of insight.

The new terminal, three miles away from the main domestic terminal, wasn't just dedicated to foreign travel. It had been crowned the *Maynard Jackson, Jr. International Terminal* with a lot of ballyhoo four years earlier. Maynard Jackson, Atlanta's first black mayor, was

Thornton's idea of the Antichrist. A fact that Jessie had learned from his ex-girlfriend.

He ran to flag down the bus as it moved away.

*   *   *

"Holy shit!" cried Ty Larkin, whose pulse rate suddenly doubled. He sat in the security station deep within the bowels of the airport. Surrounding him were screens to monitor all suspicious activity outside the terminals. This was his bailiwick on the day shift. He served on the Public Safety and Security Team. They were constantly reminded of their responsibility for the safety and welfare of the quarter of a million passengers and three thousand aircraft operations daily.

An array of radiation detectors had been installed four years before at each approach to the three terminals, a direct result of federal funding as a reaction to 9/11. Except for annual drills—when the airport worked with the alphabet soup of government agencies, like the FAA, TSA, FBI, and DHS—Larkin had never seen his radiation screen light up a red alert until now.

Now one of the three monitors was beeping and blinking like hell.

He grabbed the landline that linked directly to the office of the general manager and passed on the warning. Something emitting extremely high levels of radiation had just crossed the approach to the international terminal.

He jammed a finger into the button that started the camera scan to locate the suspect vehicle.

*   *   *

The passenger bus stopped at the international departure gates. People jumped up from their seats to retrieve luggage. Keane stood at the window and searched outside, staying onboard as it pulled away. The bus looped around to the arrival gates below. As soon as it reached the main entrance, he scrambled off.

Two three-lane roads ran in front, separated by a pedestrian walkway. The road nearest the airport entrance served taxis and buses. The access road farthest from the entrance allowed other vehicles to bring passengers in. He moved down the walkway and scanned faces among the throng. Security guards draped in orange vests struggled to turn chaos into order. He turned to walk inside when a large white van came slowly along the far road. It suddenly bolted into a spot at curbside behind a food-service truck.

He read the sign on the side of the van: *Anniston Courier Service.*

The driver, wearing a cap pulled low over his eyes, jumped out and darted across the road toward the terminal. Keane scurried to get a better view from the van's rear end. It looked damned familiar—an old Chevy G20 with the right bumper caved in and hanging at an angle.

A black Cadillac Seville pulled up just beyond the entrance. Keane ran toward it. When he got close enough, he quickly made out Crawford Selsby towering over the steering wheel.

*   *   *

Ty Larkin focused the remote-controlled camera on the van that had set off the radiation alarms. He'd run the tapes backwards and forwards on three other cameras. One plainly showed the driver rushing away, dressed in a service uniform. Larkin relayed still shots of him to the command center. The man had already blended in with the crowd and headed across the lanes of traffic toward the terminal.

Elated, Larkin clasped his hands behind his head and leaned back in his chair. At that moment he represented all the Ty Larkins of the world. All those whose job was to sit, watch, listen, stand by, stay alert—waiting for the "signal."

It all added to the reasons he'd shown up without fail every workday for the last seven years.

This is what it's all about!

He wanted to text Linda and let her know what had happened. But that was against the rules.

                    *   *   *

Keane sprinted for Selsby's car and stooped at the passenger side. He pounded on the glass and shouted, "Jessie! Where's Jessie Wiley?"

Surprised, Selsby shot from the curb with Keane hanging onto his side-view mirror and running along with the car. He twisted the mirror off as Selsby accelerated away. When Keane turned back, the driver in the service uniform stood only ten yards from the confused crowd.

With a red and swollen face, Felix Thornton was clinging to his cell phone. On the far side of the traffic lanes three police cruisers and a Humvee had stopped a short distance behind the white van. Standing close to it was a fully suited-up team of HAZMAT responders, each with his own air-supply backpack. One held a portable instrument out at arm's length, taking readings.

It was all quickly coming together. The van Thornton had parked and abandoned held a bomb—the "Big One." It had to be dirty—loaded not just with explosives, but more likely than not with a mega amount of stolen radioactivity.

Was there a possibility that Jessie could be inside the van?

Please God, no!

Keane rushed for the van into traffic, causing a cab to squeal to a stop. When he reached the center island, a cop shoved him back. Over his shoulder he spotted Thornton standing away from the curb in a corner by the terminal's windows. It had all come together. The phone call that Jessie had made to him earlier was forced upon her—part of a grand scheme to bring him to the airport, to join Jessie in becoming collateral damage from the bomb.

It was clear that Thornton was doing his damnedest to hook up with Selsby, his getaway driver. No way in hell was he going to let the two of them unite. He ran toward Thornton, but when he was spotted, Thornton quickly jostled around the throng and squeezed through the sliding glass doors into the terminal.

A cop halted Keane and the crowd while a stream of taxicabs and limos sped by. He strained to keep an eye on Thornton across the network of windows. When the traffic passed, he sprinted across the street. By the time he'd wedged inside, Thornton had disappeared.

CHAPTER 52

Jessie Wiley lay on the sharp edge of a merry-go-round, staring at the angry Clydesdale painted like a glistening rainbow—a gaudy kaleidoscope of confusion. The stupid horse slid up and down on a polished brass pole. Each time the giant creature came crashing down, a massive hoof struck the back of her head and a blinding pain shot through her skull. The merry-go-round spun faster and faster until it flung her off onto the scorching sand and jolted her awake.

Her throat was dry and raw and aching as she inhaled the stale air. Sweat drenched her neck. The sockets of her shoulders had grown numb from the relentless agony of having her hands tied behind her. She struggled to twist her head upward toward the sunshine.

If she could only climb to the window, someone might spot her. She shoved her feet against the floorboard with all her weight and gradually rose higher. When her spine rammed into the passenger seat, a concrete structure emerged outside.

She scooted backward with her elbows up the filthy seat, a fraction of an inch at a time. When she moved closer to the window, she stretched her neck to see out, but she could no longer bear the tormenting pain.

Her vision blurred. The darkness returned. Drifting away, she plummeted back to the floor.

*   *   *

Keane flew through the terminal's doors and spun around. A crowd near customs awaited arriving passengers. When he jerked his head the other way, he saw Thornton sneaking to the top of the escalator at the far end of the hall. Outside the gigantic windows three squad cars pulled to the curb, blue lights flashing. More cops jumped out with *SWAT* printed on their uniform backs. Armed with assault rifles and handguns, they yelled for everyone to move along as they spread out. Security guards patrolled the walkway and directed people away from the lone van.

Sirens screamed above the din. Police and airport security shouted orders through bullhorns. Tires squealed as vehicles inside the open parking garage raced to exit.

Keane scampered with the crowd shoving forward. Passengers scattered. A young woman in a sundress dragged a little boy by the hand while she pushed a baby hunkered inside a stroller. The boy clung to his mother's dress with a thumb in his mouth, sobbing. A heavy-set lady wearing a flowered kimono shrieked at the security guard. She couldn't run. She shouted that they were going to have to leave her be. She "didn't care if there was a damned emergency." She couldn't move that fast.

Keane bypassed the escalator and rushed up the steps alongside it, two at a time. At the top he spotted Thornton jogging into the skyway above the street. He was headed for the parking garage. But the way he clutched his cell phone as he ran through the horde of people . . . totally bizarre. It could only be for one purpose: the cell was rigged to remotely set off the detonator. If that circuit included a delay mechanism—an amateur-wiring feat—Thornton could get away safely after he punched the number into his cell.

It all made perfect sense. The isolated bomb-testing area he and Jessie found in the North Georgia woods had been dedicated to perfecting the triggering and timing.

A cop barked at Keane to turn back. He stopped and twisted around, keeping watch on the cop out of the corner of his eye. As soon as he looked away, Keane made a dash for the skywalk. A whistle shrieked from behind.

Thornton ran for the stairwell. Keane took off for another set of stairs directly to his left. Beyond the opening to the outside, he spotted Thornton's van below. It was now isolated along the airport road. The bomb-squad van had moved out of sight. From that height he could see through the passenger window the semblance of a body crouched on the floorboard. He could only make out the long blond hair.

Move, Jessie, move! Get out!

There was no way to gauge how big the bomb might be. Flashing through his mind were scenes of the blown-out Murrah Federal Building in Oklahoma City. And because she cared about him, Jessie lay trapped virtually inside a bomb about to go off, once Thornton hit the number on his cell.

He ran through the stairwell doorway and stopped. *Which way?*

He shot up the stairs to rooftop parking and shoved open the door as a jumbo jet roared overhead. No sign of Thornton. But he'd been cut off and had no way to rendezvous with Selsby. And he probably knew—as Keane quickly guessed—that his ever-so-faithful soul brother in the frigggin' cause had taken off for parts unknown.

Keane kept his head low and cautiously moved among the rows of parked cars. More emergency vehicles arrived on the terminal loop. A military van wormed its way along with the fire trucks. A snarled line of traffic stalled in the madness to escape as horns blared. With one punch on Thornton's phone, the parking garage and airport terminal could rumble down in a fireball.

A figure darted behind the last row of cars at the brink of the open roof. Keane moved toward it. When the figure scurried away, he recognized Thornton.

Keane dashed for the next row. Only one line of parked vehicles separated them. On the far side of the garage, out of Thornton's line of vision, a SWAT team sniper dove between cars. He was undertaking the ultimate risk. A bullet that didn't promptly kill would give Thornton a chance to hit the number on his cell phone to set off the bomb.

Keane spotted another sharpshooter stealing along in Thornton's direction. Another crept along the opposite wall. Thornton was squatting between the grill of an SUV and the waist-high concrete wall. His head dodged from side to side as he danced like a prizefighter, not about to make himself an easy target. The likelihood of an instant kill by one of the snipers was a hundred to one.

A helicopter in the distance thundered toward the parking garage.

Keep the choppers away! Don't startle him!

From his crouch behind a pickup truck, Keane slowly stood and attempted to spot Thornton. He was close enough to yell at him, to be heard above the mayhem that had broken loose. He stood erect from behind the truck bed and held both hands in the air.

"Don't do it, Felix," he shouted. "Let's leave here together. Just you and me."

As Thornton darted about, he clutched at his stomach with one hand and waved his cell phone as if it were a magic wand with the other. Both hands were double normal size. "Yeah, we'll leave here together, Keane," he yelled back. "We'll both blow outta here and into hell on the same train."

"What will killing more people prove?" Keane bellowed.

"That I'm in control! 'Revenge is mine, sayeth the Lord.'" It appeared that he could hardly see through the narrow slits of his eyes hidden within his swollen face.

"Revenge won't bring back your mother, Felix."

Thornton cowered behind the SUV, his back jammed against the low wall. He flaunted the phone above his head. The ungodly bastard was going to do it. He was facing his own Calvary and wanted to bring everyone into the depths of hell with him.

Only one shot—a single shot, dead on target. The only hope.

He thought of Jessie. Of her call for help, the last words he had ever heard from her.

The phone call from Jessie.

Did it come from Thornton's phone? Was it possible that her cry for help came from the same phone that Thornton now flaunted, the one rigged to the detonator?

He flicked on his cell while he crouched and brought up his phone log. The latest entry: "Unknown Number."

He had to take a chance—a totally blind chance.

He hit *Return Call* and then stood to watch.

Thornton stared down at his ringing phone. A look of shock, as if the damned device had somehow come alive. He shoved the phone to his ear. Pure habit.

That frozen second was all that was needed.

A blast from a sharpshooter's rifle echoed off the concrete walls like a grenade. The bullet blew away one side of Thornton's skull.

A car alarm shrieked. Thornton's phone flew from his hand and hit the floor. Keane held his breath as the phone tumbled.

Another bullet split open the top of Thornton's head. Fragments of bone smashed against the wall behind him and sprayed like shrapnel onto the hood of the glossy white SUV. Thornton slammed into the grillwork and slid down it. Blood and gray matter splattered the windshield.

The SWAT team swarmed out of hiding and scrambled toward the body with automatic weapons in hand. One of them reached with extended tongs, grabbed the phone, and dumped it into a bright-yellow plastic bucket of water.

What was left of the man named Thornton lay sprawled on the concrete. Blood gushed like a pulsing fountain from a hole in his skull above one ear. Amid the havoc, a helicopter hovered in, whipping up the stifling thick air.

By the time Keane had hustled down from the parking garage to the street, the HAZMAT team had rescued Jessie from the van. An ambulance had sped off with her.

He hailed an APD cruiser to give chase.

CHAPTER 53

After the ER at Grady Memorial checked out Jessie, Keane stayed by her bedside in the room where she'd been transferred. She was freed from the van, unconscious, as soon as Chief Walters confirmed that Thornton was dead and his cell phone taken out of commission. Her rescue had taken less than a minute by a bomb squad accompanied by an expert nuclear and radiological response team.

They found that the potent gamma-ray source at the heart of the bomb was shielded with blocks of lead stacked on one side next to the driver's cabin. In his warped, cowardly mind, Thornton was clearly concerned about protecting himself from the intense radiation from the center of the van as he drove. By the grace of God and the Angels on high, it was the same shielding that protected Jessie on the floor of the front seat. According to the radiologists, her total exposure was equivalent to only a few CT scans; the greater concern was Jessie's loss of blood along with her severe state of dehydration and hyperthermia. Throughout the ordeal, Keane never left her side.

*   *   *

Six days later, Keane appeared in a private ceremony in Mayor Carl Stillwell's office at city hall. He listened uncomfortably to the mayor's praises while presenting Keane with a City of Atlanta plaque for heroic action in the face of danger—his "assistance with the Atlanta Police

Force in preventing a horrific act of violence at Hartsfield-Jackson International Airport."

Keane knew that the formalities had to be kept low-key. He was an outsider who'd taken the law into his own hands—APD wasn't up to giving a lot of publicity to such deeds. Jessie Wiley had been invited to the ceremony as an onlooker, although the mayor suspected she was more than just an interested party.

During the days and nights following that fateful day, Keane had tried to ditch Felix Thornton from his head. Meanwhile, APD had assigned a dedicated team to track down Crawford Selsby. They promised Keane that "it was only a matter of time." Citing personal reasons, Suzanne Fowler had submitted her resignation the day after the incident. When they went looking for her, she'd already cleared out of her condo.

Following the ceremony, the mayor strolled over to Keane. "Once again, what can I say about your help when we needed it?"

The two men smiled and shook hands again. "By the way, Damon, what have you heard about little Ronnie Davenport's condition?"

"In my latest call to his foster parents," Keane replied, "I was told that Ronnie was home from the hospital—back in his own bedroom and doing well. He'll be returning to school next week."

What Keane didn't want to mention was the longer-term prognosis for the boy. His health would be followed closely for years.

"I know Ronnie and those Dream Valley Camp kids are special to you," the mayor said.

"I plan on spending time there for many summers to come."

The mayor carefully reached into his suit pocket and pulled out a small golden box with a white ribbon.

"Really, Mayor, it isn't necessary to—"

"Don't get all worked up now. It's not from me. The other day APD had a visit from Father Calabrese, a priest from Our Mother of Mercy at Piedmont Park. He asked that we pass this along to you."

He handed Keane the box. "He said he was aware of your role in all that's happened."

Keane certainly remembered Our Mother of Mercy Church and Father Calabrese, the assistant priest. He would never forget the anguish on his face when they had first met.

"But how could he know what I've done?" Keane asked.

The mayor shrugged. "The Lord works in mysterious ways. Who's to say that priests don't too? He told me that Father O'Shannon would have wanted you to have this. God rest his soul."

The mayor held out a hand to Jessie. "I'm delighted, Miss Jessie, to see you up and about so quickly."

She smiled faintly while keeping her other hand to her cheek to cover one of the bruises Thornton had delivered. "It took a whopping amount of courage for APD's team to come after me. That van could have blown at any moment. I might have ended up with body parts in Cincinnati."

"I understand the airport is open now," Keane said.

"Nobody's happy when you shut down the world's busiest airport for three days," the mayor said. "We called in a special team to rig some elaborate shielding around the van before they could even disarm the bomb. They brought in a crane to move it into a specially built eighteen-wheeler to haul it across the state to a nuclear site in South Carolina. I'm told they'll dismantle everything there and bury it a country mile deep."

When Keane and Jessie were leaving headquarters, he paused at the bottom of the steps. He took another look at her face in brighter light. Bringing a finger to her cheek, he brushed it lightly while he examined the bruise. He was always taken in by those remarkably blue eyes, set so wide apart above a princess nose. Just like Danielle's.

She smiled. "What about that gift from Father Calabrese?"

He pulled the small box from his pocket and removed the lid. Gently plucking out a ruby-red rosary, he held it for both to admire. "I think I'll keep this as a good-luck charm."

She shot a puzzled look. "A rosary? That's a curious gift. I mean, for you."

He placed a hand along her back, and they strolled toward his car. "It's a long story," he replied. "Maybe I could . . ."

"Explain it over dinner? I really think I would like that."

*　　　*　　　*

Keane's descent into hell and back had happened in midsummer. It wasn't until early September that the trip he'd planned since that day could be arranged. His son and daughter were always busy, but they made it happen.

Keane and Nicole sat on a blanket in the meadow, watching Andy traipse along the banks of the Big Wood River, not far from Sun Valley. Andy was performing double-haul casts out over the rushing stream, a technique he'd learned from his dad. His Buddhist robe was stuffed inside his chest waders as he attempted to catch his fourth wild trout of the day.

It was the first time in two years that Keane had even a day alone with his kids, much less four days together at one of his favorite places in the American West. He promised both that this small break in their lives—just the three of them—would be repeated as often as they could arrange it. He would be available. Nicole and Andy had their doubts—he sensed it—although neither expressed them. He knew this time it was for real. Someone once said that we live life forward but understand it backward.

That evening when they returned to the Sun Valley Inn, the woman at the front desk motioned for him. A caller had left a message and the day clerk had taken it down in longhand:

Damon,

Hope you're having a grand time. Too bad about Suzanne Fowler's fatal mishap. Have you heard?

Anyway, I know your kids are looking forward to getting back to school and the monastery. I'll be watching for them.

Warm regards,

Crawford Selsby

As he stared ahead, Nicole tugged at his sleeve. "What's the matter, Dad? You look spooked."

Quickly wadding up the note, he stuffed it into his pocket. "Not at all, sweetheart."

He placed his arms around Nicole's and Andy's shoulders and pulled them to his chest in a dual bear hug. "Let's go to my room and talk," he said. "We need to make some new plans."

AFTERWORD

The opportunity for smuggling nuclear material and using it as a weapon of terrorism today is greater than ever. According to the International Atomic Energy Agency (IAEA) in Vienna, over a recent ten-year period there have been more than fifteen hundred confirmed incidents of illicit trafficking of nuclear and radiological material worldwide. Tens of thousands of these potent "silent sources" are in private hands. In some countries radioactive materials appear on black markets together with drugs and contraband.

Experts tell us that much of the world's smuggled nuclear material is traceable to stockpiles in Russia and other former Soviet nations, where many research facilities remain poorly protected by underpaid guards, maintenance staff, and unreliable security systems. In the past, most smugglers have been amateurs looking for easy profits. But there appears today to be a surge of interest among organized crime and criminal gangs, from Russia and Eastern Europe to the continents of Africa and South America, who could realize sizeable profits from the sale of large radioactive sources to extremist groups.

Yukiya Amano, Director General of the IAEA, has said, "One of the key risks we face is that terrorists could detonate a so-called dirty bomb, using conventional explosives and a quantity of nuclear or other radioactive material, to contaminate a major city . . . clearly, the utmost vigilance is required."

The Federation of American Scientists once conducted a computer simulation to determine the effects of an exploded bomb laced with less than *two ounces* of cesium-137 in the heart of Manhattan. In the simulation, fine cesium particles spread across an area covering sixty square blocks. Cleanup and relocation following such a blast would take years to complete at a cost of tens of billions of dollars while Manhattan closes and displaces millions of people.

The ultimate purpose of the "dirty" part of the weapon is not to kill, but to terrorize—to instill fear and mayhem. The dirty bomb is a haunting weapon of psychological terror. Given the vast number of illegal or abandoned radioactive sources around the globe, many experts on nuclear terrorism have concluded that a dirty-bomb attack somewhere in the world is long overdue.

ABOUT THE AUTHOR

James Marshall Smith is a writer and physicist with a varied research career, from satellites to molecular biophysics.   He was Chief of Radiation Studies for the Centers for Disease Control and Prevention (CDC) in Atlanta for over a decade, and has served in consulting or advisory roles on nuclear and radiological threat countermeasures for the International Atomic Energy Agency (IAEA) in Vienna, the G7 Global Health Security Action Group in Berlin, London and Paris, and for the White House Office of Science and Technology Policy.   His debut novel, *Silent Source*, was one of three international finalists for the 2015 Clive Cussler Grandmaster Award.

James lives in Georgia with his wife June and their bossy Maltese, Georgie. You can find him online at *JamesMarshallSmith.com*.

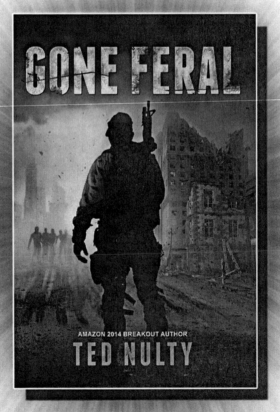

CUTTING-EDGE NAVAL THRILLERS BY

JEFF EDWARDS

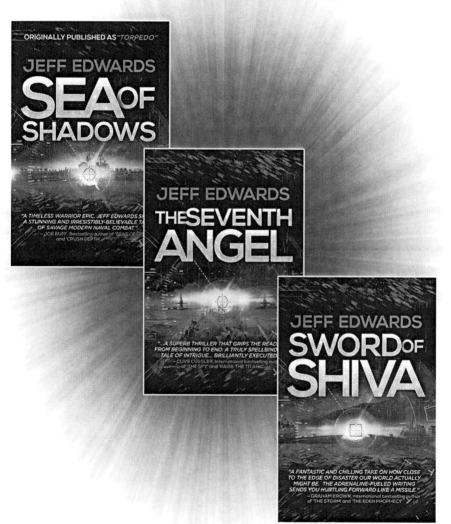

HIGH COMBAT IN HIGH SPACE

THOMAS A. MAYS

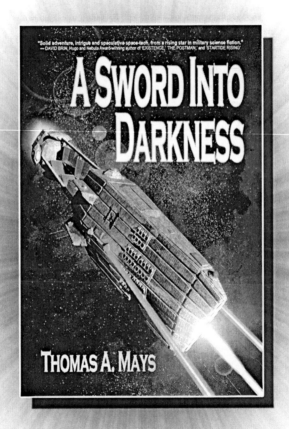

WHITE-HOT SUBMARINE WARFARE
BY
JOHN R. MONTEITH

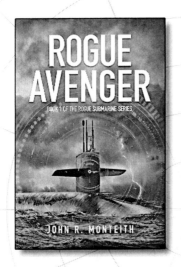

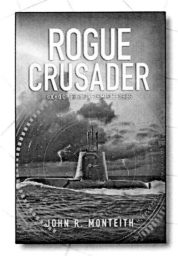

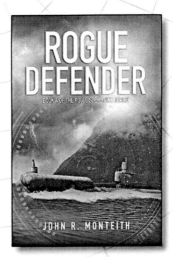

www.BraveshipBooks.Com

A THRONE WITHOUT AN HEIR...
A MURDEROUS LIE...

LARRY WEINBERG

A truth that can only lead to war...

HIGH OCTANE AERIAL COMBAT

KEVIN MILLER

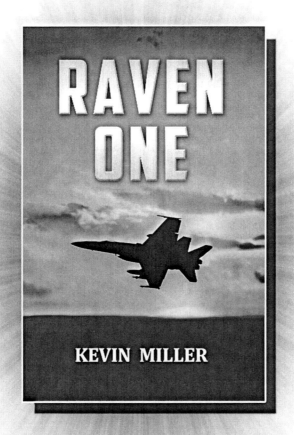

Unarmed over hostile territory...

www.BraveshipBooks.Com

PULSE-POUNDING FICTION FROM

GRAHAM BROWN
and
SPENCER J. ANDREWS

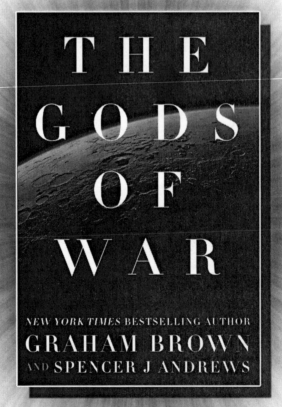

The world stands on the brink of ruin...

THE WAR AMERICA CAN'T AFFORD TO LOSE

GEORGE GALDORISI

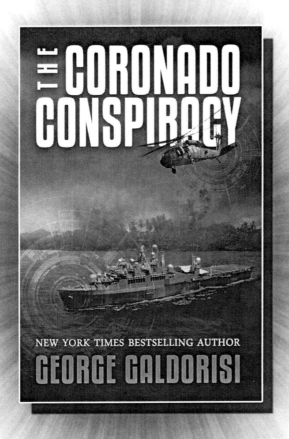

Everything was going according to plan...